D1738344

ENDANGERED
WITNESS

A Woman's Veterinary Career Turned Upside Down with Betrayal, Abduction and Murder!

A Work of Fiction

Linda S. Gunther

Endangered Witness is a work of fiction. Names, characters places, and incidents either are the product of the author's imagination or are used fictitiously. Any resemblance to actual persons, living or dead, events or locales is entirely coincidental.

Cover design by Julie Tipton.

ISBN: 0615957994
ISBN 13: 9780615957999

ACKNOWLEDGEMENTS

Special thanks to the many contributors -
To Andy Couterier for his support, to
Pam DeBarr, Kathy Buchanan, and Colleen
Garnett for their superb advice with regard
to manuscript editing and character development.

Additional thanks to Julie Tipton for her
amazing cover artwork.

I appreciate you all, and honor your commitment
to spending precious time and energy supporting
me through my second book's creation process.
It's been an exciting and rewarding journey.

*Readers may also be interested in Ms. Gunther's first novel
titled Ten Steps From The Hotel Inglaterra; also available
on Amazon in both paperback and for Kindle.*

MIXED EMOTIONS

"Lordy, Lordy, Jessi's forty." The unfortunate phrase falls out of his mouth.

"Thanks Nick. I guess I can count on you to make me feel young, sexy and beautiful." Jessi drops down on the king-size bed in the Renaissance Hotel room, feigning being shot in the heart with his insensitive words. She turns her head to take in the panoramic vista of the San Francisco bay from the 39th floor. Her head is swimming from the Vicodin she took earlier that afternoon; just after her emergency dental procedure.

"My birthday. Leave it to a veterinarian to have root canal surgery on her 40th birthday! Always something medical going on with me."

"There's a message in there," he teases as he jumps onto the bed and lies down beside her, his fingers running through her long, dark hair.

Still fuzzy from the drug, Jessi Salazar's mind wanders back to her childhood days in Panama – swimming in the pools made by breath-taking waterfalls, swinging in a hammock strewn between two mangrove trees, laughing at the howling monkeys which consistently hit the ground with a thump. Jessi spent her days in the lush rainforest running about, inventing games with her best friend and childhood sweetheart, Rico Mendez. He was the epitome of a jungle boy – an indigenous member of the local Boca del Toro Ngobe tribe. Thump! Thump! Monkeys dropped by her feet; surprising her even after years of living in the jungle with her dad, Denny, and her mother, Loretta, who left behind New York City for a rainforest life with her naturalist husband.

"Jessi. Jessi. Are you asleep? Hey 40 year old birthday lady – are you ready for your gifts? I have three of them for you. Well – two chunky gifts and one trivial, but amusing item."

Jessi shifts back to the present at the Renaissance Hotel. She feels relaxed and content in this light-hearted moment with Nick. She doesn't realize that she should treasure these next few peaceful hours, because after that, her life would morph into an unstoppable, screeching roller-coaster ride of terror.

Nick, gentle, yet playful; a technical genius in his field, with a Master's Degree in Electrical Engineering from Stanford. Impressive in so many ways. I like him, she thinks. She opens her eyes just as he flashes his nerdy smile, his unruly hair hanging down in his face, just a little too long; and his pen now almost falling out of the top pocket of his barely ironed yet fashionable checkered shirt. She likes his muscular build. An ex-college wrestler, he told me. She notices his biceps as he stretches out his arms and sits up. It's only been a little over two months dating Nick, but she genuinely enjoys his company. A welcome break from Stefan, the sex-crazed San Francisco Symphony violinist, with a following matched to that of Bon Jovi or Justin Timberlake; only the classical equivalent. Groupies always in close proximity – everywhere they went. I gave him three years; until he threw away my feelings with his crushing unfaithfulness. Slug! Ruminating on Stefan's betrayal became an obsession for Jessi, until she met Nick.

Nick slides off the bed and goes to the closet, taking out three items from his black overnight bag. He places them all on the table: a large rectangular gift wrapped in shiny gold paper, a petite square box wrapped in silver paper, and what looks like an over-sized greeting card housed in an extra large black envelope. "Nick, a black envelope? Wow. I guess I really am over the hill!" she says, rolling her eyes, then shoots him a disapproving sarcastic grin." They both laugh.

He holds up the black envelope. "This one is to be opened last!"

"Okay, I was tempted to begin with it, but if I must start with the gold wrapped item…" She attempts to shake the box, and notices that she's still struggling a little with her physical energy level, although her clarity of mind is just about restored. If this were Stefan, he'd have just one gift box for her from Saks Fifth Avenue. Lingerie. Tucked inside the tiny panty would be an expensive bauble – perhaps a strand of diamonds for her neck or a tasteful tennis bracelet from Tiffany's. He would instruct her to put on the gifts in front of him, and then watch her hunt for the hidden treasure buried deep inside the beautiful box. Everything about that man dripped sex and control. The truth about her feelings for him had hit her like a speeding bullet. Stefan's extravagance fed her hunger for alpha male attention. She tried to return the expensive jewelry accumulated over their three years together. He refused to take any of it back, wanting to keep his hold on her, reminding her of the luxurious life she'd be giving up; nothing but "the best of the best." Nick demonstrated the exact opposite in character, as far as she could tell in their short time dating. "Why am I thinking about other men when I'm in the company of one of the most caring and sincere guys I've ever met?"

The gift wrapped in gold was heavy. She rips off the paper to find a deep purple box with a large bottle of Dom Perignon champagne inside. "Whoa – the good stuff! Ooh la la, Nick. I love it!" She knew he was out of his comfort zone with the champagne and ritzy hotel scene. He was trying so hard to impress her.

"For tonight, I thought we'd indulge and celebrate. Copacetic with you?"

Jessi nods, as her cell phone vibrates on the bedside table. She glances at it, then re-focuses on her date. She moves closer to Nick and strokes his hair, looking into his large green eyes, the blended flecks of brown and blue dancing with happiness. "Nick, would you hate me if I burst your bubble just a little?"

"Hmm, depends on whether you're about to announce your need to immediately extricate yourself from this safe haven to respond to some veterinary emergency. Damn, I hope I'm so far off on this gut feeling I've got."

"Good news and bad news, Nick. No, I don't have to leave. It was just my cousin Myrna texting her wish for me to have a fabulous 40th. The bad news is, we can't drink this exquisite champagne in the condition it's in right now." Nick is totally perplexed. "Champagne, especially one of the best in the world, must be chilled before putting your lips to the glass. It sings when it's cold. Warm bubbly is never good." She can literally see his brain zipping into problem-solving mode.

"But, we have the technology. Right? Refrigerators, for example. One frosty bottle coming right up." He scans the room with his eyes. "Hmm, no fridge in this room. Weird!" Nick picks up the phone. He fakes an English accent for her amusement; upper crust. "Yes, I have a special bottle of champagne here in Room 3942 that needs chilling." He listens. "Very good. Well, hang on a moment, please. Let me ask my other half." He covers the mouthpiece, and whispers to her. "Jessi, I know we were going to have room service with this incredible view, but the hotel restaurant, very chic, is Carrington Grace; and they just decided to open tonight. They were supposed to be closed for dinner but a big wedding was cancelled at the last minute. We can get the best table, and you can even see all the way down to the Golden Gate bridge. They'll come and get the champagne, and chill it for us. Your birthday, your choice."

"Wow," her eyes open wide. That place has great reviews. Sure, I'm feeling pretty good although the Vicodin is not completely worn off. Let's do it! I think they have Duck a L'Orange. Mmm. And - I get to wear my new black velvet dress."

He speaks into the phone quickly, still with a perfect English accent; and then hangs up. "Okay we've got a reservation in about an hour." Someone's coming for the champagne. The doorbell rings. "Now, that's service!" Nick opens the door, and hands the bottle to the hotel bellman.

Jessi sits on the bed, removing the bow on the small box wrapped in silver paper. She carefully pulls out a delicate white gold chain with a beautiful rectangular purple gem hanging from it. "Nick, it's lovely."

"It's an amethyst, and those are three small peridots just beneath the stone. I'm not very good at gifts, Jessi. Do you like it?" he asks in a timid questioning tone. "I thought the colors would look great next to your golden skin, and well matched to your violet eyes."

"Nick, purple and green – my two favorite colors! You have good taste indeed." She plants a quick kiss on his lips, and jumps up, grabbing the black envelope.

"Wait. Wait. Before you open it, I have a confession."

"Oh no, there's something scary or slimy inside?" She shakes it, and then takes a sniff.

"Uh uh. I'm actually an amateur guitar player. You'll see."

"Hell no – there's not a guitar in this envelope, is there?" She shakes it again. As Jessi rips it open, she feels like she's warming up to this man; beginning to experience that easy familiarity, that casual comfort that evolves between two people where they can say and do anything. Be silly or serious. Total acceptance. She hadn't fallen in love with Nick; not yet. Sometimes she felt like that sizzle would never develop between them. Perhaps their destiny was, instead, to be the closest of friends; help each other find their next lovers and potential partners for life – but not become a couple. Her bond with Stefan was still difficult to ignore. It was holding her back with Nick.

Nick was somewhat of a geek at 41 years old, in a high profile, high tech job in Silicon Valley. He hated to brag about himself. His long sandy hair flops down in his face whenever he speaks about his accomplishments, almost like he's hiding; awkward about shining the light on himself.

As Jessi slides the birthday card out, it appears to be quite bulky. The front of the card matches the envelope, completely black with shimmering silver musical notes peppered across the scripted bold words, 'Happy Birthday.' It must be one of those musical cards, she thinks.

"Please don't hold it against me – what you're about to hear. Promise?" Nick cautions her.

A country voice with a Texas twang sings out from the greeting card. A guitar plays along – quite well, actually!

Jessi, won't you be my girl?
Jessi, won't you be my girl?
Jessi, you are such a pearl.
Jessi, you make my heart unfurl.

I wake up in the mornin'
I walk outside my door
I want to see you - just once more.
Gotta find out if you're really sure.

You're the best damn vet in the wide world
Jessi, won't you be my girl?

Nick stands on the bed miming the song, playing an imaginary guitar aligned to the words and music; as the verses of the corny, but catchy country song drift out from the card.

"Oh my God. That's your voice." She closes the card, then opens it again as the song re-plays. They both dance and sing like two kids mocking some tune on the radio. "What a talent! Do I smell a second career for you? Nicky Daniels, new country western star on the horizon!" She waves her hand in the air, as if denoting a headline. Then she tickles him until he collapses in uncontrollable laughter. She slides onto her knees and gives him a loud, smoochy kiss. "Thank you Nick. I'm having a wonderful time. I love your gifts."

"It's true Jessi. I'm falling for you. You know that, right?" His tone is serious but gentle; searching her eyes to find some return feeling.

"I know," she responds. Springing up, her head spins. Damn, that drug is still with me. "I better get dressed. You too, Tim McGraw." She takes a pillow, and playfully whacks him in the face; then grabs her black dress and shoes from the closet.

In the bathroom, while she prepares herself for the evening, she hums Nick's goofy greeting card melody. She recalls the very first day they met, only 2 ½ months ago. Nick Daniels came into her veterinary practice, dangling a cage holding a 70 year old South American parrot named Pedro; gifted to him by his grandmother who had passed away only a week before. Nick knew absolutely nothing about birds, especially parrots. Astounded to learn that he inherited Pedro, he automatically surfed the internet, and found the first vet located in San Francisco, that treated parrots. It turned out to be Dr. Jessi Salazar, her name popping up instantly on Google.

When he walked into her exam room, Jessi thought he looked like one of the lost boys from Peter Pan…dazed, confused, but curious to know more. He didn't really have a clue about the proper or safe way to hold a parrot. Her new patient's owner was attractive in an academic sort of way. She noticed his muscular arms escaping from the fitted short sleeve tee shirt, as he lifted the bird cage and placed it on the examination table. Jessi educated him in just twenty minutes on the life of the parrot; what they eat, how they sleep, tips to make them talk, their favorite things to do, signs that they are not well – the whole gamut.

Nick came back to her office four more times that week with some excuse for Jessi to look at the parrot. "Pedro seems to be always tired. His squawk is getting weaker," he said on his second visit. "Are parrots somnambulists – walking around in their sleep for hours at a time? I watch him doing this in his cage every night," he offered on his third visit. The very next day, he came back again – his fourth visit. "Pedro won't eat his food. Something's wrong. I gave him the stuff you recommended, but the colorful little guy is just not going for it." Two days later, on the fifth visit, Nick invented a story about the bird not having pooped for a couple of days. "Nada. Nothing! Should I speak Spanish to get him to do his business? Ándale? Ándale?" Jessi burst out laughing; the first time she enjoyed a hearty laugh since her break-up with Stefan.

"And what is Pedro wearing today? Jessi asked. Is that a San Francisco Giants uniform? Is he a fan?" She'd never seen a patient in costume, especially a bird in baseball gear.

"That's right. He's a Giants fan just like me. I think he used to play shortstop in his younger days for a Guatemalan team. He made that shirt himself. Quite talented for a bird, but he just won't poop!" Another round of shared laughter erupted between them.

"Maybe it's you I should be examining," Jessi barely got her words out. Nick quickly nodded in response.

"Okay, Mr. Daniels. I'd like to ask you a question. What's up with your daily visits to my office? It's not the norm around here." Suddenly, Nick Daniels took on a parrot-like persona, adopting Pedro's high-pitched bird voice. "Pedro can't sing, but he loves to dine! Would you have dinner with us? We promise NO BIRDSEED – REAL FOOD! Squawk! What d'ya say?"

"I say, you *are bizarre*! How can I turn you down? I love *bizarre*."

Now zipping up her little black velvet dress, and slipping on her red patent leather heels, Jessi feels content spending her birthday evening with Nick; although her body still longs for Stefan. She glances in the bathroom mirror. Her hair looks full, even late in the day, good curl; thick black locks flowing halfway down her bare back. She examines her face more closely in the magnified mirror. Her eyes are another story; bloodshot but a vivid, deep blue color tonight. She applies some black mascara to further lengthen her dark eyelashes. The dress looks short and sexy. Ready to finish my 40th birthday in style!

2

AN APPARITION — MAYBE!

As they approach the Carrington Grace Restaurant, Jessi is struck by the décor themed in colors of gold and burgundy, and the plushest of royal blue and gold patterned carpeting. She already spots the best table over by the picture window. She notices that the fog is starting to hug downtown San Francisco as the sky begins to darken.

Nick holds her hand, swinging it gently, thrilled to be in her company, as they stroll up to the hostess. "Good evening." The lovely older woman speaks with a Swedish or maybe Danish accent; difficult to exactly pinpoint. "Are you the Daniels couple – Room 3942?"

Jessi is a little jolted by the "Daniel's couple" reference, but squeezes Nick's hand and smiles. She's pleased that Nick has dropped his faux English accent although she had been amused by his earlier prank with the hotel staff.

"That's us," he says.

"You are very fortunate. You may have the restaurant all to yourselves this evening. Last minute wedding party cancellation."

The hostess sounds like Ingrid Bergman, Jessi thinks to herself. She is tall, blonde, slim, about 60, and dressed in an elegant black flowing dress. This woman has the smallest waist I've ever seen.

"Yes, we were scheduled to be closed for a private affair."

Nick is enjoying her pitter patter. "We heard. Does that happen often?"

"Absolutely not." The hostess smiles. "Of course, they already paid the bill and lost all the money, cancelling on the morning of the actual wedding. I wouldn't want to be in their shoes." She raises her manicured eyebrows. "Ahh, the bride's parents must be getting smashed as we speak. Oh, and since we're talking about libations, we have your champagne on ice awaiting your arrival." She catches her awkward blending of topics, and winces at herself. "Let's forget about that, and focus on you two! Yah?"

A tall South American man wearing black and white garb joins them at the hostess podium. Probably the head waiter, Jessi guesses.

The man speaks with a heavy Latino accent. "This is not a good night for dining at Carrington Grace. We have no specials because we just decided to open to the public at the last minute. Instead, I would recommend we serve you a special dinner in your hotel room. I will have the chef make it very nice for…"

The European hostess interrupts him. "Nonsense. Nonsense, Hector. Their table is all ready for them. She picks up two menus, then addresses Jessi and Nick. "Please, follow me." The disgruntled waiter mutters something under his breath and walks away. "By the way, is it a special occasion for you two this evening? Anniversary?"

"N-no, it's my girlfriend's birthday. A big one," he whispers, and shoots her a wink. Jessi gives him a gentle jab in the ribs with her black, beaded purse.

The hostess nods. "My name is Greta. Let me know if you need anything. Looks like I will have time on my hands tonight to be totally at your service."

The table setting is impressive. Beautiful, heavy silverware and expensive crystal glasses with their slender stems. The view from the large window is amazing; especially with the dash of fog hanging over the city. The sun has almost set; the sky painted with a rainbow palette of faded pastel colors framing the bridge in the distance. An antique iron sculpted lamppost is center stage, shining over the quiet San Francisco side street just below them. Looks like an old-fashioned gas lamp. Located on the second story of the hotel, the Carrington Grace Restaurant has a romantic ambiance; candlelit elegance set in a throwback art deco environment – a perfect combination.

As Jessi looks out the window, she sees a large antique clock mounted on the old bank building just adjacent to the hotel. It glows with its dated, pearl-like white face and large ornate bronze hands. 8:38 p.m. Jessi points to the clock. "Nick, check it out. Gorgeous, isn't it?"

Nick looks down at his wristwatch. "And precisely accurate."

The scene is reminiscent of the 1940's, almost timeless. Jessi can visualize the ghost of Humphrey Bogart or maybe Clark Gable standing under the lamp post below. Greta, the hostess, seats them. "I work here for 12 years now but I never get tired of this view. I hope you find the food as delicious as what you see outside your window." She hands each of them an elegant glossy royal blue menu. "Would you like a cocktail before your champagne?"

"I'm game." Jessi looks over at Nick.

"M'lady? Your preference?"

"Um – how about an apple martini with Grey Goose vodka, apple pucker and a cherry. Nothing else in it, please," Jessi requests.

"A woman who knows what she likes," Nick adds.

"It's a good choice," Greta agrees. "And for you, sir?"

"How about a margarita on the rocks, with salt? No preference on the tequila. Thanks."

He's so easy-going; a welcome change from Stefan, Jessi thinks to herself. She looks up at the ceiling. She sees a decorative chandelier shaped like an antique golden peacock. Her head seems to be a step behind her brain as she re-adjusts from the ceiling back to the table. A dizzying sensation overtakes her. Nick watches her face go pale.

"You okay, Jessi?"

"Y-yeh, I think so. It's nothing an apple martini won't cure. Ouch! I'm afraid the numbing is starting to wear off from my dental surgery." She holds the left side of her mouth, the pronounced pain taking its hold on her.

"Jessi, I hate to say this. I'm anti-drugs, but if it hurts, maybe you should have another pill. I want you to enjoy your special night – pain-free."

"You know. I think I will have one of these painkillers." Jessi opens her purse and takes an oval Vicodin out of the small vial, washing it down with a glass of lemon-sliced decorated water. Once she takes the first sip of her martini, she starts to feel better, almost like she's floating atop a fluffy cloud. She plays with the purple amethyst which hangs from her neck. She likes the feel of the smooth rectangular surface, the cut of the generously-sized gem.

"That necklace really suits you. Well, you make anything look stunning, Jessi." She giggles and then blushes, embarrassed. Nick takes her hand. "Jessi, I'd like to talk about 'us' tonight. "I'm falling in love with you." Jessi doesn't really want a serious 'relationship' conversation. She's still delicate from her ordeal with Stefan. The egotistical violinist's repeated phrase still nags in her mind: "Enjoy, relax, and simply fall forward with me. I love you," Stefan would repeat this to her regularly. He broke her heart. All she wants now is to have fun, not get heavy and mistakenly entangled with yet another "wrong" guy. She yearns to change the subject but without injuring Nick's ego.

"Can we stay light tonight, and just have a great time? I'm probably not in any condition to discuss serious topics like our feelings and the future. Is that okay?"

"Jessi, I'm so sorry. I'm being inconsiderate. It's your birthday. I want it to be memorable in a positive way. Truce. No more heavy relationship artillery from me this evening. Deal?"

Jessi appreciates his compliance. She gets up, and plants a quick kiss on his check. "You're a good man Nick Daniels. A real catch!"

"Yeh, yeh, enough accolades. Let's chow down Ms. Salazar. So - what will the doctor order tonight?" She selects the pate for a starter, and the duck a l'orange as her entrée. He chooses the Caesar salad and the filet mignon. They have animated dialogue, laugh, make several toasts, and drink the outrageously pricey, and thoroughly chilled champagne.

The waiter serves them in a brusque manner. He seems to want to hurry their meal. Nick and Jessi slow him down; Nick requesting to wait a half hour between the appetizers and entrees, and do the same between the entrees and dessert. Using her skilled peripheral vision, Jessi can see the anxious waiter complaining to Greta about the restaurant opening to the public tonight. "Everyone's already been paid from the wedding. Why open? Why? That was the agreed plan," he grumbles.

What's with this guy? Jessi ponders. Why is he so crabby and ill-tempered? Greta seems bewildered by the waiter's foul mood. She waves him off, walking away from him; escaping into the kitchen. Jessi would do the same. Maybe the chef and his staff are more upbeat company for Greta, in contrast to this guy.

As the evening progresses, Jessi gets tipsy after her cocktail, and two, or is it three glasses of the most divine Dom Perignon champagne. And then of course, there's the second Vicodin of the day kicking in nicely. Although definitely cloudy, her mind and her body embark on a culinary picnic. The food is absolutely delicious, and Nick is looking sexier and sexier. They talk about their careers, their childhood, their political views, Jessi, a proud Democrat and Nick, a committed Republican.

Nick enjoys listening to her views, whether the same or different from his perspective. "Opposites – do we repel or attract? Oops sorry, that conversation is off limits tonight." They both laugh.

She talks about her new hobby – creative writing. She's been taking a class at UCSF on Tuesday nights for the past month. Now, on her second short story, she's excited about igniting her creative side, something not often tapped in her everyday veterinary work. Jessi loves to talk, philosophize; her imagination racing like the wind. She describes the latest story she's writing for class. It's a woman's adventure, where the protagonist gets kidnapped, and then finds herself aboard a luxury yacht off the coast of Belize, spread out on the bejeweled bed of a rich, handsome prince who is visiting from an Arabian country where his father is king. Nick is fascinated by Jessi's brain – her array of talents, her playfulness. It's something he rarely gets exposure to in the technical world of chip design and hardware development.

"I guess I have no chance against a handsome prince then, hmm?"

Jessi giggles. "It's a fantasy, Nick. Just a story composed by a veterinarian."

He starts to tell her about his dream last night. It was like a full length motion picture. But then he realizes that his stomach is suddenly aching. Severe cramping sets in. Embarrassed, he excuses himself, and rushes off to the restroom.

I hope he's not upset, Jessi worries. I know his feelings for me are heating up. Is he really sick or is he frustrated? Jessi stares out the window, noticing that the fog is almost cleared; a vivid crescent moon now fully exposed. She feels at peace with the world. The streetlight shines through the haze, the scene resembling an Impressionist's painting of Paris, with the old clock beaming from the bank building, and the bridge silhouetted against the sky in the distance. Geez, it's already 11 o'clock. I've almost survived my depressing 40th birthday, pretty much unscathed; except for this fuzzy head. We're still the only patrons in the restaurant. It was our own private dining room all evening. What a treat!

On the street below, she notices several orange construction cones blocking the entrance to the road; but there's no sign of any construction in progress. Maybe it begins tomorrow. The next thing she sees makes her skin crawl, disrupts her entire paradigm of the ordered world. A red tow truck appears under the street lamp. It stops. The truck must have driven right through the orange cones. She looks back, and sees that three or four cones have been knocked down and scattered. Suddenly, a sleek, black stretch limousine drives up behind the red truck. The limo driver jumps out just as the tow truck driver opens his door and gets out. Both of them are wearing black masks. The two men seem to talk heatedly about something. An elderly gray-haired man opens the limo passenger door, and pokes his head out. The two masked men attempt to pull him from the car. The skinny old man struggles, and holds out what looks like a long umbrella, trying to jab the two men, stop them from attacking him. They get him out of the limo despite his fight.

This is crazy, she thinks, her mind, reeling. The taller masked man gets behind the old man, and plucks his eyeglasses from his face, throwing them on the ground; crushing them fiercely with two quick stamps of his left foot. The old man turns on him and strikes him hard, frantically using his umbrella again as a defensive weapon. Without any hesitation, the short, fat, masked-man brandishes what looks like a gun, and points it at the old man. Jessi can't hear what's happening. But visually, she sees the well-dressed man drop to the ground. He lays there on the blacktop. Jessi can see him move his head, and then his legs. Thank God.

Is this really happening, right there before my eyes? She doesn't want to take her gaze from the street. I need to get help. Traumatized, her eyes pan the restaurant. Completely empty. Both the hostess and waiter have disappeared. She looks back at the scene on the street and sees the two men drag the old man to the front seat of the tow truck, then dump him inside. Jessi notices the clock's reflection on the building opposite the bank, just above this horrific scenario. It's 11:18. She wishes she could leap out the window and grab the giant hands, turn back the clock to 11 p.m., and wipe out everything that she just observed. One of the masked men, the short one, gets into the tow truck while the other man gets into the limo.

Jessi runs to Nick when she sees him emerge from the restroom. "Nick. Nick. Come quickly. Out the window. Out the window!" She stumbles back to the dinner table, pulling Nick's arm – her head swimming – yanking him as hard as she can.

Nick is weak, his stomach still churning - but responds to her request, rushing back to the table with her. "Look. Look at those two cars," she yells, exasperated. She turns back to the window. It's all gone! Gone! Gone! No tow truck. No limo. Nothing but an empty, eerie tableau. Jessi drops her head down on the table.

"Jessi, what's wrong? What happened? Are you feeling queasy like me?"

"I'm feeling dizzy," she says.

He crosses to her, bends down and embraces her. "Let's go back to our room. It's late. We can sleep in a bit in the morning. I think the Vicodin may have messed you up. We drank a lot, too."

Greta approaches the table, looking concerned. Nick explains that Jessi is tired and asks if she can kindly have the dinner bill put on his room tab? The hostess nods in agreement. He hands her $30 from his wallet as a tip, then helps Jessi to her feet, and swiftly escorts her out of the restaurant, and into the hotel elevator.

After ripping off her dress, she slips between the crisp sheets. She weeps quietly. Lying down beside her, Nick is concerned. He hasn't seen anything like this from her before. "What, Jessi? Tell me what happened. I can't help unless you open up to me." Jessi feels disconnected as if she's just played the lead role in a horror movie, and is desperately trying to come back to reality. She wants to forget the whole ugly episode. When she explains the details, the magnitude of what she saw, he calms her; suggesting that perhaps she thought she saw the worst possible scene but with the drug, and all the alcohol, she may have imagined some of it. It's over now. Nobody knows that you saw anything; even if it really did happen," Nick offers. Jessi falls asleep in his arms, He gently rubs her bare back until he can hear her light snoring. He thinks about how close he feels to this woman; how he wants her to want him in the same way; but he can't force it to happen.

His heart was thrashed to smithereens three years ago when his fiancé, Lizzie, died in a car accident on the Bay Bridge. It happened in a mere few seconds. She was coming home from her sister's house where she had spent the weekend in Pleasanton. It was a lazy Sunday afternoon. They were planning on a movie in Japan Town and some sushi for supper. When she didn't show up at his house, he called her cell probably five times; miffed about her "no-show." It was a Matt Damon movie he couldn't wait to see. It never happened. Her sister, Kate, phoned him about an hour later. This is the first time since then that Nick has dated someone for more than a month. He just seems to lose interest, and truthfully he hasn't been in the "seeking commitment" mode. At the 2 ½ month mark with Jessi, he knows he's fallen in love with her. She has a light within her. It's luminescent; alive. It's a kind of magic he didn't even remember having with his Lizzie.

Watching someone sleep, and thoroughly enjoying it lets you subtly know that this one's for you. Jessi resembles a young girl when she's at rest; curled up in the fetal position, her long. shiny hair spread across her face. Nick laughs to himself. Then he gently sweeps the hair away from her lips. He would have liked to have known her as a tom-boy in the Panama jungle; something she talks about a lot. Someday. Someday it might happen. They'll travel to Central America. Still with a nagging stomach cramp, he pulls the light blanket over Jessi, then closes his eyes to dream about her.

3

VETERINARY GOTHIC GIRL

Arriving at her office the next day, Jessi's head aches. No run this morning. It would have been impossible for her. Maybe late this afternoon. It would most likely help physically and emotionally restore her energy. She's out of rhythm and her anxiety is still set on "high." Her yoga practice needs resurrecting. Ohmmmmm. Ohmmm. That never really works for me, she admits to herself. More effective for her is to just think: chill out! She barely remembered to feed her dog and cats this morning. Dr. Pepper, her Yorkshire Terrier, was not amused when he saw her hurtling out the front door. He shot her his "doesn't anybody love me" look, and began to whimper. Receiving his demand, Jessi made a dash for the kitchen, filling his bowls with food and water. The two Persian cats, Creature and Pandora, sprinted into the room, reminding her that she has two feline pets that also need their nourishment. Dr. Pepper had saved the day for all of them.

Rushing from her car and through the back door of her office, she says good morning to her 23 year old medical assistant, Sarah. No previous experience with veterinarians; but she adores animals. She wears dark eyeliner, her hair dyed black as black, her earrings long, a tiny gold ring through her left nostril, and her make-up, pale white; a noticeable contrast to the rest of her. She loves to wear black even though at first Jessi had insisted that she sport a white lab coat in the exam room. Two weeks into her job as vet's assistant, Sarah sat there in the office break room;

a forlorn expression on her face. Jessi walked in for her morning coffee, and immediately noticed. "What is it Sarah? Work or personal? I don't mean to pry, but if I can help…"

"No. It's fine," Sarah mumbled; her head still hanging down. Then, she dared to look up at Jessi and almost inaudibly whispered, "Well, actually it is about work."

"You don't like it here? You're doing an incredible job after only a couple of weeks on board. You're a natural with the animals. I've never seen anyone so young have such an intuitive skill set with every species that visits this office. You have a knack for it, Sarah. I'm impressed."

"Thanks." Then, Sarah blurted out her next statement as quickly as she could, "I just hate wearing white. There, I said it." Jessi sat down at the table with her. "Oh. I'm sorry Doctor, but you've probably noticed that I'm kind of well - gothic. It's my signature. I wear black a lot. *Everything* I love is black. White, it's just doesn't have a place in my world. Honestly, I don't know what to do. I love this job, but…"

Jessi cut in. "I get it. I get it. What was I thinking? Okay, here's my proposal. Can you find yourself a smart black lab coat somewhere? Actually, I'd rather you do a print with some black, and maybe blend it with one or two other colors." Sarah's face drops again. Jessi relinquishes. "Forget what I said – solid black is fine! Go for it."

Sarah just about shot out of the stainless steel, red leather-cushioned chair, almost throwing over the small 50's retro dining table; and wrapped her arms around Jessi. "Thank you. Thank you Doctor Salazar." Sarah danced around the break room and then said, "Wait. I'll be right back." She ran out. A minute later she was back in the break room showing Jessi her new, mid-length black lab coat trimmed with shiny silver snaps and cute folded cuffs at the wrists. Totally black, except for the silver snaps. She quickly threw on the smock and modeled it. "Is this okay? What do you think?" She did a twirl. "I've had it tucked away in the trunk of my car since the day after I started working here."

"Perfect, very stylish." Jessi had to chuckle. She was impressed with the girl's demonstrated proactivity. They bonded right there in the break room. Jessi and Sarah – a black and white adorned veterinary team!

Since then, Sarah has varied her office wardrobe. She acquired at least five different renditions of a black lab coat. Patient families love Sarah. Their pets can't wait to spend time with her.

Today, Sarah greets Jessi with an organized list of the animals to be seen; at least those who made appointments. A full schedule, except it all ends at 4 o'clock unless of course, an emergency wanders in. Then, no mercy. Jessi and Sarah could be there until 7 p.m. or later.

Jessi gets a little lift realizing that she might actually be able to get that run in today. She needs the exercise after the excess of food last night. Plenty of calories in alcoholic drinks; especially the sugar in champagne. The Embarcadero would do nicely for a 45 minute sprint at 4:30 this afternoon. Jessi loved to run. Not long runs; although she did do the Honolulu Marathon to raise money for charity, two years ago. That's probably one of those times when Stefan was unfaithful. Almost 100% chance that transgression happened while she was gone. Jessi's favorite runs lasted about an hour; along the streets of San Francisco. Lately, it gave her an opportunity to invent plot lines for short stories to use in her writing class.

As a young girl in the Panama jungle, she would run everyday. Sometimes with Rico, sometimes with her father, and often by herself. She never felt by herself even when alone in the rainforest. Animals, birds, insects of every shape and color were her partners. She'd see the same two hummingbirds each night at dusk, Panko and Taco. She knew them by their unique markings and quirky personalities. They had a distinct dipping pattern as they flew through the thick, leafy trees. There was a toucan she called Rocky who had a precise color arrangement of feathers, and a patterned beak of orange, yellow and red. Then, there was Macho Man, the giant green iguana. She named each of the regulars because they were her best friends, outside of Rico. It was her private menagerie. But it was the cacophony, the collection of sounds and smells in the rainforest that most pleased her. She'd close her eyes and try to identify each creature's unique, signature noise. Jungle Book was a children's fantasy story; but for Jessi – she lived it. It was real. The animals spoke to her. She connected with them, sketching them, watching them and with Rico, discovered new creatures. She and Rico termed it 'Whacky Wednesday," the day every week, when Rico and Jessi challenged themselves to come up with an animal, insect or bird which neither had ever seen before.

Sometimes, they'd bring an old camera which her father had given her, and captured the newly discovered creature on film so nobody would think they just made it up. Jessi would write everything down, make journals about these creatures, and paste in the polaroid under the hand-written description; as proof. She'd often go off on her own doing the same thing; content to experience the rainforest in solitude.

4

THE VELASQUEZ BROTHERS IN ENVIGADO

Rodrigo and Julio Velasquez grew up in the slums just outside of Medillín…the neighborhood of Envigado, a poor community nestled on the steep mountain slopes of the Andes Mountains. The center of drug trafficking and violence was in the city of Medellin, just a few miles from their home; inhabited by more than three million people. It was the venue for over 2,900 killings in 2010, and was revered as the "most murderous city on earth." Envigado, itself, became well-known in the mid 1990's when the top echelon of drug traffickers came together in an Envigado underground car park to discuss what to do about the police who had gunned down their leader, Pablo Escobar. The "Office of Envigado" was formed, a ruthless collection of seasoned Cartel thugs whose mission was designed to oversee crime in Medellín – settling debts between traffickers, and collecting a hefty 33% of the cocaine profits for their rock solid protection services. God help those who crossed the "Office of Envigado" once they had declared war on the police force who was attempting to clean up drug trafficking in the city. Daily killings were committed to teach Medillin cops a lesson – obey "The Office." Ignore the drug trade, or die!

Rodrigo started his criminal activities in the local Envigado comuna. His father, Gustavo, could barely feed his family, working hard as a construction worker, usually 10-12 hours per day;

then drinking each night to forget his misery and numb his aching body. Rodrigo's mother preferred the company of her younger son, Julio, because he was gentle and loved animals. Rodrigo, her eldest, was mean and stubborn. But, he was undeniably handsome, attracting the local girls like flies, with his sculpted features and his captivating smile. Often, she'd catch him gazing in the mirror at his own reflection flexing his impressive muscles. He'd flip out his switchblade and stab it into the mirror while he laughed at his own antics. Whenever he noticed that his mother was watching, he'd turn, yelling at her to get out of his room. She noticed that he talked to himself in the mirror more than he would converse with members of his own family. His mother began to fear him. Secretly, he was unhappy and hurt that she preferred his short, ugly sibling. He was jealous of Julio, who followed Rodrigo everywhere, envying his older brother's magnetic qualities – hanging out nearby, witnessing Rodrigo's devious acts, and blindly following his every order, without question.

When he was 12 years old, Rodrigo offered up his services for "free" to the local Cartel commander, his Uncle César. He was told to go away and come back when he was 13; the threshold age for even being considered as a Cartel affiliate. Rodrigo was disappointed, but he waited. In the meantime, he broke into houses and shops, committing numerous burglaries and often reaping violence on his victims. He stole computers, electronics and appliances; selling them for a few pesos on the street. Rodrigo just wanted the practice, the experience of being a criminal. He wanted to build his reputation – have his Uncle take notice of his accomplishments. He didn't mind hitting his victims in the head with blunt objects or holding a knife to a homeowner's throat. A few times he'd stab the victim; but he wasn't aware that anyone had ultimately died because of his aggression. Word got around about Rodrigo. He saved his profits and by 13 years old, he owned three guns – hiding them in a closet under the splitting floorboards in his family's unpainted, tin-roofed, rickety house.

His goal was to become one of the most famous and powerful thugs in his barrio.

One day when Rodrigo was down on his knees, proudly polishing his .45, his father found out about his son's collections of guns. "¿Qué pasa? What the hell are you doing with guns? You're 13 years old – a niño."

Rodrigo quickly turned around. "I am a man mi padre. I have already proven it. That's how I got these guns. We need protection, anyway."

"You see your father sweating all day long? Sí?" His father pulled him up from the floor, the gun still in Rodrigo's hand. "Sí, it's true. I just make a few pesos a day but I lead an honest life with your madre; not like my crooked brother, César. He is a murderer! I have no guilt – no regrets about our life. We are poor in this family but we are pure! We don't need guns."

"Stupid old hombre," Rodrigo uttered under his breath.

Annoyed, his father pulled at his sleeve. That's when Rodrigo reacted, jumped up on his feet and pointed the .45 at his father's head. "Leave me alone. Hands off. You should fear me as much as the rest of the miserable people in this comuna. I will make my mark."

His father's eyes glazed over. It was the first time one of his sons directly disrespected him. He turned away, defeated, tears of sorrow drizzling down his leathery, discolored cheeks, as he left the room.

Within a month, Rodrigo had his 13th birthday. Already with a rapidly spreading reputation, he was respected by his Uncle César, and other local Cartel leaders. His uncle had the most talented thugs train him, and then gave him the job of killing Medellin policemen. Rodrigo became a bounty hunter at 13 years old. Each "kill" would make him the equivalent of $2,000. He could make a fortune. Rodrigo immediately recruited Julio to help him in his activities, ordering the 11 year old to drive the motorbike provided by the Cartel and sneak up on a cop who walked a lonely beat. Rodrigo would whip out his sawed off shot gun from his custom designed-tummy pack and fire directly into the bewildered cop's face, before he could react and defend himself. Cop after cop met their deadly fate. He'd scream out with delight, and laugh every time he was successful. At 14 years old, he had already killed 8 cops. The Cartel bosses applauded him.

His uncle noticed the gleam in Rodrigo's eye just after he committed a murder. He started to reserve him for the most heinous of violent acts required for his barrio to stay powerful and feared. By age 19, Rodrigo was plunged into the international sector of Cartel activities, protecting drug traffickers as a hit man in a variety of countries; especially in the U.S. His uncle César had purchased a sprawling ranch on the northern California coast and wanted his family members around him. The brothers started to spend a lot of time there. They learned English from a private tutor employed by uncle Cesar, who wanted both Rodrigo and Julio to become bilingual; enabling them to upgrade their influencing and negotiating skills when dealing with Americans.

5

A VISIT FROM LANCE

Jessi buttoned up her white lab coat, ready for today's first appointment. Although not documented in her schedule, she suddenly remembered that her cousin, Myrna, and her five year old son, Lance, would be arriving soon. Lance was going to help Jessi with one of her patients this morning. She was going to begin his rehabilitation here in her pet examination room.

Only two weeks ago, he was in the park just across from his elementary school on a Saturday afternoon, running around, playing 'Marco Polo' with his friend Sammy. Mrs. Kanter, Sammy's mom went to the other end of the park with Sammy's baby sister, trying to get the little eleven month old to take a nap. She told Sammy and Lance to stay in the area; not wander off.

"Marco," Lance yelled to Sammy.

"Polo."

"Marco." With his eyes closed, Lance could sense that he was getting closer and closer to his friend. "I'm going to bust you. You're toast!"

"Polo...hey, get away. Stop it!! No!" A shrill scream burst out from Sammy. "Get away!!! Help! Get away from..."

Lance opened his eyes to see Sammy getting mauled by a huge black Pitbull. He frantically looked around. No dog owner in sight anywhere.

More screaming from Sammy. "Don't. Don't!" Lance could feel the pain in his friend's call for help.

The dog pounced on Sammy, then tugged at his pant leg; dragging him several feet along the grass, then across the pavement. Lance saw the dog start to attack Sammy's upper body. He froze for a moment, watching the ugly scene.

Sammy screamed, "No, no-o-o." The dog pulled on his friend's right arm.

Lance took off, racing to the tree area of the park where people were sitting on blankets; lunching and laughing. He spotted a man and a woman sitting side by side on a red and white patterned blanket. He screamed as loud as he could. "My friend, my friend Sammy." He was out of breath. "A dog is getting him, biting him, ripping his clothes. Help him. Please." The man immediately reacted, throwing his sandwich and napkin down on the ground. The lady he was with got up too, and quickly went to Lance.

"Show us. Take us to him," she said hurriedly.

Lance ran like the real Lancelot would have done. He wished he had his sword. Even his cheap plastic sword would be better than nothing. He could hit the dog back but I'm afraid, he thought. When all three of them got to Sammy, the dog was still pulling at his clothes. Sammy looked dead; lifeless. His sneaker was ripped in pieces and pulled off from his right foot.

The woman still had her sandwich in her hand. She tossed it to the man. "Here boy. Here boy. Food. Look," the man said. No reaction from the mongrel. "Hey boy. meat. Come. Smell this!" He held it out further. The man stepped closer so the dog could smell the layers of roast beef between the two slices of wheat bread. It worked. The dog looked up and for the first time, noticed both the sandwich and the man. The savage animal finally let Sammy go; went for the food while the woman got on her cell phone. The man raised the half sandwich in the air and threw it as far as he could in a direction empty of sunbathers or lunchers. The dog took off, following the flying sandwich. A policeman came running towards them. Then, a guy who looked like a doctor or something showed up. In the distance, Lance could see Sammy's mom coming closer, now running, awkwardly pushing the stroller as fast as she could. Another policeman went after the mad dog and seemed to shoot him or somehow get the mutt to lay down. Sammy was placed on the stretcher just as his mom arrived. She was screaming and crying. The baby sister started wailing. The policeman told Sammy's mom to go with her boy in the ambulance which was waiting on the corner. "What's this other boy's name?"

"Oh my God, yes. He's Lance Pincus. I was watching him for his mom; but I took the baby for a walk. It's my fault," she cried.

"Don't worry," the policeman said, trying his best to calm her. He would take care of Lance, get him home safely. He asked her for Mrs. Pincus' phone number. Lance ran to Sammy who wasn't moving on the stretcher. One of the policemen pulled him back, telling him he could not go with Sammy but he could visit him at the hospital.

"Is my friend alive? Is he alive?"

"He's hurt bad; but I think he will be okay. We'll know more later."

Lance's mom, Myrna, was sitting in her office, in the midst of writing an article for her company's newsletter. She bolted like a bullet when she got the call from the officer.

Lance was traumatized and still, now two weeks later, scared to walk to school, even with his mom. He never wanted to go back to the park again for fear that he will be ripped apart by some dog; just like his friend Sammy.

When Jessi found out what happened, it depressed her. Then, she became angry. What kind of fool owned this dog? He's the one they should hold responsible. "The dog learns from its master," she exclaimed to Myrna. Jessi realized that regardless of her steamed up feelings about the whole incident, her number one priority was to help her cousin's son through this horrific mess. "Myrna, how about if I have Lance assist me with one of my friendly dog patients; ease him into trusting animals again? The worst thing would be for Lance to stay clear of all dogs for the rest of his life." Jessi knew that this could actually happen unless someone is able to connect with Lance; pull him through his fears.

This morning would be Jessi's first opportunity to begin Lance's dog interaction therapy. Additionally, it provides Jessi a distraction from her own traumatic situation. Let's face it - I wasn't thinking straight when I thought I saw a shooting; the outcome of blending drugs and alcohol. Maybe I just fell asleep at the dinner table and dreamed up the two masked men, and the old man falling to the ground. I just don't know anymore.

The only bright spot from the whole fiasco was that Nick had taken some control, caring for her – making sure that she got to bed and was safely enveloped for the night in his arms. That's a real friend. No matter what happens in our future; he's someone she can depend on.

A tap at her office door. "Hey, Aunt Jessi." Lance enters. He seems timid and looks pale; not the usual rosy-cheeked, effervescent Lance.

"Come in Sir Lancelot. Come on in." Jessi stands up and smacks his hand, giving him a high five – their usual greeting. His mom, Myrna, enters just behind him. Jessi waves at Myrna but focuses almost exclusively on five year old Lance. "So, are you happy to have a week long break from school?"

"Yeah," he says without emotion.

"Lancelot, are you ready to help the great Dr. Salazar with her first patient today?"

"Um, I-I guess so." He doesn't sound very convincing.

"Good." Jessi smiles. "Well – his name is Mr. Lincoln. He's a small mutt – very friendly, with a really cool personality. I think you'll like him."

Jessi opens the door slightly, signaling to Lance to follow, and peer out the door with her. They both eye the variety of patients and their owners waiting to be seen. There's a toucan in a cage on a chair placed beside a heavy set woman, a black kitty in a small crate, a white sheepdog sitting obediently on the floor by a young Hispanic man's side. On the couch, opposite all of them is a tall, thin man who holds a small brown dog. The place is full on this drizzly Saturday morning. Jessi's silver-haired receptionist, Barbara, is busy checking in each patient.

"See, over there? That's Mr. Lincoln sitting with his master. He looks friendly, doesn't he?"

Lance blinks his eyes nervously. "Yeh, I guess so." Myrna watches from inside Jessi's office, appreciating her cousin's support for her son who hasn't slept much in two weeks; and when he did, he'd have disturbing, nightmarish dreams. He'd just crawl into her bed, clutching his plastic Lancelot sword for added protection.

Jessi's gothic assistant, Sarah, enters the waiting room from another door to pick up the stunted, short-haired Mr. Lincoln. Lance and Jessi observe the dog comically jump up all over Sarah, his tail wagging profusely. Sarah scoops up the mutt in her arms, two good-sized skull tattoos are now exposed on each of her inside wrists. She carries Mr. Lincoln into the examination room and places him on the metal table, waiting for Jessi, who had already briefed her on Lance's incredibly dismal dog experience. Like her boss, Sarah wants Lance to recognize that animals in general are good creatures – just like humans. Only occasionally is there an exception.

Jessi escorts Lance into the exam room, and proceeds to check the dog. A standard set of medical instruments has already been laid out on a white terry towel: stethoscope, thermometer, scissors, a small knife, and a pair of long tweezers. Sarah holds Mr. Lincoln while Jessi lifts his right front paw and probes it gently. The dogs jolts and howls, then pathetically whimpers.

"Uh huh. There we go. Look Lance, there's the culprit. She points to it. A cat tail. Can you see it just barely poking through the surface of his paw?" Lance winces, feeling the little dog's pain. He's still afraid to be near any animal; especially dogs. He wants to bolt, but at the same time enjoys seeing his Aunt Jessi in action, a real-life pet doctor. Jessi watches Lance's reactions closely assessing his comfort level with Mr. Lincoln.

"Lance, listen. Sarah and I have to go out of the room for just a moment to get some hot water and other stuff. Can you watch Mr. Lincoln, like Sarah's doing now? Help him feel at cared for? You can imagine how scared he is right now." Lance nervously quivers as he stands there by her side. Jessi notices his apprehension; but she wants to persevere and try out her idea for therapy. Lance looks over at Sarah and the dog. Sarah strokes the dog's back and softly talks to him. The dog seems to calm down. Lance appears to feel more at ease as well.

"Uh – okay. I guess so," Lance agrees.

"Great – you'll be our vet's assistant while we're gone for just a minute or so." Jessi nods her head, and signals for Lance to take over from Sarah. He puts one hand on the dog; hesitantly petting Mr. Lincoln. He continues stroking the dog's back, just like Sarah had done.

Jessi whispers, "You got it, Sir Lancelot. That's perfect. He likes you." She nods to Sarah. They both exit the room. There's a small one-way window where both Jessi and Sarah can observe the boy and the dog; check on how they're doing together. They see Lance standing there, his body stiff and rigid. His strokes on Mr. Lincoln's wiry coat are few and far between. Then he warms up, starts to trust the ailing hound. He leans into the dog, showing his empathy, gaining confidence with the animal. Myrna sits in the waiting room with the assortment of patients and pets, hoping things are going well, that perhaps an emotional shift results for her son. Her heart aches, seeing him so distraught. Right now, she wishes she had some of her own pets at home. It would help Lance's recovery.

Jessi and Sarah open the door to the exam room, carrying the towels and hot water. Lance watches Jessi carefully tweeze out the cat tail from Mr. Lincoln's paw while Sarah holds the poor dog, as he yelps and fusses. "It's all done." Jessi rubs some alcohol onto the paw and signals Sarah to take him out to his master. "Sarah, he needs some antibiotics. Can you have Barbara get that ready?" Sarah nods, and lifts Mr. Lincoln from the table. She puts him on the floor and the dog gets excited, starting to jump and play, as if nothing happened.

"Wow, that's amazing," Lance says with delight." He's fixed. Bye, Mr. Lincoln." Sarah takes the dog out to his owner. Lance turns to Jessi. "Aunt Jessi, do dogs cry? I mean, do they get sad and cry?"

"That's an interesting question Lance. You're so curious, and very smart. You could make a great doctor one day. What you just asked about, they don't teach in veterinary school. I don't know for sure, but I think Mr. Lincoln is thankful to us and feeling a lot better already. No more pain or sadness. You helped accomplish that." She gives Lance another high five. He feels proud.

Myrna enters. She pats her son on the back. "How did it go?"

"Good, mom. I was Aunt Jessi's assistant, all on my own! It was like I was the doctor!"

Jessi opens the door to her well-stocked supply cabinet. She takes out a bright blue, long umbrella-shaped object. "For you, Sir Lancelot." She removes a beautiful kite from the cloth covering.

"Wow. It's a fighting kite. The king of flyers! I wanted one. Mom – look!"

Myrna takes a cardboard crown from behind her back. "I crown you a knight in shining armor. Your bravery is returning. I'm proud of you." He laughs. Myrna gets something from her purse. "Hey, how about if we spill the beans, and tell Aunt Jessi about our surprise for her?"

"Okay," he beams with the fake gold, jeweled crown now sitting on his head, and the kite in his hand.

As if a trumpet has just sounded, Myrna announces, "Dr. Jessi Salazar, you are cordially invited to be our esteemed guest tonight at a San Francisco Giants baseball game. Everything's on us. Giants against the Reds. I know it's incredible, but we've landed three club seats behind home plate to celebrate your special birthday. You are hereby treated to the game and in addition, to the garlic fries; but NO BEER, after last night's dinner, and today's hangover."

Jessi jumps up, amused by Myrna's royal message delivery. "Oh my God, Nick is going to be so jealous of our club seats."

"Well, next time maybe we'll invite him as well. My personal wish is that you're still together this same time next year." Myrna gives her cousin a teasing poke on the shoulder.

The only bad news for Jessi is that she'll miss getting her run in this afternoon.

Tomorrow is always another day for exercise. The Giants trump fitness.

6

DARK DANGER ZONE

It's early in the morning and the San Francisco sky is a deep navy blue. They arrive at the building, the beat up front door covered with graffiti. When the two men enter the dank entry-way, the lighting is so dim, they'd be lucky to make it up the fuckin' staircase. "Mierda," Rodrigo commented in disgust. The Velasquez brothers hoisted the army bag weighted down heavy by the heap of the unconscious man, dropping him twice as they climbed the three flights of stairs. Dragging the sack into the apartment, then into the unkempt bedroom, they proceed to remove the load from the large musty bag, and dump the man into the cramped closet.

"He better still be fuckin' breathing, Julio," Rodrigo says with annoyance. "Imbecile! Why did you shoot him in the stomach? We said we'd only plug him in the leg or the arm if we absolutely needed to take a shot to get him into the truck. We didn't want to try to kill him. Dios mío!"

Julio is shaking; scared that he may have committed murder, when that was not the plan. He tries to sit the old man up against the wall in the closet, kicking his own shoes out of the way. Rodrigo starts to pace the room. "This is a kidnapping, a bribery you stupid fool! Not supposed to be a murder!" He smacks Julio in the head, disgusted with his younger brother. Rodrigo was the taller sibling, blessed with a deep, sultry voice. He was also the much better-looking brother, usually the rougher of the two.

But this time it was Julio who took the violence too far last night, shooting the feisty geezer.

"I didn't try to kill him. El hombre was gonna hurt you bad with his sharp dagger umbrella. I had to do something fast. So, I shot him. It was a reflex. A defensive move."

"Sí, but you almost killed the fucker, you dummy. Now what the hell do I tell the judge bitch daughter we're bribing? She's not going to sway a murder trial jury if she thinks her gringo daddy is dead." Rodrigo storms out of the bedroom to grab a beer from the broken down fridge which couldn't really keep anything cold. This place, on the nasty edge of the Tenderloin, was their hideout away from their Cartel leader uncle's mansion which sat on a hill overlooking the coast. They did the dirty work out of this dingy, centrally located two room apartment. Rodrigo hated this place. It was dismal; but admittedly convenient for their devilish deeds.

Julio stands up, looking down at the old man; getting worried, more nervous about what went down. Did he really kill this 75 year old millionaire? He shot him in the stomach, not through the heart. He shouldn't die. Julio bends down to look more closely at the skinny man propped up in the closet. "Ven aquí. Ven aquí. Rodrigo, he's movin'! I saw his hand move; and now his leg. Ven aquí!" Rodrigo rushes back into the room. He bends down and notes that the man's shirt, tie and pants are soaked through with dark blood. Wearing an expensive, fashionable suit, the dying gray-haired mustached man is wet with sweat. He smells rank.

"Julio, you lucky bastard! He's comin' around."

"I want my daughter," the old man mumbles. "Mar- Martina." The pain on his right side aches like hell. He groans. He wants to scream; but can't get any sound to come out.

"Julio. Ándale! Get the masking tape. Come on. Get it! He's conscious now. We need to shut him up quick."

Julio runs to the tiny kitchen, tries to open the squeaky paint-peeled drawer to get the tape out. Mierda!" He yanks it so hard, the drawer springs open; a load of other junk popping out, falling to the linoleum floor. "Ahh good, the tape!"

Rodrigo wraps the wide gray tape three times around the man's head, covering his mouth. "Go to the pharmacy, Julio. Buy some rubbing alcohol and some thick bandages. We're going to try to keep him alive. I don't know what the hell I'm doing but he better not die, for your sake – my brother." Rodrigo kicks Julio in the leg. "Move Julio. And get some breakfast stuff. It's almost morning. I'll call the fuckin' daughter after I get something in my stomach; give her instructions to follow if she wants her father back. That's what she gets for being a judge. That's what I'll tell her," he sneers.

Opening the door to the apartment, bandages, alcohol and pastries in his hands, Julio struggles to turn the key in the damaged lock. He fiddles with it, Finally, the door opens.

"About time!" Rodrigo yells out from the kitchen. "I just heard from César. He wanted to know if we got the old man last night. He said there was a fuckin' witness who saw us from that high class hotel restaurant window. I guess Hector, the waiter, informed César that there was some woman, sitting alone, watching the whole thing from her table."

"Qué? What do you mean, Rodrigo? The place was supposed to be closed for the night." Julio is panicked; his hands now clammy.

"Sí. She's some animal doctor who works in the city. We know who she is and where she lives. Her name is Dr. Jessi Salazar. I need to catch up with that woman – put her on the right path. You know what I mean?" Rodrigo checks his jean jacket pockets for his pistol.

Julio weakens, hearing this news. "Mierda, someone saw us with our masks and everything that we did? Fuck! We're cooked, Rodrigo! I'm not sure if the old man is still moving." Rodrigo sits down, rips a pastry out of the bag, and starts eating.

Julio slides down in the chair, his head in his hands. "I'm not the only one screwing up. What about Hector? He was supposed to make sure nobody dined in that restaurant last night. Damn it! What kind of back up is that?"

Rodrigo devours another pastry. "I need to call that Judge Wells, and find that veterinarian woman before the end of the day."

7

JUDGE WELLS PRESIDING

Judge Martina Wells presides over the Vicente Rodriguez murder trial. The defendant sits in the chair, his legs in chains. Eyes narrowed. He has long, slicked-back hair, thick eyebrows and a patch of dark fuzz protruding out from just under his lower lip. He looks mean, shows no emotion, as if he's bored with the process and with the players. Next to him, his fat attorney thumbs through papers and files. If things go as planned, Vicente would be out of here in a week or so. The Velasquez Cartel family would make sure of it.

He had weakened in the jewelry store, and killed the Asian sales girl. A stuck up San Francisco bitch. She deserved it. He decided to kill her when she didn't hand over the 10 carat diamond necklace – the whole reason for the robbery. The other booty was just a dollop of whipped cream on the ice cream sundae. I asked her twice, the bitch. She didn't think I'd do it. I could see her dark eyes widen in total surprise when I pulled the trigger. It was 5:03 p.m. He saw the clock on the wall above him reflected in the mirror. Shot her in her pretty, painted face; knocked her over in less than a split second, her red blood splattering on the glass behind her. Vicente immediately went for the back door. Bad luck. A cleaning woman was there, just outside the ritzy jewelry store, waiting for it to close. He had managed to disable the camera in the store; blocking any videotaping of his actions. But the cleaning woman was not predictable. She had all her gear, including a large rolling cart sitting there right next to her. When Vicente opened the store's back door, ready to bolt, he tripped over the equipment and fell to the ground, his gun sliding away from him; the cleaning woman now yelling in Spanish at the top of her lungs. Twisted his fuckin' ankle. The sales girl must have hit a button just before he shot her.

The police found him laying there on the ground. The cleaning woman's dirty bucket of water spilled all over his pant leg, the diamond necklace in his jean jacket pocket along with five pairs of expensive ruby earrings, four emerald rings, and three diamond bracelets. The young policewoman bent down next to him, flashing her badge in his face, while the male cop grabbed his hands from behind, locking them in handcuffs. Vicente reacted like a wild animal and lunged at the bitch cop, taking a bite out of her exposed inside arm just after she raised her metal badge again, pressing it against his cheek. She screamed. Wailed. He was satisfied with her response. He could see the dark red liquid sputtering out of her arm. He could taste it; almost sweet, warm on his tongue. The male cop quickly came from behind, and punched Vicente head on in the face three times; angry with himself for trusting any "perp" in his possession. Vicente felt the crushing pain, the blood dripping down from his nose. Bastard! "Mistreatment of captors," Vicente yelled out. "Fuckin' cops." He wanted to punch him back, but the cuffs were tightly secured. His leg was killing him. He was trapped.

Today, at the San Francisco Superior Court, Judge Martina Wells is hungry to nail this guy. Life imprisonment – minimum, she thinks. Both she and the D.A., Sanjay Dalla, were both anxious to get the death penalty in this case. Jury selection looked good, and Dalla's team was ready to pounce on the defense attorney who was already squirming, nervous defending his client, son of a Cartel leader. Dalla's skilled prosecutor, Max Dunlop, would certainly be triumphant. The evidence appeared straightforward and concrete. Martina needed to check herself, careful to keep an open mind. New evidence could possibly crop up.

She needed to try to maintain a balanced view throughout the process.

The actual trial would officially start tomorrow. The press couldn't wait to begin reporting. The sketch artists were on hand to draw portraits, documenting the reactions and expressions of both sides. Cameras would be permitted only when the verdict was read. A group of 5 or 6 tough looking, tattooed Latinos, several of them shaved bald, filled the chairs in the spectators' gallery. The victim's Vietnamese family members huddled together, most of them in tears; tissues under their noses.

An announcement is made. "Her honor, Judge Martina Wells will now address the court." Already seated, having observed the finalization of the jury members, Martina speaks with confidence and gravity. "We are here in the San Francisco Superior Court to embark on a murder trial. The accused, Vicente Rodriguez, is alleged to have murdered Sienna Vo at the Miracle Jewelry Mart location, approximately two weeks ago. The prosecution is seeking the death penalty in this case. For that reason, I anticipate that courtroom proceedings will be quite intense. For jury members, I have some direct guidance before we embark on this case, which is expected to take 1-2 weeks of your time. Defense attorney, Gregory Harris and prosecuting attorney, Max Dunlop, will each deliver their opening statements first thing tomorrow morning at 9 a.m. My advice to you is to listen carefully. Stay alert. Don't miss a thing presented. As we move through the trial, please take my comments and guiding orders very seriously. Evidence will be thrown out by me if it doesn't meet the standards set by the court. Objections will be made the attorneys. Some will be sustained and others will be overruled. I trust in your care to discard from your mind something that is thrown out because it is deemed as inadmissible. Have I been clear? Are there any questions?"

The twelve jury members look around at each other, 4 men and 8 woman. Some of them scan the room, and others peer over at the two attorneys who are standing behind their chairs.

Gregory Harris, the Defense attorney, already looks tired from the day's events. It's been a long one; including the final hammering out of the agreed selection of jury members. Sanjay, the DA, appears ruthless, ready for Max Dunlop to rip into Vicente, the evil-looking defendant.

Martina speaks into her microphone with one closing comment. "Remember, you will be asked to make the best decision possible, based on all the facts you hear in the case, to determine one of two things; whether the defendant is guilty of murder beyond a reasonable doubt, or whether there is, in fact, insufficient evidence to convict on the murder count. Please rest tonight and be fresh in the morning to start listening carefully at 9 a.m. sharp. See you then." She bangs her gavel twice and stands, stepping down from her elevated desk area. She eyes her court clerk and says, "I'll be in chambers, Corey. I have a lot of work to do before tomorrow."

8

A SHOCK IN CHAMBERS

Martina slings off her black robe, hanging it on the antique iron coat rack by her office door. Just under 110 pounds and at 5'3" tall, she could never find a judge's robe that fit her well from the choices available in the stock catalogues. She'd been meaning to have her admin. look into having a few customized robes designed for her petite frame. At 6'3" tall, her father towered over her. Martina's mother had passed away from heart failure, almost three years ago. She had been frail, standing just 5 feet tall. Martina inherited her mother's body type – slim and petite, with unusually small hands. Sometimes in court, it appeared as if she were a little girl in the midst of imaginary play, pretending to be the judge; until she spoke. Then, it was crystal clear that she was masterful and in total control of the courtroom.

Eager for this murder trial to begin, Martina is determined to read every brief, every document, every shred of evidence and any information she can get her hands on this afternoon. Her father is taking her to dinner at Les Saisons, a trendy new, French restaurant with good reviews; featuring an inventive new chef who specializes in exotic sauces. Kicking off her tight high heels and laying back in her leather-cushioned mahogany desk chair, she reaches for her tortoise shell reading glasses. Her cell phone rings, the classical Mozart ring tone wafting across her office. Her legal clerk walks in holding several thick files for her perusal. "Corey, can you hand me my cell phone from the robe hanging there? I left it in the side pocket." Corey retrieves the phone and passes it swiftly to Martina. "Here you go, Judge."

"Good afternoon. Judge Wells, speaking."

The voice on the other end is deep, with measured phrasing; the Latino accent instantly locking in her attention. "Are you alone, Judge Martina Wells? Because I have important news about your father, and it's not good!" Shaken, her hands start to tremble. She struggles to the hold the small phone, her right hand barely cooperating. Her brain bending, she imagines the worst.

"Corey. This is a private call." She says this a little too abruptly with a stern command. Corey is startled. She signals for him to disappear. The hefty court clerk nods and tiptoes out of the judge's chambers, closing the door behind him.

Rodrigo, the felon on the other end, notices her pause. "Bueno. Bravo. Sounds like you handled that well. Got rid of your visitor. Hopefully, you will continue to take my directions very seriously." He chuckles. She has a visceral reaction to the sound of his voice. "Who is this, and what about my father? Where is he?"

"Sí, the old man. Nice suit. Too feisty. That's my personal opinion. A fucking elitist snob!" He laughs again, the guttural sound coming from a deep, sinister place. "Oh, pardon me. You are a lady and a judge. Lo siento. My regrets. I almost forgot about the status of your position, your power."

His evil undertone cuts straight through her body. Her neck is stiff; cramped up.

"Oh my God. Is he okay? Are you with him?"

Yes, of course, we have him here, although he's all tied up right now. I'm afraid he cannot talk to you. His mouth is well-taped. Do you want him back or should I kill him?"

"What?" She's horrified.

"Sí, hard to believe, but sometimes a family member may decide no, just kill him. Gracias." Rodrigo laughs again as he stands with one foot pressed down on the ripped up plastic seat cushion of the cheap kitchen chair; playing with the long metal keychain which falls from the belt loop on his jeans. A cluster of heavy keys jingles along with a pen knife, its metal cover etched with the Cartel's insignia. He flips the knife open and begins digging out the dried blood from under one of his fingernails, putting his phone on speaker mode so he can use both hands.

Martina disintegrates in her chair, breaking down; a foreign sensation for her. Her usual confidence is melting away. Tears drip onto her burgundy desk pad. She tries to mask her emotions, her throat tight; constricting.

"Sounds like I have your attention," he says in his thick accent.

Is he Mexican, Columbian, Peruvian? I wish I knew. Martina has no idea what this man wants but she's sure it has to do with money. Ransom. He must be "kidnapping" for money, targeting her real estate tycoon father's millions. She has access to his money, and this guy probably knows it. Parker Wells made sure of that about a year ago. "Yes, you have my attention," she responds.

"Bien. Now, I will give you the targeted mission and clear instructions. If the goal is accomplished, you get the old man back. If not, your loving padre, Mr. Parker Wells, is dead at the end of the trial. The **day** the trial ends. Comprendes?"

She can't talk. The trial? The murder trial for Vicente Rodriguez. Oh shit, she thinks. She sits in silence; her world turned upside down.

"Sí?" He commands her to answer.

Martina snaps out of her shock. "Y-yes, I understand." She tries to hold it together. "I understand."

"Bien. You will sway the jury. Achieve a 'not guilty' verdict any way you can. Throw out the DA's evidence. Find excuses for the jury to not consider some of the facts. Guide them! Do whatever is needed. Stay professional, entiendes?"

"S-sí."

"Leave no doubt in anybody's mind. You have a reputation as a commanding and tough judge. So, this time, be tough on the prosecution! Vicente Rodriguez must get off, be acquitted. The DA must not be able to prove he committed the murder."

Her grip on the cell phone tightens, her chambers swirling around her as she continues listening to this hateful brute. "But I can't. My integrity as a judge is on the line. I don't have that power, anyway. It will be too difficult, too obvious. There must be a…"

"Shut the fuck up! I was trying to be nice, but I can get very nasty. Nasty, Sssssss - like a poisonous snake; commit unthinkable acts, like shooting daddy right in the head. Bang! Bang!" He grins. "I'm a good actor. Please listen carefully, Judge Wells. I want to see steady progress or I will start cutting. Snip! Snip! Let's see, I think a *pinkie*, that's how you say it in English, correct? Si, the right pinkie will go first. Tomorrow you will start influencing, using your charisma. Oooh, I love that word, don't you? *Charisma!*" he yells. *"Charisma!"* he whispers. It must have a Spanish derivation. It's so beautiful! He pauses. "So - you understand the plan? We have an agreement then, for the sake of your dear father?"

Martina cannot speak; shocked at what she's just heard from this strange man. Her head spins into a disoriented orbit she never knew existed; her integrity beginning a hasty slide down a dark tunnel of no return.

"Don't make me repeat my question." Rodrigo screams into his cell phone, almost jolting Martina off her chair. "Say yes, pig judge! Worse than a blood-sucking lawyer!"

The old man lays crumpled up inside the small dimly lit, smelly closet. He hears Rodrigo's yelling from the other room. He recognizes the voice. It's coming from the tall one. A moment ago, he thought he heard his daughter's voice. Martina. How? That's impossible. Those assholes. I should have poked his eyes out with my umbrella before the other one shot me. Shit! The pain. His legs seem to have numbed up. He notices that his breathing is steadily becoming more shallow as the minutes pass; in the process of his life slipping away. The blood puddle on the floor is dried and sticky; and more blood seems to keep spreading over his clothes and across the stained carpet in new directions. Parker can't really move to do any further inspection of his condition. *If I didn't have this damn tape on my mouth, I could plead with them to take me to a doctor. Is it my money they want?* Something tells him it's more than that.

Exhausted, Martina pleads. "Yes! Yes, I will do what you say. I beg you, just don't hurt my father. He's frail. He has medical issues. How do I really know he's okay? Give me some proof. God, please, pl…"

Click. The dial tone cuts her off.

9

PICNIC AND BLUEBERRY PIE

Holding hands, as they exit the De Young Museum situated in the middle of Golden Gate Park, Nick leads Jessi to his car. "Impressionism – you gotta love it!" He smiles, then rolls his eyes.

"Well, I actually enjoyed it; especially Monet's rendition of the setting sun over the River Seine." Her preferred artists included Monet, Renoir, and Cezanne – all Impressionists.

"Yeh, but did you see the review from the art critic posted above that painting, written at the time it was actually done? It read something like, 'Monet, the so-called artist's setting sun looks more like a slice of tomato slapped up and pasted into the Parisian sky.' That was hilarious."

Jessi frowns.

"I'm just teasing you, Jessi. I know the reviews were up there to highlight the absurdity of the critics' comments regarding a great talent such as Monet. But sometimes I like to see artists use right angles. I'm an engineer. Impressionism seems to favor round, curved shapes – no hard edges; and fuzzy people. This is why I like Picasso or Kandinsky; even Warhol. Clear edges, lots of solid primary colors." Nick lifts the picnic basket and the blue plaid blanket from the trunk of his Volvo.

He's so practical, she thinks to herself.

"We both like blueberry pie, right? Even if we have different preferences in art. I made the pie with my own hands," he boasts. "No hazy impressions used there – the authentic required ingredients utilizing right angled baking tools. Okay, okay, I'm exaggerating. There *was* the roller for the dough – kind of cylindrical, hmm?"

"See. You used curved objects after all." She pokes him in the ribs. He almost drops the picnic basket.

"Hey! Hey! You're going after a man with his arms full." He leads her to the perfect picnic spot under a sprawling oak tree. Jessi spreads the blanket on the grass while Nick sets out the food and the wine.

She takes in the variation of foods sitting before her. "A feast for the eyes," she says, impressed.

He nods. "Yes, you are an incredible feast for the eyes. Look how cute you are with that black and white-ribboned hat, and that pretty patterned sun dress." He playfully pulls her down to the blanket.

"This old thing? $20. I bought it in Santa Cruz, at a flea market. But I love the compliments. Keep them coming!"

He takes her hand and gently molds it around a clear plastic wine glass. "Yeh, I went all out creating just the right ambiance for today's lunch." She giggles. He pours her some chardonnay. "So, looks like you're recovered from the other night's mixed birthday dinner and events." He clears his throat in jest. "No, seriously, Jessi. Is everything back to normal for you? I haven't seen any news about an abduction or shooting in San Francisco over the past two days. Not on TV, not in the papers, not even on the internet."

She takes a long sip. "I've been looking for that too! Nothing! I do have an imagination and who knows, maybe I was a little buzzed and high from the pills; just fell asleep and had a bad dream, like you said. All is good!" She toasts him. "Here's to me feeling much better – no tooth pain and minimal emotional stress compared to the other night. Cheers!" They drink. "And by the way, the Giants took it big time last night. What a fun belated birthday event. Only bad thing is that I ate every last garlic fry at AT&T Park."

"Don't remind me. You went to the game, and I worked until midnight. You brat!"

Her cell phone rings out. Flight of the Bumble Bee ring tone. It's a phone number from her past. It's Dierdre, her ex-boy-friend's grandmother. I wonder if Stefan put her up to that. The elegant Dierdre Van Oeterloo, now in her late 70's, an esteemed member of San Francisco's symphonic society. Dierdre, so proud of her talented grandson, the orchestra's premiere violinist. Despite her awareness of his constant deceit and weakness for attractive women, his grandmother still loved him uncondition-ally. He was her jewel. He dedicated his life to the violin, and to juggling females. Of German-Austrian descent, witty and classy, Jessi had enjoyed the connection to Dierdre, who had always been kind to her throughout the three years she and Stefan were a couple. Dierdre was disappointed when they split up, suspect-ing that Stefan's incessant unfaithfulness must have been the ultimate breaking point for Jessi.

"Nick, I'm sorry. I need to take this call."

"No problem." He gets up. "I'll take a little walk."

"No. No. Stay here. It will be brief. I'm sure of it." He sits back down and pours a little more wine for himself; then tends to slice his prize pie.

"Hello. This is Jessi."

"Oh. It's really you, Jessi. I miss your optimistic voice; always so cordial. What are you doing right now?"

"W-well, I'm in the park with a friend. We just visited the Impressionist exhibition at the De Young."

"That's lovely, dear. You are such a class act, always appreciat-ing the beautiful things in life. I don't want to keep you, but I have a favor to ask."

"Sure. Anything." Jessi missed Dierdre; especially just hang-ing out at her mansion with her two Springer spaniels and play-ing gin rummy late into the evening while both of them sipped hundred year old brandy. The old woman was ruthless; played a mean card game.

"Today, I turn 80 years old. Can you imagine it? I'm what they call a genuine octogenarian." Her voice cracks a little with the multi-syllabic word.

"Congratulations, Dierdre. That's right! We're both Virgos. My birthday was a couple of days ago."

"Yes, dear. I'm so sorry I missed your birthday. Well, I'd still like to celebrate with you. That's why I'm calling you. You see, tonight at Golden Gate Fields, there's a private birthday party for me at The Turf Club. Yes, a real dress-up affair. I plan on crawling into the giant chasm of extreme old age with my dignity in place, and having a good time. I want you to be there to enjoy it with me. A crazy old woman's request, I know. Sorry for the last minute invitation. First, I thought it might be awkward, because of you and Stefan; but when I woke up this morning, I had this overwhelming urge to call you. You are the number one person I want to have at my party. I miss you."

"Oh Dierdre. I miss you, too."

"Tell me, dear, how is your veterinary practice doing?"

"Uh. Fine. In fact, it's thriving!"

"Fabulous, my darling girl. You are beautiful and successful, as usual. So, you will be there tonight? Yes? I'm sending a limo for you at 7:30. Same address as before?"

"Yes, I haven't moved, but…"

"It's only one o'clock in the afternoon. You have several hours before the car arrives. Just enjoy your day. We'll have plenty of time to catch up tonight."

"Okay, Dierdre. It's good to hear from you." Jessi melts with happiness. Estranged from her cheating father and her mother now having passed away, she had appreciated Dierdre's motherly care and attention.

Jessi could almost smell the fragrance of Dierdre's unforgettable Chanel number 5. The woman is always regal, charming and consistently authentic. "See you tonight then." She disconnects before Jessi can say anything else.

"I'm so sorry Nick. That was an old friend. She's turning 80 today. I hope that I have near her vigor and vitality when I'm 65; let alone when I'm 80 years old."

"Whoa. Jessi, there's no need to rush life along like that." They both laugh. She takes a bite of his heavenly blueberry pie, loving the fact that he bakes, and she doesn't.

"It's getting warm. That sun is hot. I don't need this jacket," he says. Standing up, he mimes, as if stripping for money; slowly removing his navy blue cotton golf jacket. Dum dum dum de dum dum dum." He takes off the jacket one sleeve at a time. Under it, he wears a Hawaiian style button up silk shirt. But instead of palm trees scattered about the pattern of the shirt, there are colorful feathered parrots sprinkled everywhere, all set upon the lush leaf-green background. Nick sits back down on the blanket.

"Nice shirt!" She feels the creamy fabric. Then suddenly, her eyes cannot believe what she sees. "Nick, is that Pedro, your parrot, all over your shirt? Oh my God. And what the hell! Are those word balloons, with little phrases coming out of Pedro's mouth? Wait, is that a picture of you feeding him?"

He nods nonchalantly as if bored with the shirt; and gobbles down a chunk of blueberry pie using his fingers. He's tickled that she's so amused, hopefully impressed with his ingenuity.

Jessi starts reading the shirt, going from one word balloon to the next. She laughs as she speaks, almost losing control. She reads the first one, "Nick wants pie! Nick wants pie!" The next one, left side on his chest, reads, "Nick loves Pedro!" The one on his right sleeve reads, "Pedro rules the rainforest. Squawk! Squawk!" Laughing so hard, she rolls Nick onto the blanket with her, tickling him until he can't take it anymore. "How in the world did you get this shirt made?"

He sits up and proudly blows on his fingers, brushing them against his shirt, beaming from his creative accomplishment. It worked! He got her to have a great time today, despite the other night's emotional trauma. "I had the shirt designed especially for me, and Pedro. Uh huh! My parrot has a shirt exactly like this one. You've got to see it!"

"No! Stop it! You're kidding!" She collapses in stitches again, just visualizing the bird wearing it.

He whips out his iPhone and pulls up a photo. "Damn – it *is* Pedro!" she exclaims. "And, he's wearing the identical shirt." She can even make out the captions inside the miniature word balloons. "You have fallen over the edge, down into the crevice of craziness, Mr. Daniels. I better call the medics. You need help!" She falls over in tears - her wine spilling everywhere on the blanket.

"A sloppy drunk I see. I have no idea what may have caused this behavior, Dr. Salazar." He roots around in his wicker picnic basket and brings out a plastic bag with some fabric inside. "And look what I found in here for you." He pulls out an identical Hawaiian Pedro shirt.

"Nick! She holds it up. "My size! It's ideal for the office!" She hugs him. "Oh, I'm so sorry. I hate to rush you, but I've got to leave soon. I said 'yes' to my friend's birthday party tonight, and I have no idea what to wear."

He drives Jessi home from Golden Gate Park, taking short-cuts to expedite their journey; both of them in carefree moods, He gives her a kiss before she gets out to walk up her mosaic-trimmed front steps. He doesn't really know where she's off to tonight except that it involves a party for Jessi's 80 year old friend. "Enjoy yourself Doc; and congratulate your friend on her formidable feat!" He wonders if it has anything to do with her ex-boyfriend, Stefan. At this stage in their relationship, it's still not quite his business. "I'll buzz you tomorrow, and maybe we can spend the evening together, gazing at the stars. I have a special viewing place. How does that sound?"

"Um, sure Nick. I hope it involves your homemade baked goods. I'm stuffed from that gourmet pie but I love your treats! So delicious." She pecks him on the cheek.

"Great. How about if you also come by tonight after the birth-day party? I'd love to snuggle."

"Oh, I'm not so sure. Depends on the time; but I'll call you later. I promise."

Disappointed he didn't get a clear "yes" for tonight, he drives away thinking maybe he's being too needy. Man up, Nick Daniels! You're just falling in love. Damn it!

10

PENSIVE BEFORE THE POUNCE

What the hell should she wear tonight? The outfit selection for this evening with Dierdre needs to read simply elegant, and formal! Ahh, what about the velvet emerald evening gown, decorated with an edging of small crystal rhinestones across the plunging neckline? She snagged the pricey Calvin Klein designer frock at Neiman Marcus; their annual Evening Wear sale – about a year ago. She wore it for her friend's dreamy wedding held at Wente Winery. Dierdre hasn't seen it and for that matter neither has Stefan. Why even think of Stefan? She knew he'd be front and center at his Grandmother's "once in a lifetime" 80th birthday shindig. I guess it's a way to see him without making any direct contact beforehand. Jessi still ached for his touch. She also hated him.

She refused to take his calls since that dark day at Symphony Hall just four months ago. Does he know that Dierdre invited Jessi to share in the occasion tonight? Or, was he pulling the strings behind the scenes, manipulating his own grandmother with the goal of connecting with the now elusive Jessi Salazar? Of course, Dierdre was equally cagey, one of the richest women in California; matriarch to a large German conglomerate. As the Chair of the Board of Directors, she didn't need to be actively involved everyday in the business; but she was clearly in the company's power seat. She controlled the family fortune, owning 80% of the two billion dollar privately held food company, left behind by her husband, who passed away over 15 years ago. 20%

of the company was owned by Stefan, her only grandchild. Her plan all along was to leave everything to Stefan. His inheritance would be extraordinary, and he knew it! Dierdre had her concerns about how he might handle such an extraordinary windfall. But, that's life.

Jessi gazes out her condominium's bay window. She has a bird's eye view of the Bay Bridge. She preferred this bridge to the more famous Golden Gate; and now they were lighting it up at night, like a diamond necklace. Lucky for her! Dr. Pepper jumps up on the printed, cushioned chair, and then leaps onto the table.

Stefan had ripped her heart right out; in a blink. She trembles now when she thinks of him; painfully recalling the very last time she saw him. Her plan, that day, was to surprise Stefan with a delicious lunch at Maxwell's, just across the street from Symphony Hall where he was in rehearsal.

It was almost noon as she opened the door to the theatre. The musicians usually broke for lunch just before noon for about two hours; then had a quick meeting after lunch before all musicians went away to relax and change into their black tuxedos and evening gowns. The theatre was empty when Jessi entered. She walked down to the orchestra pit and climbed the stairs up to the stage. Her plan was to surprise him in his dressing room. He liked to be alone in there; connecting with his violin, practicing his solos or cleaning the Stradivarius with his special tools and fluids. As the lead violinist, Stefan was given his own special suite away from the other musicians. Like the conductor, he got the royal treatment – both of them with scads of adoring fans. Stefan was also featured on the marquis; top billing.

Jessi never made it to his dressing room. Pushing through the stage's heavy red curtain, there he was with Claudia, the young, sexy French cellist. Sprinkling her neck with kisses, it appeared that he was ravaging her right there in the wings. Anyone could walk by. Why wasn't he at least in his dressing room? Jessi stood there silently and watched for a few more moments. Stefan teased Claudia's breast, squeezing it, as she moaned with pleasure. Then, he heard something, and turned around. Their eyes connected.

"Spoiled pig," Jessi screamed. "Bastard." She ran, tripping on the stairs, falling down. Picking herself up, tears streaming down, she managed to bolt from the theatre. She knew Stefan was a flirt, but hadn't realized that he was an absolute cad.

He ran after her, grabbed her by the arm. "Jess. Jess. Stop! Listen…that was nothing. She's nobody to me. Zero." He said it in his confident upper class German-Swiss accent. "It was just a dalliance; a meaningless flirtation!" He attempted to plead with her, but wasn't very convincing.

Did he think she was an idiot? That she would say "Fine, Stefan. No problem. Thanks for telling me or better yet thanks for letting me know, by accident." He could see that she was devastated, but he was somewhat puzzled that she hadn't realized before that he possessed more than a wandering eye. Had she been blind? He stood there, bewildered.

Jessi broke loose from his grip, and darted down the busy San Francisco street. He phoned her more than twenty times, sent dozens of texts; even had Dierdre call her. She did not respond. A stake had been shoved into her heart. It was the story of her father all over again.

Jessi had adored her father, Denny Salazar. He taught her everything about the rainforest; the animals and plants. Jessi also loved being with her best friend, Rico. She had a crush on him; but if she had a choice of spending an afternoon with her father versus Rico, she would choose her father in a split second. Denny was charismatic, brilliant, compassionate, and made her giggle with delight. He told the goofiest jokes; but he was always made her giggle. He called Jessi the mini Dr. Doolittle of the Panama rainforest; because she spoke the language of the jungle creatures. He admired the undeniable natural bond she had with all living things.

Denny, who left New York City to become a jungle guide, was proud of his talented daughter. He would point out to the tourists how the animals naturally flocked to his daughter; parrots, macaws, iguanas, snakes, monkeys - all of them. She was an animal magnet. She was relatively unaware of her innate skills even when her daddy made a big deal about it. In total awe of Denny, she followed him everywhere, accompanied him often on his guided expeditions with tourists. He'd say, "Jessi, my little jungle girl, will now talk to you about the Panama tree sloth. She is the pre-eminent mini Dr. Doolittle. Just listen to her and watch, as she describes and imitates the animals. She can spot a sloth in 30 seconds. She'll demonstrate that to you today. I'll put money on it!" Then, he'd step back giving Jessi a deep royal bow, handing over the rainforest stage to her.

Jessi thought about the times she had with her father at Rainbow Lodge, a special nature resort owned by her father's good friend, Tikko. Denny often took her to the lodge in the deep jungle, an hour's walk from her own house. The most memorable time was one day when she was about six years old. They were at the lodge spending the afternoon. Tikko and her father sat relaxed on the porch, sharing wild jungle stories. Jessi was playing with Tikko's two pet parrots, Zsa Zsa and Benny. She was happily swinging in a hammock, just a few feet away. Tikko's wife, Cora, brought out some special treats gifted to her from a family of tourists from Oregon – a plate stacked with Oreos and Mint Milano cookies; almost impossible to purchase in any grocery store in Panama. She served them up with some home-made mango punch. The smell and the taste of the cookies and punch stayed with Jessi for years. Cora sat down on a rocking chair next to the hammock, chatting with Jessi about the various birds in the rainforest; teaching her how to differentiate their sounds, then having Jessi imitate each distinct species of bird. Jessi followed Cora's lead as they reviewed a laminated card which detailed the local birds; including a colorful picture of each one. Denny and Tikko were busy, discussing new ideas for nature excursions and sharing tales of frightened tourists, who came to explore Panama but were often intimidated by the plethora of multi-colored insects and animals; even scared of the standard iguana. At the end of the afternoon, Jessi put on a show for her father, Tikko, and Cora; describing the birds one by one - what they liked to eat, their daily habits, and their primary mode of protection against bigger birds or animals which typically preyed on them. Then she transitioned into the dramatic part of her show, mimicking each bird's unique call; its typical chirps and sounds. Her audience applauded after each and every one of her bird imitations. She remembered how her dad laughed so hard that day; his tears flowing down his cheeks as he drank a beer and enjoyed the day with his friends and daughter.

That night, Tikko invited Denny and Jessi to spend the night in the open air, top floor lodge room; the most expensive of all his small resort accommodations. A rich couple from Chicago had cancelled their stay at the last minute. It was there for Denny and Jessi to enjoy. The room featured a king-sized antique wrought iron bed, a huge flowing, white net surrounding it. Jessi and Denny accepted Tikko's invitation, and spent most of the night awake in the bed, with a flashlight they shined on the array of colorful insects taking off and landing on the net's surface. Denny pulled out his book of Panama insects, and identified every insect clinging to the net. Jessi's life with Denny had consisted of one learning experience after another; non-stop.

She truly felt like a princess; not only because of her father's handsome smile, not because of the accolades from group after group of tourists who had been thankful to escape their mundane urban jungles. No, it was because of her father's pride in his little mini Dr. Doolittle; how he lit up every morning when she came into her parent's room, jumping on their bed, eager for the day to begin.

Her mother, Loretta, was quiet and reserved; a contrast to Denny. She consistently responded to her husband's needs; took good care of him, was his loyal follower; rarely an initiator of activities or family outings. From the day she gave up her financial career on Wall Street, she dedicated her life to making Denny happy; supporting his wild desire to become a naturalist. Denny called all the shots in the household. Before they left New York for the rainforest, he had completed his Master's Degree in Animal Science at Columbia University while his wife gave birth to Jessi, and worked ten hour days for two years after her daughter was born. Upon graduating, Denny announced the big move to Panama. Loretta was more than happy to leave the city and become a full time parent to her daughter. They looked forward to their new life.

Then, one day in the wet rainforest, when Jessi was almost 13 years old, she made an ugly discovery. It was one of those days when Jessi was spending the afternoon with recently turned 13 year old Rico, together swinging in a hammock, teasing each other just like every other day. But what was different that day was that Rico had kissed her; just a quick, sweet peck on the lips. His lips were moist and soft. They confessed their feelings for one another; vowing to stay together forever. For an hour, they sat there quietly, each creating a special ring for the other from the various colored marsh reeds in the swamp. Rico made her a ring which resembled an engagement ring, with a little knot on top, imitating a sizable diamond. She made him a simple band; of four or five different colors and tones of reed. They used branches to cut the reeds and shape them into woven cylinders. They giggled and joked as they crafted their promise rings. After placing the ring on the other's wedding ring finger, they rocked together in the hammock, taking in the sounds of the jungle; gazing up at the thick canopy of trees, spotting a monkey here and there, then a small flock of brilliant feathered parrots. Today, they held each other for the first time; romantic confessions now out in the open. An early teen couple in love. Rico thought about touching her breast, but changed his mind, not wanting to frighten her or think he was going too fast.

The Panama sun was setting. Jessi had committed to her sick mother that she'd be home well before dark. Loretta had been ill for some months with a serious lung disease; possibly cancer, which she hadn't explicitly shared; but Jessi had read about it when they went to the village, on the library's old computer. Her mother would cough all night, and the roof would shake. Alone in her bed late at night, Jessi would cry. Wave a magic wand. Anything. just please God, make her better. Her father told Jessi that Loretta wished to be private about her ailment; not spend time talking about it which would probably only make her feel worse.

"Rico, I'm afraid about what my parents might say if they find out about us kissing and…"

"I understand, Jessi."

Rico pulled Jessi out of the hammock and placed the second kiss of the afternoon, on her young lips. Then, he led her to the base of the mangrove tree. "Before you go, let's put our rings in a safe place." He took out a small pouch he had crafted while Jessi had been busy finishing up his promise ring. The pouch was made of two thick slices of tree bark and threaded with a narrow reed, woven between the parts like a shoestring. "Each day, after school, we'll fetch our rings from this pouch, and wear them while we swim and play; but only 'we' will know they exist. It will be our romantic secret.

"Yes, I like it," Jessi beamed. Rico buried the pouch with the two rings in a deep hole at the base of the tree. They left each other that afternoon after dozens of intimate promises, going in different directions to their homes on the opposite edges of this patch of rainforest. Usually only a 20 minute walk, unless it was raining hard, Jessi decided to take her favorite shortcut. She could feel the threat of an imminent downpour as the rainy season was about to break in Panama.

There he was, her father, tucked under a lush tree, basting some woman with his kisses; the female body's clothes tossed aside. Oh my God, it's Rico's mother, Carina. It was the end of the world as she knew it; as if the light in her heart was instantly burned out. She could almost hear it in her head; just like the second when a light bulb snaps; making a faint, little sound. And then, it's suddenly black. The hot rain started pouring down. She stayed out of sight. Even in the deluge, they continued their feverish kissing, moving in their syncopated, coupled rhythm. It didn't seem that either Carina or Denny had any idea that Jessi was close by, that she was watching them as they wriggled around on a ragged hemp cloth in the dirt; their love-making, frantic. Then she heard her father whisper, "I love you Carina, my beautiful Carina. I love you, my angel. You are my *real* woman." Carina was born in Panama, into the Ngobe tribe. Her husband, of the same tribe, went off for weeks at a time to the cities, selling his local crafts. She was alone a lot.

Jessi ran away when she heard her father whisper those words of love to Carina. "You are my real woman." Am I his real Dr. Dolittle? Is my mom his real wife? The rain burst through the trees, in buckets. Jessi's hair instantly turned into long, dripping strings; slapping her in the face, as she ran faster and faster through the rainforest. Muddy puddles and rivulets sprung up everywhere. She cried and slipped; cried and slipped again; becoming muddier and muddier, as she navigated the final steep slope up to her weathered house. How can I live with him any longer? What can I do to get away from this place? Get away from Panama. Disappear. I hate him.

The very next day, she cut off her relationship with Rico, finding him down by the lagoon just opposite her favorite waterfall; their designated meeting place. Jessi hurriedly explained that she realized that she was just too young to get romantically connected. Being friends anymore was also not a good idea, since he had already kissed her. Their romance was simply a mistake, a bad mistake. Rico was bewildered, pleaded for her to spend more time discussing it; but she resisted. This went on for weeks. He tried to talk to her and she ignored him. He finally backed off, but from afar, he watched her day after day; his heart aching for the return of the days before their kiss.

Her cat, Pandora, nips at her earring, bringing Jessi back to the present. Her eyes flood with tears. Why do I always go after bad boys? Why? Stefan and my two boyfriends before that also turned out to be unfaithful. Her thoughts chew her up as she watches the traffic go across the bridge. Is it because of my cheating father? The father I am estranged from now, the father I left behind when I was accepted at UC Berkeley? The father who watched my mother die just seven months after I came upon that torrid scene in the rainforest? Is that why I attract men who disappoint me?

She needed a shower, to refresh herself, then get dressed for Dierdre's party at the Turf Club. The limo would be here to pick her up in an hour.

11

THE TURF CLUB AND THE TERROR

Dierdre met Jessi personally at the Turf Club's entrance. The 80 year old "birthday girl" was immaculately and elegantly dressed. She wore a black chiffon gown with a brilliant diamond brooch at her throat.

"Jessi – my dear, you look stunning in emerald green. Your hair is lovely! With just a few hours notice, you walk in here like a princess. I'm without words, my dear." Jessi and Dierdre enter the party area together, arm in arm. Dierdre hugs Jessi's sleeve, grateful for her presence. They stop, each taking a champagne filled glass from the waiter's tray.

Just a few feet away, he stands there staring at her. Poised and polite, Stefan greets Jessi with his raised glass, sporting his self-assured, yet personable smile. Dierdre notices Stefan's gaze. She pulls Jessi to the side, away from the other guests. "Jessi, Stefan has been so upset for almost four months since the day you two parted. I've seen him break down and cry, dear. He regrets his indiscreet, hollow transgression with that musician. He's in love with you Jessi, and he wants you back." She notices Jessi's discomfort as her words spill out. She's said too much, and immediately goes silent.

"Dierdre, I don't know what to say."

"I understand your pain. Believe me dear. But I want to tell you a secret; something you don't know. Stefan had already bought you an engagement ring, planning to give it to you just a day after you found him embracing Claudia. I think Claudia had been constantly enticing him. She wore him down. He just weakened, probably nervous about popping the question to you. Scared that you'd turn him down. Let's face it. My grandson did a stupid, unsophisticated thing. But, I still love him and I think you do too."

"It's not that black and white, Dierdre. I was degraded, demoralized and I've moved on with my life. I'm in a good place. But I wanted to be with you tonight, just as you asked." Jessi takes the woman's delicate hands and looks into her beautiful blue eyes.

The violin starts to play. The crowd circles around him. Stefan is in his element; his eyes closed and his body swaying to the music, as the notes from his instrument float out across the huge glassed-in room; which has been decorated with tasteful lavender balloons and streamers. The instrumental is by Massine, titled Meditation. Jessi recognizes it. It's one of her favorites. He used to play it for her privately. Sometimes in the middle of the night, he'd surprise her; standing on the bed naked, his slender, yet muscular body over her. Each time she lay there waiting for his choice of melody, she hoped he would play Meditation! And he would satisfy her. "If this were heaven," she'd lay there and think, "I want to die!" The music would take her out of her body, back to her childhood in Panama and then back again into Stefan's bed. Even though he stood there playing the violin in the dark, she could feel him at the same time moving his body over hers; playing her like his treasured Stradivarius. His power, swirling around the high-ceilinged bedroom. He was always in tune, hitting the notes perfectly.

Now, at the Turf Club, he does it again. She fights it with her every fiber; but even standing there, surrounded by a hundred people, she can feel his hands move over her as he plucks and slides his fingers across the strings. Perhaps she imagines it, but she senses that he knows what she's going through even though his eyes are closed, and he's emotionally enraptured in the music. Then, she notices one moment where he opens his eyes and scans the room to place Jessi's exact location. He turns slightly more in her direction, closes his eyes again, never pausing his music. Nobody but the two of them realize that he's sending her a personal message through the lilting notes. "You've come back to me. You are here. Don't fight it, Jess."

Once he ends the mesmerizing piece, he carefully places his antique violin back in its case. He turns to move to his grandmother. A red-haired woman pushes past Jessi and Dierdre, running over to Stefan; wrapping her long arms around his neck, sprinkling him with small kisses. The woman runs her red lacquered fingernails down the front of his tuxedo. She doesn't stop at his waist. She slides the tip of her index finger down past his black cummerbund, almost publicly fondling him. He smiles and pushes her hand back up to his chest, a little taken aback by her bold move. Jessi remembers how women react to Stefan. Even Jessi had been guilty of this. With his cocky charisma, he owns every room he inhabits. Jessi was herself, magnetically attracted to this man.

When they were a couple, sometimes before Stefan would enter a room, Jessi would feel lifeless – like a pile of metal nails waiting to be swept up by his magnetism. When he was near, within reach, Jessi would come alive, feeling the heat of her raw physical attraction to him, just like this red-haired woman who threw herself on Stefan tonight. She understood it. Unfortunately, during their relationship, Jessi had become jealous and even angry when she'd witness women thrusting themselves at him. They seemed hypnotized by his European style, his streaked blonde hair, his crystal-clear ice blue eyes, his intelligent yet playful nature, and his giant musical talent. Every woman's fantasy.

Dierdre takes Jessi's hand and leads her over to Stefan. They are close enough now that they can hear the red-haired woman whisper in his ear, "Stefan, your talents go beyond the strings of your violin and I *fully* appreciate it." She reaches for a glass of champagne from the waiter, and hands it to Stefan. She smirks, strokes his chest again, and gazes into his eyes with her dirty expression.

Stefan nonchalantly throws her off and heads closer to Dierdre and Jessi. He raises his own glass of bubbly. "To my enchanting grandmother on her 80th birthday. May you live forever and a day!" Dierdre and Jessi raise their glasses, and sip in unison. His grandmother leans into him, "Stefan, who is that red-haired woman and what was she doing to you, my dear?"

"I've never seen her before. Personally, I think she resembles some alien species from another planet." He laughs. "She's probably just another violin groupie. They seem to be multiplying around me lately. It's my curse!" He smiles down at Jessi. "There's only one groupie I want in my life." Jessi can't help but be amused by his arrogance. That's how he greets me after all of these months. Cocky! He just can't help himself, she thinks. Somehow it heightens her attraction to him.

Jessi hears something unexpected come from a man standing just behind her, mumbling in a hushed tone to a woman next to him. "Yeh, that toast he just gave is not only for her 80 years on the planet but for her two billion dollars, a juicy inheritance for Stefan once she croaks." Jessi turns towards them and sees the painted botoxed face of his date. He looks rich and she looks cheap. The woman slaps the fat man on his wrist, and giggles at his sarcastic remark. Stefan notices Jessi glaring at the couple and gently pulls her over, engaging her, and his grandmother with his flattering question, "How are the two most fascinating women here? Grandmother, did you like the Massine piece I played? It was just for you." He winks at Jessi. She blushes.

"Most definitely, Stefan. You surprised me with it. I haven't heard you play that for ages. "You seem more energized and alive since Jessi has arrived. Dierdre gives her own toast. "It's been too long for you two to be apart." Stefan drinks to the toast. Jessi is perplexed about what to do, feeling uncomfortable with this interaction.

"Nightcaps at my Victorian in the city. Yes, ladies? Let's sneak out of here in a couple of hours. We must seal grandmother's celebration with a very special private toast this evening."

Jessi responds, "Um, listen Stefan, I-I." The dance band begins to play an old classic, "The Way You Look Tonight."

"No, no, no. You must say yes, yes, yes," he raises his voice over the music. "Otherwise, our birthday girl will be very displeased. She may never recover. Look at her." Dierdre pouts, feigning depression; then shoots Jessi a pleading stare.

"Of course, then." Jessi hugs Dierdre. "I don't want to disappoint my very favorite friend on her 80th birthday."

"Très bien. Très bien!" Stefan breaks in. "But for now, let's dance. Grandmother?"

"Stefan – would you do an old woman a favor? Dance this one with Jessi."

He raises his eyebrows and kisses his grandmother's neck, then her cheek. "Jessi, may I glide you across the dance floor to satisfy our birthday lady? The song is almost over now so I'm afraid you'll need to commit to a few more dances with me." He locks her in with his blue eyes and his saucy grin.

She chuckles at these two connivers. "Yes. Let's glide!" When he touches her back with his long fingers, chills tiptoe through her body. The evening flies by. She talks to many of his friends, having not seen them for months. His conductor is there with his own entourage. Everyone seems delighted to see Jessi, asking her about her practice, the animals, interested to hear any funny animal adventures she might have had over the past few months. Dierdre doesn't leave Jessi's side, introducing her to numerous people from the upper crust San Francisco art society. At about 10 p.m. Stefan assembles the three of them. "It's time for us to make our break back to my Victorian. I have the limo waiting for you both downstairs."

"Now, without saying goodbye?" Jessi asks. She looks from Stefan to Dierdre. They both nod.

"Yes, we'll just sneak away without any fuss," he says. "I'm driving the Audi; so I'll meet you there. I'm fast," he beams. "I'll be waiting for you." He kisses both of them on the cheek and strokes Jessi's long, dark hair, lightly brushing her earlobe. Jessi smiles, tingling inside, feeling her legs weaken beneath her. Then, he leaves.

Politely excusing herself, she tells Dierdre that she'll meet her outside the lobby where the limo will be waiting. "I just need to make a quick call and visit the restroom."

She finds an alcove where she phones Nick. He doesn't pick up so she leaves him a quick message, giving her regrets about not making it later tonight.

As she turns to the lobby entrance, a man from behind speaks in her ear, immediately commanding her attention. He has a Latino accent; a deep voice. "Ms. Jessi Salazar. No, don't turn around. Stay exactly as you are." Jessi feels something pushed into her back, a hard object. It could be his hand, or… Oh my God! Her mind races. She freezes. The guttural sound of his voice precipitates her panic. He sounds evil, chilling. Her heart beats like crazy. She can hear it in her head, pounding. Pounding.

"You saw nothing! Let me repeat. You saw nothing! Don't forget it. Don't make yourself or your close friends sorry. You know what I mean?" Then his tone softens. "If you agree to erase any incident involving trucks and limousines from your memory, then you will hear nothing more from me. Agreed Ms. Salazar? If yes, simply nod your head."

He pushes the object harder into her back. Jessi nods twice. Then – silence, except some jingling of keys or chains walking away, further and further away.

Jessi is suddenly back in the hub bub of people around her, all in the process of leaving Golden Gate Fields. She can make out dribbles of conversations not directed at her – comments about parties or company functions just attended. Jessi stands there; stunned, numb, scared. Her mind fractured, spiraling in all directions. She turns to see if the man is still in sight – anywhere in the vicinity. She has no idea what he looks like. She sees nobody suspicious. She moves hastily to the lobby entrance. Then she suddenly stops, fully internalizing the man's message. The two masked men abducting the old man. The horrible scene observed from the window. It all happened! It was real! Not just a bad dream, not some hallucination.

As she pushes the lobby door open, she sees Dierdre standing at the curb waiting for her. Did he mean he would hurt Dierdre or Stefan or …? Oh God. What about Myrna and Lance? Damn it! She approaches Dierdre, who looks pleased to see her. The old woman places her age-spot marked, yet graceful hand over Jessi's trembling hand. She doesn't comment on Jessi's distraught condition. Just as Jessi's about to explain that she needs to leave, go home – not take the limo to Stefan's house, Dierdre unsteadily leans into Jessi, losing her balance.

"I-I'm feeling faint. Oh my. Please. Please help me into the car."

"Yes, of course, Dierdre." Jessi opens the door to the limo and carefully seats her safely inside; then slides in beside her. "Are you okay, grandmother?" She reflexively calls her grandmother, like she used to do.

"Oh. Forgive me. I- I think I'm fine now, dear. Just a bit tired. I'm so happy you made it to my soiree, and now having a nightcap together at Stefan's; it's the best birthday present I could wish for." Jessi manages a smile in response and doesn't push the intent to excuse herself. She pats Dierdre's hand as they sit there in the back of the posh limo. Jessi shivers in her seat, still distracted by the Latin man's threats. After three glasses of champagne, she's feeling tipsy but perseveres to stay upbeat with Dierdre. The man said he wouldn't be back if she kept her mouth shut. That's my plan, she thinks, and looks straight ahead at the hazy street lamps as they move through the soupy, gray San Francisco fog.

12

THE SENSATION OF THE CELLAR

Stefan's magnificent Victorian sits high on a hill. The face of the house is like a fairy tale. He stands there at the tall, massive oak double entry door. He's changed his clothes, now wearing a pair of slim, off-white linen slacks and a navy blue cashmere v-neck sweater. A few strands of his blonde-streaked hair flop down in his face. He stands there ready to greet Dierdre and Jessi. He takes her breath away, holding the same exact stance she'd seen on the cover of San Francisco Magazine with the bold caption which read *Stefan - Violinist For All Seasons!* He was perfectly posed at the open Victorian door, his tall, thin body leaning to the side, Stradivarius violin in one hand and his bow in the other hand; an audacious smile on his face. The photograph appeared on the front of San Francisco Magazine just two months ago; two months after they split up. When Jessi saw it on the corner newsstand, her heart stopped. She bought two copies and stuffed them into her Louis Vuitton computer bag, rushing down the street to her office so she could close the door and dig into the article all about Stefan. Tonight, he wore the same outfit and stood in the identical pose featured in the magazine; except no violin in hand. Instead, he held two splendidly shaped brandy glasses.

"My two favorite women! Welcome!" Jessi helps Dierdre up to the door. Each is handed their filled brandy glass by the handsome master of the house. He leads them into his favorite room, where a wood-carved Italian fireplace roars with the most brilliant fire. "It's getting a little chilly out there; so I thought Louis XIV brandy in front of the fire would warm us up."

Jessi can't help but notice that the glass she's holding is of the finest crystal stemware. The artwork spread around the room is impressive. An original Rembrandt hangs above the mantle and a Turner on the wall behind the sofa. The coffee table is made of brown and gold etched leather books, stacked atop each other. Two velvet burgundy chairs frame the beautiful black leather sofa, all imported from France. It feels as if the room had been dipped in gold leaf; gilded frames, side tables and gold-edged vases, fresh flowers sprinkled everywhere.

This man's taste matches his ego, Jessi thinks, as she sinks into the sumptuous sofa; a place where they made love at least a dozen times over their sex-charged three years together. Dierdre eases into her favorite chair near the fireplace, her grin reflecting how satisfied she is that they are together again – the three of them, in Stefan's home; having a drink, the fire warming her.

Jessi is still shaken by the stranger's words in the lobby of Golden Gate Fields. She eagerly takes another sip of the hundred year old brandy. When she dated Stefan, he just about had this pricey stuff on tap. So smooth. So fine! The liquid crawls down into her stomach, soothing her everywhere inside. Her nerves slowly lose their frazzle; softening the edges of her mood. She wants to erase the brutal scene from the hotel restaurant window and the man from earlier tonight; but both scenes are still trapped in her mind.

Jessi, Dierdre and Stefan chat about new furnishings in the grand sitting room, the re-designed fireplace, and the season coming up for the symphony. Stefan pours more brandy for each of them. Dierdre talks about her recent travels. She recently returned from a trip to Vienna where she attended her company's Board of Directors' meeting.

Dierdre – a ruthless businesswoman! Most impressive to Jessi is her philanthropic trailblazing. Animal rescue is Dierdre's favorite brand of charity. She gives thousands of dollars every year to the ASPCA. Her benevolent nature, sincere concern for the treatment of animals, and her ability to inspire others to generously donate, had cemented an instant and unbreakable bond between Jessi and Dierdre.

Stefan sits down on the sofa next to Jessi; his long legs extended out onto the leather book coffee table. They chat, floating from subject to subject. Jessi is content listening and watching; adding something here and there about her veterinary practice. Dierdre loves her animal tales. Jessi briefly shares the story of Pedro, the parrot, who came in some weeks ago outfitted in San Francisco Giants baseball gear. Dierdre and Stefan chuckle with delight. For them, Jessi's animal vignettes always seem to top their own travel and symphony stories. Dierdre starts to fade, sinking further into the comfortable chair. Then, she drifts off to sleep.

Stefan pops up and finesses the brandy glass out of Dierdre's frail hand. He takes the lap blanket which sits by the fireplace, and molds a cocoon around his sleeping grandmother, tucking in the sides of the fabric around her petite body; then placing the ottoman under her feet. He dims the lamp, the blazing fire bright. He moves to the sofa, sits down, and takes Jessi's hand. Your gown is divine. "You look like an emerald." He slides his long index finger across her neckline to the center of her chest; just flirting with her breasts. Her skin sizzles from his touch. She shifts away, but only slightly. "Stefan. I'm not here to…"

He looks down at her leg which escapes from the long slit of the green velvet gown. The tiny rhinestones lining the opening sparkle by the light of the fire. Her black patent high heels show off the shape of her muscular calves; one thigh now exposed by the deep slit. He whispers. "Please, don't get the impression that I want to do anything with you that you don't want yourself. That is simply not my style. I promise to be on my best behavior. My very best." He takes her hand and lifts her from the sofa, like she's royalty. "Let me show you my new wine cellar. You haven't seen it. Everything imported from Florence and other beautiful places in the world. The décor will make your heart stop. She nods.

He leads her through two rooms, and then escorts her down an unfamiliar winding, black iron-sculpted staircase. "This wrought iron is French, imported from Lyon." I had it custom fitted as the entry to the Italian cellar. My preference. I love French wrought iron." She follows him; but has some trouble navigating the stairs with her 4 inch heels. Stefan takes the cue and stops, carefully removing one shoe at a time. "Safety first. I'm looking out for you." His skirting touches distract her. On the final step of the twisting staircase, she trips, almost falling. He gracefully catches her, like a knight would in some castle far away. "I have you Jess." She straightens up and they both stand facing one another in the wine cellar.

The room features plenty of rich wood and stone from top to bottom. A soft plush area rug spreads out in front of a heavy wooden tasting table, regal high back leather chairs around it. A ceramic Florentine candle centerpiece sits atop the table. Stefan lights the candle using a long match stick which he takes from a box set on the stone fireplace mantel. The lights dim as the candle glows. "How did he do that? I didn't see him click a switch. She grins and rolls her eyes at him.

He laughs. "Like magic. Yes?" He guides her over to the oak cubbies designed into the wall, full of hundreds of wine bottles, their labels clearly visible; one section of whites and another area of burgundies, pinots and cabernets. He beams. "All different temperatures; precise levels. Variety – it's the spice of life when it comes to wines. To get the most from a wine, it must be stored at the right temperature. Then, it will sing to you."

Each section of the room is separated by a wall of deep cinnamon-colored stones. "The stonework came from an old church being re-modeled in Florence. These original earth-colored stones were to be removed and destroyed. Can you fathom it? Sometimes we, Europeans, like you Americans, can be too quick to get rid of things most precious and beautiful." He opens a bottle of red wine, from the section closest to the tasting table. She recognizes the label. "I know you love this one. Silver Oaks Cabernet," he says.

"Hmm. It is my favorite." Her eyebrows raise in delight.

She missed it's fruity, full flavor; its texture, its blend of sweet berries and special spices. It was expensive stuff. She hadn't indulged in Silver Oaks for awhile. She had become used to stopping at Trader Joe's and picking up a bottle of J. Lohr, an adequate pairing with her lasagna; something she occasionally prepared for Nick.

"It must breathe just a little before we savor it," he says with an almost philosophical tone. He places the two glasses on the table. Jessi eyes the elaborate crystal chandelier hanging above them. He slides his hand down her back, stroking just below her waist. Looking up at the ceiling, he says, "that is my piece de resistance, plucked out of an Italian monastery.

She's in awe of the creativity he's channeled into decorating and furnishing his house. "Stefan, always finding something new and beautiful. How do you make time to search for these treasures?"

"Believe it or not Jess, I've had a lot of time on my hands since we parted. I lost my most prized treasure and replaced it with these meaningless material things. Not a good trade, my love." He hands her the glass of Silver Oaks. With the drinks at the Turf Club and the brandy just awhile ago, Jessi knows that this silky red wine will be her undoing. But she takes a hearty sip, then another; enjoying every drop as the liquid touches her lips, and soaks into her tongue.

"You look stunning; red lips, emerald gown, deep blue eyes, long, raven black hair. He touches her hair, running his fingers from her forehead through the long curls down her back. "Every woman at the Turf Club tonight wished they could be you. I could see it in their eyes."

She enjoyed feeling sexy. He knew this about her and in response always made her feel desirable; commenting on her clothes, her hair, her eyes, the way she moved. She drinks more wine; then puts the glass down on the table, telling herself, that's enough. I'm feeling it a little too much. Before she even finishes that thought, he leads her over to the bottled red wine collection. He points out his impressive "finds" of clarets and pinots. His slender fingers slide under the thigh high slit of her dress. Each move of his hand goes longer down her leg and then higher on her inner thigh than the previous one. She moans a little, longing to surrender, but still a degree of resistance. She didn't plan on losing control this evening. Like a wizard, he touches her private area; just a fleeting brush at first. Then again. She tingles. He pushes her gently up against the cold stone wall. Jessi flinches at the sudden chill just as he takes her arms and slowly pulls them above her head, propping her up to the wall. She's giving in.

"It's been five months and seven days since the last time I touched you like this. Are you aware of that, Jess?" He whispers; his breathe warming her body.

She mumbles, "I didn't know the numbers, exactly." Her head starts to get fuzzy, her mind morphing into her physical body; feeling every nuance of his touch. His hands move to her breasts.

Suddenly, a flash of the man's threatening voice from earlier this evening invades her mind. Stefan kisses her neck, her ear, her breasts – then, pushes her just a little more upright on the wall. She feels the simultaneous, contrasting sensations that only Stefan can evoke; the cool, rough stones on her back, the liquor warming her body, the hot feathery feel of his slender hands all over her. The complexity of what happens to her in his presence and under his physical influence – a unique collection of smells, textures and sensations almost levitate her from the floor. Her body takes over; her mind retreats. He releases her arms. Jessi drops them around his neck, helpless, like his plaything, to do with what he likes; without any objections from her; his soft, compliant life-size doll.

There's music, soft violin music accompanied by a cello. Nice melody. When did he turn on the music?"

Stefan takes hold of her arms again, this time putting them tightly at her sides and pushing his body into hers just a little harder. His pelvis pressing, his hips moving, his intent clear. He changes it up. Now each time he presses into her, he resists just a little, holding back, only slightly making contact; taunting her to want him more. He has perfected the game of foreplay.

He reaches down and strokes her exposed leg, with a sly hint of hesitance, as if he's going to stop. His fingers slow and then he continues, now with deliberation. He appreciates her moans of pleasure as he withdraws his fingers from her skin, and then wanders them back again. He can sense how much she's missed playing cat and mouse. Her reactions are his drug. Once his ego is happily nurtured, he craves additional control.

Jessi begins to move to the music, her back now almost flush to the wall; as if she's glued to it, but only in one spot.

"Yes, keep moving, Jess." He steps back to admire her. She moves her hips back and forth in slow figure eights; feeling the tiny undulations of every cool stone against her back. Delighted at the view, he smirks. "Hmm. I like it, Jess." He takes a long sip of his cabernet.

"You like the Silver Oaks. Don't you Jess?" She nods, her eyes now closed, as she keeps her hips swaying. He catches her by surprise; and takes hold of her waist, sliding her to the floor. Ahh, the plush rug feels like crushed velvet under her, as the soft texture makes contact with her excited body.

She opens her eyes to see Stefan reaching into his glass of wine which sits on the floor close to the rug. He gives her a taste, placing his wet, dripping finger first on her lips, and then in her mouth. He takes three fingers, and immerses them deeply into the wine glass, then again, on her lips and into her mouth. The drops slide down, coating her throat. "You want more?"

She nods in response. The music winds her up, coats her brain, seeps into her soul. Gregorian chants spill into the cellar, blending perfectly with the violin music.

He sits beside her, as she lays there on the deep piled rug. He hikes up her long velvet gown. "Ahh, you remembered Jess. The garters. The silk stockings." Delighted, he snaps the garter against her leg. It stings. It stings her with pleasure..

She can't speak. Trembling, she waits for his next move. She opens her eyes and sees that his fingers are wet once more with the crimson wine, but now he moves them high up between her legs, pulling down the thong panty; craftily entering her wet vagina. Warm, magical. She continues to move her hips to the lilting strings. She recognizes now that it's him playing the violin. It's him who also plays her like his other sweet instrument. She gets lost, as he explores her. A series of tiny shudders release; and her fears, her pain and all problems that need solving, completely melt away. Each shudder takes her deeper and deeper into nothingness. He moves over her, his pants now thrown off, his shoes tossed aside; entering her, moving with his own special brand of passion. She immerses herself in his wonderland of lust. Of body, and yet not of body. As he leads her to the brink, she savors the sizzle of their union.

"You saw nothing. You saw nothing." She hears the accented voice from the crowded racetrack in her head. But this time, each word brings her satisfaction, no threat. She wants to hear those words again; even say those words. "You saw nothing. You saw nothing." she hears it again.

She repeats the words aloud, but with a slight twist, as Stefan continues to slowly move his hips above hers. She looks into his aquamarine blue eyes and whispers to him, on the edge of consciousness. "I saw nothing. I saw nothing."

Stefan grins, bending down to kiss her neck. He's amused by her whimsical words, as they both start on their path to climax. What is she thinking about? He wonders. "I like that. I like that, Jess."

13

MORNING MANIA

As Jessi awakens in her own bed, alone the next day, she recalls the experience still burning inside her from the prior evening's events. The fast tempo of the Turf Club party, the ominous threat from an unseen man with a heavy Latino accent, and her total abandonment, entwined around Stefan; lost in an orbit of physical ecstasy. They were a perfect fit, like the double helix strands of a DNA molecule. She couldn't keep denying it, which was what she had been doing now for months. Stefan escorted her out to the limo early this morning, both of them tiptoeing past his sleeping grandmother, like mischievous little children.

Jessi had been eagerly consumed by this hungry man! On one hand, she felt some regret but much stronger was her joy at having him take her, in every way. Maybe, just maybe, they could try to make the relationship work. How could she possibly turn her back on what felt like her sanctuary; where she was meant to be. He missed her, confessing his loneliness, his regrets about his foolish infidelity, and the emptiness he had been feeling ever since their abrupt separation. He whispered his apologies all night long, after having carried her up to his king-size antique bed, undressed her, and placed her gently on the cool, inviting sheets. He told her he loved her, and couldn't bear to lose her again.

She slept like a princess, falling off to the sound of Stefan's smooth voice, reassuring his love and commitment to her. He could hypnotize her with his voice. She stirred around 4:30 in the morning. He asked her if she needed to get home. "Yes, she needed to feed her pets, make some work calls and then an early lunch with Myrna, all leading to a late day of scheduled animal patients.

And then there was her promise to Nick for tonight which didn't mention to Stefan. She didn't want to leave Stefan this morning. She snuggled up to him and asked him for just another half hour of his warm embrace. He gave her more than that, feasting on her body before she ever finished the request. When she got home, she crawled into her own bed. I just need one more hour of sleep.

Dr. Pepper jumps onto the bed and nuzzles Jessi; wetting her face with his nose, prompting her for his breakfast. "Alright Doc. Just a minute. She wrestles his little body into the blanket. He rolls over and wants to start the game all over again. Pandora and Creature, the Persians, show up, trying to sit on her head while she plays with Dr. Pepper, who sometimes behaves more like a cat than a dog – imitating his feline housemates. He must be a little confused. Jessi laughs to herself. That's what it's like rooming with three females, I guess.

She still has some time before her first scheduled call with the owner of an Amazonian Hyacinth Parrot. The bird was having trouble swallowing his seed over the past week. Jessi planned to check in on Palomar, 15 year old patient, just a baby in parrot years.

Her mind shifts to Nick. What, if anything, would she share with him about last night? She had just demolished their sexual exclusivity, although there had been no explicit agreement with Nick on this. Jessi didn't really want to give him up, but would it be possible to re-set his expectations without breaking his heart? She loved his company. The spark is just not yet ignited. And now with Stefan, the contrast was too great to ignore. Nick was slowly seeping into her life, with his breezy sense of humor and in his rambunctious, yet understated manner. She risked losing him completely if she confessed her transgression with Stefan;

especially since she had confided to Nick how shattered she had been when she discovered Stefan in the arms of Claudia. Jessi is now as guilty as Stefan had been four months ago.

The phone alarms her. She looks across the room; resting her eyes on her long emerald green evening gown now hanging limp from the ledge of her white-paneled bedroom door. The whole night with Stefan plays back to her in an instant. She needs to take the dress downstairs and hang it back in the "dressy clothes" storage closet. No, it needs to go into the hamper for things to be dry-cleaned. Where's that ringing cell phone? Her head aches. I hope it's not Nick calling. Dr. Pepper locates the source of the ringing, under the other pillow, the little polka dotted encased phone falling out of Jessi's black satin evening purse. She must have tossed onto the bed early this morning. "Thanks Pepper." She clicks it on. "Myrna. Good morning. Yes, I'm still good for 11:30 at the Buena Vista. I'm starved."

Myrna sounds beyond excited, and talks at a fast clip; a special lilt in her voice this morning. "Jess, I met such an attractive man. It already feels like a relationship. It's crazy. I think it can get serious. Oh my God, I can't wait to talk to you more about him. Do you want the details now or later?"

Surprised by this news, Jessi opts for the beans to be spilled during the crab benedict entrée please, while sipping a pot of very strong coffee. She's feeling the hangover; but admittedly, less than expected. "I've got to run Myrna. I have three work calls to make and I desperately need a shower first." Her cousin has no idea about Jessi's hot evening with Stefan. I'm going to keep it under wraps until I decide what to do with Stefan; if or how we move forward. Myrna would be concerned about Jessi putting her trust in a man who showed so little respect for her; only a few months ago. Myrna had been Jessi's number one supporter during those rough times; seeing her through the tears, and the pain.

Jessi nourishes all three pets. She tries to plan for when she can possibly get a good run into her schedule; doesn't matter "where" it will be. The challenge is "when" can she make time for it. It would give her a space to think about the stranger's threats; whether she should do anything about it; tell anyone. She agreed to keep quiet; so that's what she'll do for now. It just nags at her.

She doesn't hear the phone ring as she steps into the hot shower. It's her land line. She hardly uses the number much any more for outgoing calls, relying mainly on her cell phone. Not that many of her friends even have her home number. It's usually only solicitation calls from the phone companies, or insurance agents or cable providers, all trying to sell something new. The deep Latin voice leaves a cryptic voicemail. "It never happened. It never happened." He laughs his evil laugh. "Just checking in with you, doctor." He hangs up. Jessi forgets to listen to her house phone messages before she makes her morning calls, and then leaves home to meet Myrna. Just as she picks up her car keys, her cell phone rings. Oh God. It's Nick.

"Jessi. Good morning. I'm just going into a meeting; but hey, are we all set for tonight? I'll pick you up at 8 o'clock for a scintillating evening under the stars. You haven't forgotten, right?" He senses Jessi distancing herself even before she speaks.

"Uh. Nick. Yes, sure. I-I'll be home by 7:15 and then change. Very casual, right?"

"Yes – the shortest shorts you can find would be okay. Just kiddin' Jessi. Jeans please – you won't believe how casual this will be. But bring a jacket, just in case needed. You're sure you're up for it? I know you had your friend's birthday party last night."

"N-no. I mean… yes. Sure. Let's do it." She didn't want him feeling bad. Maybe she would talk to him about the stranger. I think that Nick is someone I can trust.

Myrna almost leaps out of her chair at the Buena Vista Bar and Grill when she spots Jessi coming through the front door. She's already seated at the table, stirring her coffee, gazing out the window at the cable car making its turn. The crowd of anxious tourists is ready to pounce on board, jockey for one of the limited number of prized seats. Myrna notices something different about Jessi. She looks especially radiant, her cheeks blushed; her smirk, coy.

Anxious to talk about the man who just appeared in her life, Myrna gushes out the story of how she met Rod yesterday in the park – the one directly across from Lance's school. It was another unfortunate dog experience for Lance. They were sitting on a blanket, sharing some milk and cookies. Lance jumped up, trying to get his new kite off the ground, running around, doing the best he could to raise it into the air. Suddenly, a huge black dog came out of the blue, racing across the grass, and almost knocked Lance off his feet. The dog looked vicious, and seemed fully intent on yanking the ball of kite string out of Lance's hands. The animal nipped at the kite which had fallen down on the ground; then lunged for the ball of string, knocking Lance flat on his back. Jessi started to panic, listening to another bad dog tale involving her nephew.

"Myrna, how is he?"

Myrna sighs. "N-no. No. I'm sorry. Lance is just fine. This gorgeous hunk of a man saved the day. He came running, scooped up Lance and instantly frightened that dog away. I didn't see an owner anywhere. That mongrel shot out of the park like a bullet; disappearing from the scene."

"Myrna! You almost made my heart stop. Thank God Lance is okay."

"His name is Rod. He plopped Lance on to our picnic blanket and said, "He is all yours Miss. At first, Lance was screaming and then Rod got his attention with some little magic trick he did right there, with some colored balls he took from his pocket. He distracted Lance into ignoring what had just happened with that crazy dog. Then he taught him the secret to his trick; and gave him the four little balls. "I swear, he bonded with Lance in less than ten minutes; well not only with him," She grins. "His accent was so sexy. I melted. Honestly, I'm still melting. Just so damn good looking, tall and such an incredible hero for Lance."

"Thank God."

"I know. I was scared Jessi. I hugged Lance and then the stranger who took off his dark sunglasses, smiled, and asked if he could possibly help Lance fly the kite. He said that he was an expert at sailing those flyers and could easily teach Lance. He introduced himself as Rod from Cartagena. It sounds almost musical, doesn't it? Rod from Cartagena."

"Wow. You are floating on some cloud. I feel like splashing water all over your face." Jessi playfully spritzes some in Myrna's direction; hitting her on the nose.

"You!" Myrna gives Jessi a handful of spray back, hitting her chin.

"You wanna step outside?" Jessi puffs up. They both giggle.. The waiter doesn't look amused, as he stares at them from the next table. Then he curtly takes their order. "Two crab benedicts and keep the coffee coming. Oh, and please, can you make sure that the muffins are lightly toasted." Jessi makes the precise request. The waiter seems a little annoyed. Jessi and Myrna raise eyebrows, winking at each other as he continues; His snooty façade is fully in play as he picks up each cup and brusquely fills it with coffee, some of it splashing down on the table. Jessi softens and adds before he leaves them, "Thank you, sir. We're sure that our crab benedicts will be unforgettably superb just as usual." She raises her coffee cup to him and beams. He actually leaves sporting the hint of a grin.

A beep from Jessi's phone. It's a text message from Stefan. "Don't think I forgot about you. It would be impossible!" Something tingles inside as she reads it.

Myrna watches Jessi's expression transition into blissful reverie. "Hmm, I knew there was something different about you when you walked in here today. What's up Jess? Your reaction to that. Was it a text? You went to another place. Nick?" Then it clicked for Myrna.

"Busted." Jessi takes a deep breathe. She didn't want to divulge the actual source of her stirred, less than pure thoughts, now exposed to her cousin.

"Myrna, I literally wish it were Nick, but…" Jessi takes another sip of the full bodied coffee. She could use another two or three cups of the stuff. She hangs her small, up-turned nose into the cup; a signal familiar to Myrna. Now distracted, Jessi looks away, staring out the window.

Myrna shakes her head with disapproval. "Not Nick? That means, oh no. It's Stefan." She says it in disbelief. "But Jess, how could you? He drove you insane! You were shattered when he…" She stops almost in mid-sentence and swallows hard. "Okay, I understand. I get it. He's irresistible."

Jessi looks down, embarrassed, sorry that she had attempted to keep it a secret from the only relative she's still connected to these days: and more than that, from her best friend. She gulps down more coffee, finishing off the cup.

Silence. They both gaze out the window at the hoard of tourists boarding yet another loaded cable car.

"I won't pry Jessi. If you want to talk about Stefan, I'm here." Her distaste for the man cannot be suppressed. "The letch! Oh God, Jess. I'm sorry. I know you have a weakness for him. I just can't watch you go through another betrayal! It's like some amusement park ride; constantly up and down." Myrna is annoyed. She loves Jessi, and likes this new guy Nick. He's downright hilarious, and quite handsome! He's not one to simply throw away. Not at this stage!

"Damn Myrna." She reaches across the table and touches her cousin's hand. "Thanks. No really. Thanks for caring so much. It's not just Stefan that's thrown me off here for the past couple of days. There's more. Oh crap! It's so complicated. I'd like to put it all on hold for today."

"No worries, Jess. You can listen to me. I have plenty more about Rod."

"Good. I'm interested!"

Myrna's eyes light up again. "I'm planning a thank you dinner for Rod; simple – just some good old-fashioned spaghetti and meatballs. It turns out he's a Facilities Director for a company on the peninsula, a huge pharmaceutical site with dozens of buildings. He has a lot of responsibility." Muscles, great personality and intelligence on top of it." Myrna blushes as she describes him.

"Oh yeah, you're really focused on this guy's brain. I can see that." Jessi takes on a more serious tone. "I'm happy for you. Look at you. Your eyes are lit up like two dancing fireflies. But listen…are you sure you want him at your house, Myrna? You just met him and you're a single parent with a five year old."

"Jess, I have such a good feeling about this man. It's kismet or something. You know I don't take dating lightly. He's already bonded with Lance. And it was magical from the second he spoke to me. His voice is so deep and sexy. You can see that he loves kids. He flew that kite with Lance for over an hour before he ever sat down and visited with little ol' me."

"Hmm. Okay, Mryna. You know what you're doing. I guess."

Jessi's second sense was taking over. She was happy for Myrna; feeling somewhat concerne about her jumping into a relationship like a speed demon. She hadn't dated anyone seriously since her husband passed away 4 years ago from Leukemia.

"Jessi, you should have seen Rod expertly manipulating that kite – up, down and across the skies; throughout the entire expanse of the park. He had it doing a mambo in the wind. What a showman! He actually drew a crowd. The guy is skilled, good with his hands. Mmm, evidently very good from what I could surmise." They both break into laughter. The waiter shoots them a stern "quiet down" look.

Jessi glances down at her watch; a black-faced Movado, gifted to her by Stefan on her last birthday. "Myrna, I'm so sorry but I have to leave. My first patient will be at my office in 30 minutes and I need to thoroughly review that hound dog's file before I see him today. Waiter, excuse me. Can we have our heck please! She gushes, giving him her friendliest smile. "It's on me, Miss 'schoolgirl in love'. Just take it slow with this guy. Okay? Promise me?"

14

IN COURT AND IN CHAMBERS

"T his court is now adjourned until Monday morning at 9 a.m.
Please arrive promptly." Martina Wells bangs the heavy gavel twice. She feels the blow as hard as it sounds on the mahogany
desk. Her head is throbbing. "Oh God, help me," she screams inside her head. Escape. She wants to escape from the courtroom.
She can barely breathe.

The DA, Sanjay Dalla, springs up from his chair, flying over
to Martina, spitting angry. It's too late. She's disappeared from
the courtroom, dodging any conversations with the stakeholders
from either side. That bitch, he thinks. What the hell's with that
woman? He had been side-barring that same question throughout the day to his prosecutor, Max Dunlop; who sat there with his
usual stoic expression. Sanjay knew that Max was really drenched
in sweat, anxious and agitated by the shenanigans being pulled
by the bench. It was an alternate Judge Martina Wells residing
today. He'd known her for five years now and yes, she could be
tough, a stickler for accurate detail; but had consistently taken
a fair, objective approach, suitably applying her power as judge.
Today, she had been unusually ruthless, her dictatorial remarks
to the jury were almost entirely targeted at the prosecution. She
ripped the policeman as he overconfidently sat there on the
witness stand. Martina pointed out that his harassment of the
defendant at the crime scene may have actually provoked the
defendant enough for him to bite the policewoman. Unusual
behavior for a judge, but she did it anyway.

Martina darts into her chambers, the cutting stare of the bald-headed juror #4 hanging on her mind. She had been successful today; the jury dutifully taking her guidance. But the last witness who took the stand today for the prosecution had been the cleaning lady, Mrs. Alvarez. At the jewelry store heist and murder scene, the woman had been standing outside the back door when the alleged killer, Vicente Rodriguez, ran out; almost colliding into her as she was preparing her cleaning bucket with suds. Today, the woman sat there nervously, presenting a different re-count of the details than she had given at the crime scene. Martina pounced on the opportunity to overrule the entire testimony of Mrs. Marisol Alvarez. The woman struggled with her English vocabulary, perhaps causing her to vary the facts from one sentence to the next. It was obvious to all that she had never been in or near a courtroom; possessing little understanding of the protocol or importance of staying consistent with her story. Martina requested all members of the jury to discard every bit of the frazzled woman's testimony. But that bald-headed juror number 4 didn't appear to buy it. His hands sat on his fat belly, his thumbs twiddling, searching in his mind for the rationale behind Judge Wells' emphatic direction to the jury. The other jurors had been immediately obedient, almost like they never heard the meek woman's testimony in the first place, readily tossing it out like yesterday's junk mail. At least, that's the way Martina read their body language, their expressions of awe whenever she addressed them; their instant compliance. Exactly what she was hoping to achieve from this jury.

Then, the shapely, pixie-haired juror number 3 had placed her hand on the bald-headed man's knee, locked eyes with him, nodding her agreement with the judge's guidance; sexually influencing him to succumb to the instructions given by Judge Wells. He shrugged his shoulders, then raised his eyebrows, as if starting to consider her point of view. He looked down at her hand still on his knee. With a hopeful grin, he nodded his head. She had 'sold' him. Juror number 3 patted his knee again and without words, transmitted the message, "Yes, now you see that the judge did the *right* thing, throwing out that confused cleaning woman's testimony. Martina noticed the transaction. My God. Maybe those two jurors actually knew each other before this trial ever started. They seem too familiar. But the outcome of their strange intimacy seems to have gone in Martina's favor. Her mind darts in several directions. She doesn't really care whether they are somehow related to one another or are even sexually involved. They could be in cahoots with the kidnapper. Her thoughts return to one singular focus; the Hispanic man's threat on the phone yesterday. "Sway them or else your father is dead."

Once in her chambers, she collapses into her swivel chair. She drops her head in her hands, shaken by her proven ability to fake it in the courtroom. Her phone rings. She jumps. Sanjay Dalla is steamed. "Judge Wells, I need to see you now. I'm just down the hall."

"Sorry, Mr. Dalla, I'm up to my ears in meetings for the rest of the afternoon, and then I have a dinner engagement. We'll need to connect tomorrow. I'll give you a call when I'm free but it may not be until after tomorrow's proceedings." Her voice was beginning to crack. Lies. Lies. All lies. She was already tired of the façade. "I'm late for my meeting. Good-bye, Mr. Dalla."

Leon, her assistant, walks in. "Judge, sorry, but the DA has been trying to reach you. He's hoping to get a few minutes with you this afternoon."

She erupts. "I know. I know! I just spoke to him. Okay? Back off Leon. Got it?"

Tense. She's very tense. She needs to hold back; keep it inside.

Leon backs off. "Uh. Oh, sorry Judge Wells." Usually they're on friendly terms, much more casual than this. "Is something up? Can I help?"

His sympathy only makes her feelings of guilt soar. Her nerves grind. "No, I just need some time alone. I have a dozen things to do before tomorrow. Please, Leon." She lowers her voice emitting to more of a whispered plea. "I'm sorry. Please."

Her cell phone rings. It's his voice again. "Judge Wells. Are you having a nice California day?"

Martina covers the phone. "Leon, I need to take this." Without hesitation, he quickly exits the office. "Y-yes?" She takes a drink from the water glass sitting on her desk from early this morning.

"Tell me, what do you get when you cross a court judge with a billy goat?"

"What? What do you want?"

"Martina! Answer the question!" he demands.

Tears run down her cheeks. She cries. "I don't know, what?"

"Baaaaaaaaaaaaaaaad blood. Baaaaaaaaaaaaad blood. You get it. Right? You and I - we don't want baaaaaaaaaaaaaaaad blood." He laughs. In the background, she can hear some jingling of chains or similar. His signature sound. What is that? A long chain attached to her father?

Another Hispanic voice. "Rodrigo. Hey Rodrigo. Ven aquí." Martina now realizes that at least two men are involved. Julio's yell was a slip-up. Rodrigo missed failed to respond quickly enough to cover the phone. For a second, he gets nervous; annoyed at his idiot brother for yelling his name while he's on the phone. Did the bitch hear his name? He gets back to business, regaining his command.

"A reminder for tomorrow, Judge. Keep it going. You had a good start today. But only a start! Throw out more of the DA's evidence. Sway them; if you want your father to live! Your goal is no conviction! Have a good evening."

"But h- how do I know he's okay? What proof do I have?"

"You don't! But you understand the consequences. Sí? Sí Martina Wells – big shot San Francisco judge? Time for me to go."

"Wait! If I do swing the jury to not convict? How do I…"

Dial tone. "Damn it. Damn it!" She throws her phone onto the desk, and watches it drop onto the carpet.

Sanjay Dalla suddenly bursts into her office. "Trying to avoid me? You've succeeded Your Honor, but time's up!" He sits down on the straight backed chair. "Your behavior was ethically unacceptable today. Why did you throw out solid, valid evidence presented by my prosecutor? It's a clear Code 187 Homicide, straight out of the California Penal Code. Vicente Rodriguez is guilty of murder! You know it!" He leans across the desk. "You must have overruled over two dozen sound objections from me. Are you running some kind of circus out there?" He stops himself, realizing that he may have gone too far with his sarcastic, rhetorical question. He lowers his voice. "It's not like you, Martina."

She puts on her best cold, 'in power' persona, instantly recomposing herself. "I'm the judge – right? Right?" She struggles inside; but perseveres; confronting him back. She stands up, and gets in his face. "That's what I do when I think evidence submitted is not legitimate. I can't talk with you personally about my reasoning for every move I make. You know that." She looks away from him. Martina feigns writing; working on something else highly important. Trying to look like she's got a lot to do. "Now, go! Please leave Mr. Dalla! I'm expecting another attorney. We have a conference in five minutes."

Sanjay is furious. He wants to push her further; then realizes he better leave or it could completely throw the prosecution's case, and viewed as attempting to harass the judge. He turns around, slamming the door behind him.

Tears of fear and frustration slide down her cheeks. Flawless ethics have always provided the compass for her life. But, her father is her father. Her flesh and blood. He's supported her, immensely impacted where she is today. She started out as the underdog in high school. Now, she's on top because of her father, Parker Wells. He gave her a winning strategy for success; coached her like his protégé, his favorite corporate intern; shaped her intellect so that she would stand out amongst hundreds of potential future candidates for judgeships.

Then there was Sanjay. She met him during a trial about five years ago. She was instantly attracted to him; a man of equally high ethics. A man continuously fighting for justice. She had somewhat of a secret crush on him. They both graduated from Stanford. Now their evolving relationship was on a path to destruction. The sun set over San Francisco. Martina sat there in the dark, waiting for something to light the way.

15

PROOF OF LIFE, POR FAVOR

Finishing up her last appointment, Jessi wanders into the break room. Sarah sits there gulping down an energy drink, sporting her latest black smock design, this one with small metal studs edging the collar and cuffs. Her hair is blacker than yesterday, and her eyes outlined with an even darker charcoal pencil. "Hey Doc. What did you think of that chinchilla? Sarah flashes her forearm; two long red scratches apparent. "Looks like he likes me, huh?"

"Ouch. Did you put something on that?"

"Yeh, no worries. It's barely bleeding now. I'm fine."

"Those chinchillas are just like foxes and raccoons. Completely unpredictable, whether house pets or in the wild. Next time, you need to wear an arm shield, Sarah. Please. Top shelf in that cupboard." Jessi points.

"Will do Doc. Got any plans for tonight?"

"Uh, yeah. Doing some star gazing with a friend; maybe a little picnic somewhere with a good view. He's surprising me."

"Hmm, sounds radly romantic Doc! Need to get me a new boyfriend." She takes a long sip from the can. "Honestly, I'm more into girls these days. Oh, I don't know. I guess I'm just exploring my sexuality." Sarah is suddenly embarrassed by her own words.

Jessi retrieves a diet coke from the fridge. She needs some caffeine. Not into energy drinks yet, she goes for the classic 'pick me up.' She sits down and joins Sarah at the table. "What about you? Your plans tonight?" Jessi's cell phone rings. Maybe it's Stefan. Nope, unknown caller.

His voice sends her reeling. "Dr. Salazar, I hope you got my message earlier this morning." Her heart races. Her face turns chalk white. Sarah notices that Jessi's blue eyes have instantly doubled in size. She still looks awesome even though evidently alarmed. Sarah marvels at her boss' beauty; her own heart skipping a beat.

Jessi speaks into the phone. "What do you want with me? Why are you calling me?" Now more concerned, Sarah has never heard anything close to this tone coming from Jessi; not even when she's been super tired after tending to ten or more consecutive patients.

She mimes Jessi a question, doing a walk with her fingers in the air. She whispers, "You want me to leave?" Jessi nods. Grabbing her purse from the reception area, she can't imagine what's happening with the Doc, but it doesn't look good.

Jessi pushes her hair back from her face; wishing he would just leave her alone. She hasn't said anything to anyone since that night. "You've got my word. I've forgotten the whole thing already!"

"But, how can I depend on your word, Dr. Salazar?" He yells into the phone. "What collateral do I have that you won't squawk?"

"I-I don't understand." Now in a panic, Jessi grasps for what message he's trying to transmit; what he's asking for.

"You were lunching or brunching, whatever you call it, this morning at the Buena Vista. Friend? Relative, perhaps? A very pretty lady!

Shit, Jessi thinks. She wants to call Myrna immediately and find out if she's okay.

"Did you tell her about what you saw from the restaurant window? Oops. Correction…what you *thought* you saw; *imagined* you saw…"

"No. No! I said nothing."

"Well, somehow, I must be convinced, and stay convinced." Rodrigo sits in the dimmed kitchen. He enjoys taunting his prey: as he takes his long belted chain of keys, and raps them on the already damaged formica table. Maybe, he should just eliminate this smart ass doctor, the only witness to the old man's kidnapping and shooting.

She shakes with fear and can hear the violent metal thumps of some kind of chains on a hard surface. I'm dealing with a maniac, she realizes. Her head fills with images of what he might look like in person.

He smiles and thinks, it's so easy to take these high class bitches to the edge where he can almost feel them flinch and wriggle, desperate to escape his trap. "Good afternoon then Dr. Salazar. Just remember - stay silent. Your life depends on it; not to mention your sexy cousin's life. Yes, I know she's your cousin. But don't worry too much. I'm beginning to believe that you won't talk. Good girl." He disconnects.

Julio runs into the kitchen from the bedroom, heading for the refrigerator. He grabs a cold Corona. He's overheated, his armpits sweated out, his forehead dripping wet. "I got the old man's clothes off. Fuck! It took forever and it's hot in there." He places the beer bottle on his forehead for some relief. "Those stinking bloodied clothes. Mierda!" He had to cut them away from the man's body while the geezer moaned in pain. He even had to cut off the man's soiled underwear. The smell had become just too unbearable; stinking up the tiny apartment.

"He's getting worse Rodrigo. I wiped him up and put a sheet over his naked body. But you better take a look at him."

Rodrigo erupts. He smashes his chains down on the kitchen table, in a rage – thrash after thrash. Little chunks of the formica table fly onto the floor. Mierda! He storms into the bedroom. The skinny old hombre is crumpled up on the floor under the frayed blue sheet. "Looks like he's shivering under there, Julio," he yells out. "Get in here. Ven aquí!"

Rodrigo kicks the man's feet to see if he will react. "Hey, Señor Parker Wells. You awake? Nod your fucking head!" He kicks him again, but this time in the right leg. Parker is barely able to move his head, sliding in and out of consciousness. He's lost the concept of time; little idea of how long it's been since these thugs threw him in the tow truck, then dragged him up a staircase and shoved him in this closet. Through bits and pieces of their conversation, he's gathered that it all has to do with some trial; and Martina is in serious danger. He wishes that he could somehow kill these imbeciles. Wipe them out. He wants to tell them that he can give them money if they would just leave his daughter alone. But his mouth is taped and his body is getting weaker. He's debilitating at an accelerated pace; losing the battle to live.

Bending down, eye to eye with the old man, Rodrigo speaks to him again, "You don't look good." He laughs, amused by his understatement. "You look like a street bum, not a billionaire. You shit in your pants, amigo! When is the last time that you did that? You're a pig! A pig! Oink. Oink." Rodrigo gets down on all fours and snorts like a pig; jumping around in front of the pathetic man. "You can't even see very well, can you? We crushed your eyeglasses a long time ago. You're hopeless!" He snickers.

He turns to his brother, yanking Julio by the throat. He pushes him up against the wall opposite the closet. "He's going to fucking die Julio, and it's your fault. I should kill you for this," he screams. He comes at him again, with the palm of his hand; full force. But instead of hitting Julio in the face, he smashes something on the wall just next to Julio's head, then rubs his forefinger and thumb together. "I just killed a spider. Look at him." Rodrigo holds up his forefinger in front of Julio's eyes; the dead spider now just a smudge. "He's crushed to death. It could have been you." He backs away from Julio, and smiles. "I was getting ready to jam my hand into your nose and push it right through your tiny brain."

Releasing him, Rodrigo begins to pace the room; gradually calming down. "We'll work around this. The judge will complete her mission. She has no idea that her father's almost dead. My plan will succeed. Our cousin Vicente will get his freedom; and if he doesn't, more people will pay. Right now, I need insurance from that bitch, Dr. Salazar. She's a fucking endangered witness! He raises his arms in the air, impressed with his own brilliant twist of words. He looks down at the decrepid half-human, who lays there, his ass hanging out of the ragged sheet. "Julio – take the tape off his mouth. Give him some bread and water. I'll be back late tonight. Don't forget to tape him up again, right after you feed him. Three minutes – tops!! If he speaks a word when the tape is removed; no more food or drink. It will be his choice to either shut up or die." He looks down and winks at the dying Parker Wells.

16

LANCELOT OR COWBOY?

His bedroom theme is Lancelot. Everything in it is based on the Renaissance tale – the bedding, lamps, curtains, wall hangings, even the dresser, chairs and round table by the foot of the bed. A knight in shining armor greets you as you enter the room. Another one on the other side waves good-bye as you leave the room.

Myrna sits beside five year old Lance, who is snuggled in bed, under the covers, his pillow case covered with elegant horses topped by knights holding their jousting poles, posed and ready to fight. The window is open halfway. The wind starts to blow hard, howling around the corner of the building. Myrna considers herself very lucky to have found such a perfect, two bedroom condo in a great section of San Francisco – a little off the beaten path, but only a fifteen minute bus ride to the flurry of Union Square and Market Street. The only drawback is that the condo sits on the first floor of the building. Sometimes she gets concerned about safety and security; a single mother, with a young child.

Lance's bedside lamp is turned down low. He plays with his miniature knights and horses, crashing them down on the blanket and then raising them into the air, ready to fight each other. He provides his own unique sound effects, including gallops, jabs and collisions. Myrna takes the plastic toys from his hands and puts them on the side table. "Let me tuck you in Mr. Lancelot. It's already 8:30. Time to shut those big brown eyes."

"But mom, it's Friday night! Can't I stay up later?" His Blue Flyer kite from Aunt Jessi is spread out on the tall-backed Lancelot chair opposite his bed. Since Rod, mom's new friend, coached him on flying, he and the fighter kite have been inseparable.

"Tomorrow night, we'll make popcorn and watch a movie," she offers as a consolation trade. "You can stay up until 10, how about that? Special treat!"

"Yay! Yay!" He claps with delight "Mom! Mom! Do you hear that dog barking? Do you? He sounds mean. Mom, what if he comes in here and gets me? Bites me, takes me away." The dog barks louder. Lance starts to whimper. "Mom, I'm kind of scared."

"Hey, little man," he says, walking into the room, raising his hand to 'high five' the cardboard knight standing at the door. Rod approaches, and sits on the other side of the bed, next to Lance and across from Myrna. He gets up close to the little boy's face and tickles him in his tummy. The boy can't help but giggle; but is still concerned about the dog who continues his incessant barking. In his Latin accent, Rod whispers in the child's ear, "Lance, my new young friend. No dogs will come here into your house unless, of course, you personally invite them." He reaches across Lance and takes Myrna's hand. "Your mom and I are both here to protect you. No harm will come to you."

"How can you be so sure?" His little voice is timid and full of fear. The dog barks again, sounding closer, more vicious.

"He's getting closer!" Lance yells out. Myrna quickly goes to shut the window all the way, to cut the volume of the dog's bark. That dog does sound large and fired up, she thinks, as she pushes the window down.

Rod comforts Lance. "You're okay. No hay problema. You know, maybe you should change the whole Lancelot thing, and instead, become a cowboy. Cowboys have lassos, sharp spurs and guns. Very powerful. No dogs ever mess with cowboys, amigo. I've never heard of it happening, not even once!"

Myrna is a bit surprised at Rod's suggestion, but she knows that Rod is just trying to distract her son, give him confidence, help him forget about the barking dog. Whatever it takes for him to overcome his recent "bad dog" experiences. She sits back down on her son's bed. "Wait a minute. Lancelot has a big sword. Isn't that enough to shoo away bad dogs?" She looks over at Rod. "Lance probably doesn't need a gun like a cowboy."

Rod considers her point. "A sword? Hmm. It's okay, but a gun is faster, more reliable and can make a bigger impact. You know what I mean?" He imitates a cowboy shooting a target. The two adults continue their animated debate across the bed. They look down at Lance to get his opinion. "Cowboy or Lancelot?" Myrna inquires.

The boy is almost asleep, still holding one of his plastic knights in his hand. He mumbles, "Yeh, maybe I'll become a cowboy. Maybe." He drifts off to sleep. They can hear his gentle snoring. Myrna turns off the lamp, and heads to the door.

Rodrigo kisses Lance gently on the forehead, and rises from Lance's bed. He thinks to himself, I could kill this bitch right now, but no. I want to have her. Yes. I'm hungry for that piece of ass. He admires her standing there in the doorway, silhouetted by the light behind her. She looks tasty. He moves to her, taking her in his muscular arms. He tells himself to slow down. Be a gentleman. He kisses her slowly; arousing her. She closes Lance's bedroom door behind them, leaving it just a few inches ajar. He kisses her wet and long, as he backs her into the living room. He feels his cell phone vibrate in his back pocket. He kisses Myrna; as he pulls out his phone. He holds it behind her head, his eyes fully open. Her eyes are closed. She's floating on a cloud. He reads the text message from Julio. "We lost the old man. Fuck. What next?"

Rodrigo finesses the phone back into his pocket. He slides her onto the brown suede sofa, kissing her neck, stroking her hair. He reaches under her bra, and with his other hand, he turns off the lamp behind him. Myrna likes the feel of his manicured hands. She whispers. "Ahhh. Thank you Rod, for getting Lance's mind off that barking dog. That was perfect."

"Myrna, sweet Myrna, the pleasure is all mine."

While he enjoys himself, Judge Martina Wells sits in the dark of her chambers, drinking whiskey. Slugging it down. Beating herself up for what she will need to do tomorrow to save her father.

17

BODY INFLUENCES BRAIN

Friday night. Nick would arrive in just ten minutes. It was already 9:30. He was going to be delayed; crisis at work. "It's fine. Stargazing is best late at night," he told her. "Especially in the special location I've has yet to divulge." She stares out the window at the bridge, a bright half moon in the sky; a few stars twinkling. Yes, it could be the perfect night for watching the skies, especially in the right spot.

Dr. Pepper stands there on the chair, peering out the window with her. He jumps down, retrieves his stuffed squirrel from under the coffee table and nudges her with it. "One throw Pepper, then I need to get my jeans and sweatshirt on zip pity zap!" She throws it for him. He runs after it. Jessi wants to phone Myrna to find out if she's okay. The creep on the phone backed off in the end on threatening her family and friends, once she re-committed her silence. But she doesn't feel safe. He's got me in an emotional torture chamber. Did he shoot that old man? Kill him? I must forget it, she sternly coaches herself, as she looks in the mirror and refreshes her make-up.

Her mind shifts to Stefan. If he would only call her. Texting was not enough. She knew he had a new symphony debut going up tonight but she longed for his attention; that gravelly, Swedish voice turning her upside down, inside out. I can't tell him about the Latino man, but if I did, I think he'd know exactly what to do with such a bully. Nothing takes control of Stefan.

What a week it's been! Fortunately, her veterinary practice operates with one Saturday on, one Saturday off; and this was an off weekend. No veterinary office hours unless an emergency demands it. Her receptionist, Barbara, would be there in the morning to administer medicinal refills if necessary, and book appointments for the following week. This means Jessi could sleep in tomorrow for an extra hour and then maybe take that "run" on the Embarcadero; with Stefan's violin music in her ear, as she passes the mimes on the street, street artists entertaining the kids before they board ferries to Alcatraz, and the thousands of tourists that swamp the restaurants, bars and ferry building to find unique San Francisco mementos.

Picking up her cell phone, she hits the button to call Myrna; but gets voicemail. Damn! Her nerves are jumping. She tries Myrna again. She answers this time. Thank God she's okay. Myrna speaks in a slurred, slow voice.

"Were you sleeping.? Sorry, I didn't mean to wake you. I just…" Myrna giggles, then in a hushed tone says, "Jess, n-no. Listen, can I call you later? I'm-I'm, well, you know, I'm kind of…" Her voice trails off.

"Yes. Sure. No problem. Call me later or in the morning – that's fine. I just wanted to check in on you." Myrna sounds occupied. Jessi's never heard that tone, that sultry, primal voice coming from her cousin. Sounds like she's with her new man; distracted and indisposed.

A text comes in. It's Stefan. "I'm calling you now. I need to hear your voice before my big solo." Her phone chimes, simulating a melodious violin. It's the special ring tone assigned to Stefan. She had never removed it. He whispers into the phone, probably in his dressing room or somewhere backstage in the wings. "Tell me you can't wait."

She smiles. "It's what I've been thinking about too! Stefan, how's the new symphony going so far?"

"It pales against the violin strings being pulled in my body right now. The ones that want to play with you. How about we leave next Friday for the weekend and fly to L.A.? I have two nights off, Friday and Saturday; since the Russian ballet is here at Symphony Hall. We can stay in my suite at the Hotel Roosevelt; enjoy Hollywood. I know a sizzling late night club. Kind of a dirty dancing scene. You know how we enjoy that. Remember that night in New York City, right after my Carnegie Hall debut? The black lights, the 1950's retro clothes you wore on the dance floor, your hair in a long ponytail of black curls, your lipstick - deep red and your hips moving with mine." She remembers the passionate love-making that followed.

Oh my God, how does he do that? It only takes a second for him to fire up her body; whisking her back to heated passion. Her seeing it, feeling it, being there. She gathers herself. "Yes, I remember it well."

"So? Pronto. Pronto. I go on in three minutes. Please – have mercy. You'll go with me next weekend? I want to hear the 'yes' word."

She exhales, giving in. "Yes. I'd love to go. I'll need to get a back-up vet for next Saturday morning; and well, there's something else I need to take care of right away."

"I agree. Cut him off. He wasn't right for you anyway. Too boring."

"What? Who?" She never told Stefan about any new man in her life; nothing about Nick.

"Forgive me. I'm guessing, my love. Somebody must be trying to get into those delicious panties, and then there's your incredible brain. A delectable recipe, especially in this town." He takes a pause. "Come on Jess, isn't there another man whose heart you've already captured? Admit it."

"Um. Maybe. Yes. I do need to talk with him, re-calibrate our relationship back to a friendship, not a romance. I want only you, Stefan. I can't fight it any more."

He smiles; relishing his victory! There was a slight chance it could go the other way with Jess. He had previously screwed up but the fire between them could not be denied.

Pandora and Creature circle her feet while she talks on the phone. They swirl around her ankles, their long tails brushing her legs as they move around her. A kitty tail massage, a modern dance of the felines. She smiles down at them, loving their sense of mischief and play.

"Drop him Jessi. Tonight. Drop him, so we can fully re-ignite our romance, pursue our union. And Jess, I have an important question to ask you next weekend. I'll wait until we land in L.A., and when we're settled on the sofa, sipping brandy in our suite; the lights dimmed, I'd like to show you something I've been keeping for you." He catches himself, and chuckles. "No, no, I mean something other than that." They both giggle. He's so bad, and it's so good.

Without warning, the Latino man's voice shoots back into her mind. "Stefan, I have something else I'm dealing with too. It's heavy. Seriously, it's been weighing me down this week. I can't really talk about it, but I wanted you to be aware of what's going on with me."

"You can depend on me anytime. Of course, you know that. If it's a family thing about Panama or your father, I'm ready to listen. If it's something negative about your insane violinist lover, well, then save it, my sweet!" She can sense the crafty grin on his face. "By the way, Dierdre sends regrets that she didn't get a chance to say good bye the other night. She misses you already, like I do." He walks out of his dressing room, phone in hand and pulls back the heavy stage curtain to sneak a peak at the audience. "Ahh, there she is. Jess, I can see her now sitting in the lower balcony box just next to the mayor. They are jabbering as usual. She's such a flirt. My grandmother is in her element." He laughs again. "A bientot. I will talk to you soon. My solo is coming up." He hangs up.

Stefan, she thinks. She hadn't been quite ready to re-commit to him before this call tonight. But her body responded for her. She had to be with him again. She had almost fully committed her life to him the last time, before his cheating, his *mistake;*

that's what Dierdre called it. Merely a *mistake.* Jessi plays with his name. Mrs. Stefan Van Oeterloo. Nice sound to it. Dr. Jessi Van Oeterloo. Sounds strange, but I'm hooked.

She needs to prepare for tonight's discussion with the other man in her life. So much to enjoy about Nick. He's funny; and a good friend. She needs to be honest with him; straightforward about her feelings. But, it's tough because lately she had been steadily warming up to him, his wit, and his caring, almost protective nature. Maybe she could talk to him about that evil man threatening her; but it was risky for her to say another word to another soul about what she accidentally saw from that window.

18

THE NIGHT SKY

Nick's plaid blanket is spread out on a high San Francisco rooftop. The night sky is crystal clear, the half moon embedded in the midst of a deep blue umbrella filled with thousands of stars, some twinkling and others barely visible. The picnic basket is open and two plastic glasses are filled with red wine. Packages of unwrapped half-eaten deli sandwiches and other delicacies sit within arm's reach. Nick is exhausted and at the same time, relaxed. It had been a tough week in chip design, he explains. His CEO wanting to move up the development cycle and project deadline by two months. His team is now expected to "kill it" until late into the night for the next eight weeks. "Sure, my team members will all, most likely, receive a hefty Project Completion Bonus, but the question is at what cost to their family lives? At least I got approval to alternate free pizza and hot sandwiches to be brought in each night. Over the last couple of days I've been adding my own homemade pies to their pantry of snacks. It's a hard-knock life for engineers in Silicon Valley." Nick stops talking; noticing that while he's been babbling, Jessi has been sitting beside him, nervous and on edge.

He makes his best attempt to re-engage her. "I've been missing you, Jessi. How was the birthday party? You haven't mentioned it. Must have been a blow out, having it at Golden Gate Fields?" She sits there, but is a hundred miles away. "Jessi – you're okay, right?"

"Oh. Sorry, Nick. Yeh, it was an elegant party. A memorable occasion. Dierdre was glad to see me." The guilt piles up as she stumbles her way through the end of her response. "It was nice to re-connect with that family." Her hands fidget in her lap.

She looks up at the never-ending night sky, feeling very tiny, barely a speck on this planet Earth.

"So, how does it feel to be sitting on top of the world on the 51st floor? My friend Mark was able to get us up here. His dad is superintendant of the building."

"I feel limitless; no boundaries. I was actually wondering how you landed this view." Changing topics, she says, "Nick, I have some bad stuff going on right now. I'm in trouble with one thing and in a quandary with another. I think I know which direction to go on each of these dilemmas but my mind is still strugglng with exactly what actions to take. I need to…" Something brilliant suddenly shoots across the sky. A huge long, wide, and very colorful streak of light. "Oh my God, Nick. Did you know that was coming? A comet! It was a comet, wasn't it? I've never seen anything like that. Did you time it?" She is awestruck.

"I thought maybe we missed it because we got here so late." He reaches across the blanket and gives her a tender kiss. "That one in particular, only occurs once every hundred years or so. It happened tonight for a reason. He moves closer to her.

"It was stunning." Her next words spill out awkwardly. "Listen Nick, I think I need some space. I-I've been…." Her cell phone buzzes. She tries to ignore it. Exactly the wrong time for an interruption. It's Myrna. She had been wanting to talk to her all day, just in case she's in danger after that man mentioned Myrna's name on the phone "Sorry Nick, it's Myrna. Maybe I should…"

His bubble had already been burst tonight. Jessi seems concerned about something else. "Go ahead Jessi, it's your cousin."

"Myrna. Hi. Everything good with you?"

"Yes!" Myrna is ecstatic and chatty, singing her words into the phone, but in a hushed tone. Someone else must be close by. Maybe Lance is sleeping. "I think I'm in love. I have to talk low.

My new guy is in the other room. Oh Jess. We're going away for the weekend, Rod's treat. He has a special place to take us; a sprawling dude ranch in Salinas owned by his family. It will be good for Lance. We're taking him to an old-fashioned rodeo tomorrow. Can you believe it? From Lancelot to Roy Rogers. I just woke Lance up to tell him and get him ready to go. Very impromptu. Rod suggested it, some time after dinner tonight. Lance was already in bed. We got him up now, and he's thoroughly excited. We're leaving within the next 30 minutes."

"Myrna. Myrna. Slow down. You're talking about Rod, the man you just met? That's not like you. And it's so late to go out anywhere tonight – especially way down to Salinas."

Still whispering, Myrna continues. "I know. I know. It's fast for all of us to go away together. But he's the one, Jess. You know how long I've waited for this." Nick can't help but sense Jessi's disbelief at whatever her cousin just told her; his eyes fixed on her, shooting her a puzzled, questioning expression.

Myrna oozes. "Rod is great with Lance. Jess, honestly, I'm dazzled with this hunk of a man. He takes charge. I love it. I gotta go Jess; just wanted to connect before we disappear for the weekend. We don't want to get there too late. I told Rod that I needed to call you before we took off. He's helping Lance pack right now. He just came back from grabbing his clothes from his house. We'll get there after midnight at this rate. Bye, Jess."

"Myrna, wait, there's something I want to…" She's interrupted from the other end, by Lance, yelling out, "Thanks for the kite, Aunt Jessi." The overtired boy zooms around the room, holding the fighter kite high in the air, whisking past Myrna, as she sits on her bed next to her almost-packed suitcase. "I'll call you Sunday night when we get back." Lance hijacks the phone. Jessi hears some long chains or keys jingling in the background. "Bye, Aunt Jessi!" Dial tone.

The phone disconnects. Jessi is perplexed. "What the hell is happening with Myrna?" She stares down at the silent phone. Something tugs at her. She doesn't know what it is.

"Jessi. You okay?" Nick takes her hand. "You look like a ghost has just given you the hebee jebees."

"I'm fine. I guess Myrna is in love." For a moment, Jessi's mind travels back to a simpler time. She's 13 years old, running through the rainforest, playing tree tag with Rico; before the day she found her father cheating on her mother. She was happy then, innocent; not yet jaded, not at all cynical. A sadness overtakes her here on the rooftop. "Nick, I don't mean to be morbid, but I have a strange question for you."

"Shoot. The weirder, the better."

"How long do you want to live?"

Not prepared, since he'd never been asked this specific question in his life, he fumbles for a response. "Yes, strange question between two people on a dark rooftop."

Jessi can't help but chuckle at his retort. "You're always such a wit! But seriously, would you like to live until maybe 95 or 96, or 100? What age?"

"How about 42 for starters?"

"Yeh, you're right. That makes sense." More quick wit from Nick. "Well, did you know that studies show that when asked, most people just want to live to their average life expectancy – no more. They don't want their mind outliving their handicapped physical body. I often see the same thing in older animals who come into my practice. A dog's eyes sometimes tell me that he's ready to go. Like Pinky, this 14 year old greyhound I had last week. He came in limping, incontinent, unable to climb stairs, had a hard time even walking into the exam room. I saw it in Pinky's eyes. He was ready. But his owner wasn't willing to let him go. It's understandable. Meanwhile, the dog suffers."

Nick sits up, hugs his knees to his chest, pondering Jessi's veterinary scenario. "Wow. I never thought about it. I guess I'm not around life and death everyday like you. My mind doesn't go there."

"Sorry Nick. I don't know why I'm even thinking about such an extreme topic. I was upset by Myrna's call and for some reason, it led me here, to this issue."

He nods, appreciating her intelligence and ability to consider the deep questions in life. That's why he's fallen in love with her. Nice body, yes! Beautiful face, indeed! Spectacular brain, without a doubt! Big, big heart, most impressive! This combination was like quicksand for him. You can't turn back love, he thought to himself.

"On a lighter note," he says. "With my luck, 70 year old Pedro the Parrot will most likely make it to 110 ten years old. Damn!"

She takes him seriously for a split second. He rolls his eyes. They both burst into giggles. Nick adds, "Nah, I'm actually getting used to the little guy. He's imitating me now."

Jessi playfully jabs him on the shoulder, shaking her head. "Why am I such a nut case tonight, Nick? I mean, how can you stand it?"

He takes her hand and holds it in his, pressing it to his chest. "Jessi, I want to say something."

"Okay."

"Look, I know that I'm not the number one man in your life right now." Jessi's guilty feelings heat up her face. "But I want us to hang in there. I think more can develop between us." He opens up her right palm under the night sky. He turns on the lantern beside him, so the details of her palm are clearly visible.

Jessi is intrigued by his unexpected actions. "What are you doing, Nick?"

"I'm looking at your lifeline. My sister taught me this when we were kids." He runs his finger diagonally across her palm, following the most pronounced deep line. "You will live a long life. See that? Now, look at these finer branches, sprouting out from your main lifeline. You see them? And these little breaks?" She nods, enjoying the moment, his childlike playfulness. "These little branches are like hiccups that happen to us in our lifetime. But look here at the end, this little rogue branch merges back into the main lifeline, solidly re-connecting again. That's the Nick and Jessi line; right there – happily together again until the end of time."

He places her hand down on the blanket by his side. Tears well up in Jessi's eyes. She doesn't want him to see her reaction. She's embarrassed; feeling guilty about her night with Stefan. Technically, she cheated on Nick, just like Stefan had cheated on her. She's conflicted.

Nick turns to her. "What I'm suggesting is this – let's stay close. I have faith in our future – our partnership. In the meantime, do what you need to do, Jessi. You don't have to tell me the details. Believe me," he kids her. "Just know that I'll be here for you, waiting; if the time comes when you're ready for more. We can still have fun together like this." She tries to blink the tears away, so they don't run down her cheeks.

He knows that something has happened, maybe with Stefan, or maybe with some other guy. He forgives her. His intent is to grant her carte blanche to do whatever she needs to do. Explore. Find out who, and what, she really wants.

Jessi puts her head on his shoulder and decides to lighten up the mood. No need for her to say more about their relationship. "Hey, Nicky Daniels, got another sour pickle in that picnic basket?" He reaches into a plastic tub and like an experienced magician, produces a bulky, oversized pickle. She crunches into the dripping green object. They transition into a tickling frenzy. The pickle goes flying down the slope of the building, and then shoots off the rooftop. Their relationship is now saved from complete destruction. She rests her head on his lap and gazes at the stars.

19

MISSING, MAYBE DEAD

He tries to keep his composure as he says good night, but feels like he's already lost her. It's the right thing, but it still hurts. "Nick, thanks for an unforgettable evening and for that light show! I'll always remember it." She pecks him on the cheek and gets out of Nick's Volvo.

"Sleep tight," he calls out from the driver's seat. He drives off. She needs a good night's sleep. Jessi unlocks the front door; and turns the antique iron doorknob which reminds her of Stefan – the polished iron railing leading to his wine cellar. I wonder what he's doing right now. The grandfather clock in the entryway chimes just as she opens her door. It's 1 a.m. She shouts out to her three pets. "Are you hungry, you guys? Pandora? Creature? Dr. Pepper?" She beckons them.

As she moves to the kitchen to retrieve some pet food, Creature and Pandora come prancing in, their tails high in the air; as if royalty. Dr. Pepper is nowhere to be seen. She glances at her cell phone. There's a text from Stefan. Funny, she was just thinking of him. He writes, "Silver Oaks cab - ready for our next encounter. I must see you again. Has to happen before next weekend. I can't wait." She smiles. Nick's long face before she left his car tonight disrupts her thoughts of Stefan.

She hunts around for Dr. Pepper. "Pepper – come and get some chow, you hungry puppy. Are you playing hide and seek with me? I hope not; I'm really tired. I have a treat! Pepper!" She notices some dark smudges on the floor and on the doggie door which leads from the kitchen to her patio area. Opening the back door, she flicks on the outdoor light, and walks down the path behind her house. She falls to the ground when she sees what looks like little paw tracks of blood on the paving stones. "Dr. Pepper!" she screams." He's not there. She looks everywhere outside. Nothing. She rushes back into the kitchen and examines the doggie door again. Oh my God, he's not here. What happened to him? Is he hurt? Blood. Blood means attack.

Collapsing on the kitchen floor in a heap, tears drip down her face. She hugs her legs; then rocks back and forth. Then, it clicks. That man! That Latino voice. He's got Pepper. Oh God. Jessi's cell vibrates from her purse on the kitchen counter. It moves across the slippery granite surface with each vibration. Fearing the worst, she doesn't want to answer it. It stops. She's shaking out of control. "Pepper. Pepper!" She keeps repeating it. "Pepper. No." she whispers to herself, and rocks. The phone vibrates again. She unsteadily rises, and picks it up; placing it hesitantly in her ear.

"Dr. Salazar, do you know where your canine is? Your precious Dr. Pepper?" The Latin voice laughs, an icy, hollow laugh.

"Is he safe? Please. Please." Jessi screams as loud as she can into the phone. "Where is my dog?"

"Calm down, Doctor. Keep one thing in mind. It's only a dog. It's not your cousin Myrna or your nephew Lancelot. Yet!" She freezes. "Now, you understand how important your silence is to us. My pet name for you is 'my little endangered witness.' You understand what I mean? Sí?" Rodrigo stands in a sprawling living room, which has a western theme, unconsciously clanging his long chain of keys on the rock fireplace, as he taunts the pathetic vet. "Good night, my little miss endangered witness!" He hangs up.

"Fuck you!" Jessi throws the phone onto the floor, hoping it will smash into miniscule pieces – so that she'll never have to answer it again. This freak even knows Lance's fantasy name. "Oh my God! I wish he would please let me bury my dog. Please." She falls to the floor again, and rocks back and forth. "Dr. Pepper. I'm so sorry."

Rodrigo walks into the bedroom where Myrna waits, wearing a short black nightie. She sees his tall, sexy frame in the shadows of the doorway. "What are you doing Rod? You must be tired from all that driving."

"Tired? Me? Maybe, but I'm hungry for love." He growls and slips out of his jeans; which fall to the floor jingling, his chain of keys still attached to the belt loop. Wearing only his tight, black tee shirt, he slides in next to her and squeezes her leg under the sheet. "Señorita, you are nice and warm in here. I like it. Come over here."

She rolls into his arms. It feels so natural. "Sorry, Myrna, I was just checking on Lance. I gave him a special cowboy hat I found in one of the closets. It's perfect; fits him well. He's sleeping with it right by his side, ready for tomorrow's rodeo."

"He really has taken to you, Rod. You're magical therapy for him."

"Sí, I think you are right. And, for you?" He wiggles his manicured fingers inside her.

Aroused, she tingles, barely getting her response out. "Yes, magic; magic for me, too!"

"Ahh," he whispers. "That was exactly my plan for you."

At about two in the morning, he checks to see if Myrna is asleep. Her hair, disheveled across the pillow, her nightie on top of the sheets, the covers bunched up near the foot of the bed. Yes, she's certainly a good piece of ass, he thinks. A prime cut for someone just like me. He slips out of the bed and walks back into the room where the fire is still flickering. Naked, he sits down on the warm stone, cell phone in his hand. "Answer the phone, you idiot. Answer!"

"Sí?" Julio mumbles.

"Rodrigo! Where are you?"

"At Javier's ranch in Salinas. He's in Cartagena doing business."

"The old man is dead. Did you get my text?"

"Sí. I'm with the bitch vet's cousin. I'm going to kill her if the Doctor says anything before the trial ends. Eh, I might kill her anyway. She knows nothing right now. I'm fucking her brains out and she loves it."

"What should I do with him? He's still laying like a smelly heap in the closet."

"Get some giant black plastic bags. Double or triple them up. Wrap him in the bags. Then put a black tarp around the whole thing. Tie it up with some twine. Put him back in that giant duffle bag we used to get him up the stairs. Then, put the bag in the bathtub until I get there. I won't be back until Sunday, maybe not even until Monday. You better go out to the all night market, and get the stuff now. Spray some Lysol and air freshener into the bag. Do that every so often."

"Shit, Rodrigo! It would be good to get some help."

"Pendejo! Imbecile! This is all your fault anyway, Julio. Sleep in your own bed! Know what I mean? I'm taking care of important business with the judge and now with the vet's collateral – her dumb cousin. It's a good thing I have the skills to achieve results. The goal here is to have the judge somehow get Vicente released, and keep the vet's mouth shut. So, just do as I say until it's over."

"Sí Rodrigo. I will do what you say. But, then what?"

"We leave California; go back to Cartagena. Lay low. Take a long holiday. You need some color, hermano. You're beginning to look like some white bitch these days. I want you to find that vet – Dr. Jessi Salazar. Her home address is on the kitchen table, written in the matchbook. I almost killed her fucking dog tonight before I left San Francisco. I shot him. I intend to send her a message; one pet at a time. But the little bastard got away when I tried picked him up and put him in the truck. He was bleeding a lot. By now, he's probably dead somewhere on the road. Enough on the dog! Julio, get to her house early, by 7 a.m. I want you to follow her all day tomorrow, see what she does, who she sees. Listen to what she's saying. If needed, deal with anyone she talks to about the old man. That cannot happen; and if it does, it will be stopped. Comprendes?"

"Sí. Sí, Rodrigo."

"Bien. Call me immediately if something comes up."

20

THE CREAM CURDLES

Pandora and Creature meow, nudging Jessi's legs, then move up to her head; simultaneously purring in her ears. She had managed to get from the kitchen to her living room sofa, not making it all the way to her bedroom. She feels gritty, still in her jeans and light jacket from last night. Numb, disoriented. Her life is in shambles, now controlled by a sick megalomaniac. She drags herself to the shower, tries to wash away her despair. Run. Run, she tells herself. I need to run, get myself together. Figure out what to do next.

His demand was for her not to talk to anyone, keep her mouth shut. How could she do nothing? Her dog is probably dead, her cousin in jeopardy. Is she next? Who else will be targeted? At least Myrna and Lance are out of town, away from the eyes of this evil force. She was happy that her cousin was in love, out of harm's way.

She feeds her cats, embraces them, appreciating their sweet feline sounds and the texture of their soft fur. She opens the back door, and lets them out of the house to pursue their choice of strolls through the neighborhood. She doesn't usually encourage her cats to go out on the prowl. But this morning, she is petrified that the murderer will come back, and finish off the rest of her pets. She wants them to be out there, not in here, provide them some safety. Pandora and Creature would always return home. She locks the doggie door.

After a quick shower, Jessi is dressed in her shorts and halter top, a light-weight sweatshirt tied around her waist. As she starts off on her run, she almost trips off the first curb. Strength. Strength is what you need, Jessi! No time for wimps today. Her cell phone sits in the inside pocket of her running shorts along with $60 in cash, just in case of an emergency. Her standard operating procedure. Faster. Faster, she tells herself.

Her mind drifts back to the jungle. Suddenly, she's running, running home after kissing Rico, after exchanging their handmade promise rings. It's raining. She's running fast; slipping and sliding. Slipping and sliding. And then she sees him, entwined, in the arms of Carina. Her father, moving his hands up and down the woman's long, brown, slender body. Jessi wanted to throw a rock at his head, shock him out of touching that woman; Rico's tramp of a mother. Jessi remembers thinking to herself. I hate that woman. I hate my father and I hate Rico! Now, running down the San Francisco streets, she finds herself moving faster than she ever thought possible. Tears stream down her face.

The streets are starting to populate the downtown area. She speeds up; the image of her father and Carina slipping out of her mind. She realizes where she is; just one block from Stefan's Victorian. She's run so far, up steep inclines; all the way up to Nob Hill.

I need him. He loves me, and he has power, strength, stamina. I can talk to him. He'll know what to do about this whole mess! He'll give me confidence and direction. It's Saturday. He doesn't go to Symphony Hall for rehearsal until later in the afternoon. I'm going to him. She struggles up the stone steps to the massive mahogany door. His Audi is parked in the paved driveway. Thank God he's home. Once she rings the doorbell, hears the beautiful clock chime, all she wants is to feel his arms around her; protecting her. No answer. He must be there. Please! Maybe he went down the street to Starbucks for a morning latte. He loves hanging out in his sun room on Saturday mornings, so he should be here. She rings the bell again. Finally, she hears his footsteps coming down the staircase. Her wish is granted. He's there!

Stefan opens the door but only slightly. He wears an over-sized violet bath towel around his waist. His hair appears half-wet; a small matching towel in his hand which he uses to wipe his forehead. "Jess! It's you! Uh – what's up?"

"Stefan, I'm in trouble. I need to talk to…" Fuck. It's Claudia standing behind him who edges the door open; her long, curly blonde hair falling onto her shoulders, her fake breasts almost falling out of the sheer, white robe. She strokes Stefan's bare arm as he stares at Jessi. It's the same cellist from before. The woman seems cocky; smiles, beaming, happy to see Jessi taking the fall, again. "Sorry, we were just up late last night," she purrs. Too much brandy, I guess." Her tongue sweeps across her lips, as if in slow motion; like she's tasting him.

Jessi pushes the door in, almost knocking Stefan down, who, for the first time in their history, appears powerless. He jumps back, surprised at her physical force. She's angry, incensed. Behind Stefan and Claudia, there's someone else. Another tall woman; this one, wearing a skimpy black sequins-covered teddy, and spiked high heels. She has a short, straight-bobbed black haircut. Her red lipstick is smeared. Stefan's blue and black paisley tie hangs askew, around her elongated neck. Her eyes dark, her make-up features thin black lines outlining them; completely smudged.

"Oh God!" Jessi mutters, almost inaudibly. She feels dizzy but can't help to take another look. This girl is maybe 20 or 21 years old. She seems familiar to Jessi. Oh God. It's the French intern from the symphony, who plays the flute. The girl looks scared and tries to dart away to another room. Too late. A tableau Jessi will never forget now embedded in her mind. She did it to herself. Now, she's caught him a second time; this time she's interrupted sex with not one, but with two women. The younger one could be his daughter.

"You're pathetic! Pathetic!"

"Jessi. Jessi, this is not what you think. I was just...."

"Shut up! I should have known you're still an asshole!"

She takes off. The rope of his tangled deceit tightens around her throat. She can barely breathe. To think she trusted him. To think she wanted to confide her disastrous circumstances to him. I'm a total loser. Her eye catches the attic window on the top floor of his house. She knows it's the window to an exquisite wallpapered guest room, with matching drapes and bedspread; one you might find in the heart of England. A face is in the window. It's Dierdre, peering out at her; probably having heard the commotion downstairs. The window is ajar. Jessi's grandmother surrogate, watching over the whole scene, like a madam pimping her slutty prostitutes. How could she be in the house when Stefan is clearly having sex with two women at a time?

Running, escaping down the street; Jessi almost crashes into an old man coming out of the neighborhood Starbucks. He's Asian, and small. He's holding a cane. Having dropped his newspaper, he bends down to retrieve it. She quickly apologizes. "Please, please let me help you. I'm so sorry." He can sense her panic, her distress. She kneels down and picks up the paper, handing it to him. She stands up. He looks into her eyes, placing his hand on her sweaty arm. One of his eyes is clouded over, all gray and murky. Maybe he's blind in one eye. He seems so serene, although she had almost knocked him over.

"Remain calm, dear girl. You will come through everything." He smiles, his white teeth in perfect alignment, except for one very yellow, crooked metal-capped tooth in the lower front of his mouth. "I thank you for being here." He looks down, then starts walking away, now tapping his cane. She watches him hobble down the street. He's careful, measured, cautious; feeling his way to his next destination.

21

A CALL FROM THE JUNGLE

She runs. She mourns. She rips herself to shreds with her thoughts. Her legs feel weak; but she doesn't stop. Jessi Salazar; you're such a child, she thinks, beating herself up for her profound stupidity. Her addiction to Stefan is now curtailed once and for all. What was she thinking? She can see the cement steps up to her house; the beautiful roses in painted ceramic pots on either side of her bright blue front door. On any day, after seeing too many pet patients, all she can think about is going home to see her own pets. She has a one track mind about animals. Like Jessi, the young girl living in the Panama jungle, animals remain her safe retreat. Turning the key in the lock, she's shivers; praying that her cats are waiting for her outside the back door. Oh God, I hope they haven't been hurt or kidnapped by that freak; like Dr. Pepper. If I cave and go to the police, that man may kill Myrna or someone else close to me. I need to wait; not make any moves to expose him. Not yet. He has me backed into a dark corner. I must be strong.

Her cell phone rings out. She's wary. Terrified. Rushing to the back door, Jessi is relieved to see Pandora and Creature, through the glass window of the kitchen door. "Meow. Meow." She can hear them. They rush in as she opens the door. She simultaneously clicks to answer the phone but doesn't say a word. Whether it's the evil Latino man or Stefan calling her, she wants nothing to do with either of them. But at the same time, she's insane with worry about her dog. Maybe she can get the man to tell her what happened to Pepper. She can't be dead. Gone.

"Jessi? Is this Jessi Salazar?"

"It's a Latino man's voice. He sounds different, but it must be him! "What the hell do you want now? You already have my dog. Where is he?"

"Jessi? This is Rico…Rico Mendez from Panama."

"What? Rico? How…How do I know it's you? I'm sorry, but…"

"Si. I understand. Well, let's see. You remember the promise rings we buried in the rainforest? The ones we made from marsh reeds; and then put in a little pouch made from tree bark?" The warmth of his voice is clearly reminiscent of Rico. A scene from her teen years snaps into focus. Rico and Jessi stand in the rainforest. The young girl smiles, her eyes glistening with teenage love for the wide-eyed boy.

Could this really be Rico on the phone now? A lump forms in her throat, her eyes fill with tears of joy, content to re-connect with the best thing from her childhood. But it doesn't stop another wave of doubt passing through her.

"My phone number. Rico, how did you get it?" She wants to be absolutely sure it's him. Still panicked, she thinks the man who injured her dog may be attempting to trick her. Maybe, somehow, he found out about this boy from her past.

"Lo siento, Jessi. I'm so sorry. I-I called your office phone number. And, well, it referred me to your cell phone number for veterinary emergencies. Should I call back later or maybe you can contact me at my hotel? I didn't mean to upset you. Sounds like you're busy right now."

"Your hotel? Sorry, what hotel?" Surely, it's him. It is Rico. She recognizes the lilting music in his words; the way his sentences end in such a sweet, gentle tone. She had dreamt about hearing Rico's voice again, but feared contacting him after she had so abruptly dropped him from her life. "Rico, it's so good to hear your voice."

"Bueno. I'm here in San Francisco." He's happy that she now believes him. But why is she so troubled? What's going on with her dog? He can picture her pretty face, her long dark curls, her flawless complexion.. As soon as he found out he was coming to San Francisco on business, he jumped on the internet and googled Dr. Jessi Salazar; finding plenty of information regarding her veterinary practice, including her professional photograph. There she was, almost life-size and in color, on his wide screen; her sea-blue eyes with that same twinkle, her raven hair even longer than when she left Panama. She stood there in the photograph, smiling, surrounded by a menagerie of pets – two dogs, a parrot, a rabbit, a cat. It was the coolest advertisement he'd ever seen for a veterinarian. She looked smart, kind, and happy; the way he remembered her just before he gave her a first kiss that day in the rainforest.

"I'm sorry Rico. I thought you were someone else."

"Jessi, you don't need to explain anything. Are you around today?"

Should she see him? Jessi still feels painfully guilty. She had ended it just after she had witnessed her father lying under the mangrove tree with Rico's mother. She conversed with Rico only one more time after that painful day. The very next morning she found him kneeling down by the waterfall, pitching stones into the shallow end. She remembers calling his name, and then coldly telling him what a mistake she made letting him kiss her the day before. She couldn't tell him the ugly truth. Why break his heart? Why lead in to the ultimate moment when they would both look into each other's eyes, awkwardly silent, grasping at what to say next. Without a doubt, they would have both opted to back out of their promise to be together forever. Instead, Jessi ended their relationship with a simple, "It was just a mistake; a big mistake. It will be tough to stay friends. I'm sorry, Rico." She kept her head down when she spoke, dreading any eye contact that would give her away her true feelings. She left him standing there in a daze; the stones he was pitching, still in his hand. She heard their blunt thumps as they fell to the ground, as she walked away. She had said goodbye, even though she'd fallen in love with this boy, who openly cherished her all through their young years. For the next 12 months after that scene, she focused on planning her escape from Panama. A few years later, Jessi left for California, embarking on the journey which would lead to her future career as a capable veterinarian. She knew Rico was broken-hearted; but she had vowed to set him free. She also knew how much he revered his mother. She couldn't be the villain to burst the bubble.

Rico clears his throat, feeling a little nervous on the phone. "Jessi, I'm at Ghirardelli Square hanging out with some colleagues from Panama City. I'd love to see you. Honestly, I can't wait to see you. It would be a dream come true to get together, even for a couple of hours. But it sounds like maybe it's a bad time for you. Are you still snubbing me after all of these years?" He chuckles. "Just teasing, Jess."

She smiles and then the sadness creeps in again. "Rico, it wasn't about you or anything you did. Something happened there in Panama. I never told you about it. It was hard for me. The way I dealt with it was to cut you out of my life and then finally leave Panama. It would be good for us to talk."

Her mind races. This was the absolute worst time for him to show up; in the midst of her chaos. Life tosses us some bizarre scenarios, criss-crossed circumstances. Stefan flashes through her mind, the extreme contrast to Rico; each of them exact opposites in terms of character and style. Rico is more like Nick. They would like each other; maybe even strike up a friendship. It seems that I have a pattern of rejecting the "best" men in my life, she thinks, while Rico waits for her either to accept his offer or blow him off.

"Yes, I'd like to see you Rico. Of course! What are you doing later this afternoon – let's say 4 o'clock? I have something urgent to do first, early this afternoon. You can help me with something, if you don't mind."

"Sure. I'm available any time today. I also have something important to talk to you about," he says.

"Can you meet me at a small boutique hotel bar on Market Street? It's called the Rubik Cube in the Hotel Metamorphosis. It's close to the Embarcadero. Can you find it?

"Dios mío, I will finally see you, jungle girl. I am the luckiest hombre in San Francisco. I will be there at 4 o'clock sharp. Hope I recognize you."

"Yeh, you will. I'll be the disheveled looking veterinarian." Her troubles seem to melt away. It feels so good to re-connect with him.

22

RISKY DECISIONS

Before she gets in the shower to wash away the emotional turmoil she was thrown into when Stefan opened his door. Her paranoia overwhelms her. What if that man returns when she's in the house? In the shower? She double locks the front door; and places a chair against the back door to the kitchen; the sight of the bloodied pet door screaming at her. The cats watch her with curiosity. No sign of forced entry.

Jessi welcomes the hot water which soothes her tired body. No more tears for Stefan. She is determined to wipe it from her mind, with bigger troubles to sort out. During her talk with Rico, a lot more was happening to her than renewing the relationship with her lost friend. She was simultaneously processing her current suffocating situation. She wants her life back. There is only one way out. It's risky. Very risky. The authorities need to know about this. He threatened her personally; including her friends and family. But what is likely to result, even if she goes along with keeping her mouth shut? The terrain looks rocky. She trembles, thinking about what lies ahead. It's also impossible to focus on her vet work with this hanging over her. And, she has a critical surgery on Tuesday which she needs to perform well; save the life of a 3 year old cat. It's a delicate operation; involving his heart.

Just as she turns the faucet off and reaches for her towel, she says, "Pepper, you can lick the tub now." But he's not there. Her dog usually patiently waits for her right outside the shower, sitting on the bathroom rug, his little brown tail wagging back and forth. As Jessi would step out; Pepper would get up on his hind legs and lick the top lip of the tub. "Pepper, where are you?" she cries out, then falls to the cold tile floor, clutching her bath towel; wishing she knew what happened to him.

I'm going to the police. It scares me; but it's the right thing. Maybe that old man is dead or in a ditch somewhere, half-alive. I think he was shot in his stomach. I'm not sure. And what about his family? They must be flooded with fear. Still, it's odd that this story is nowhere in the media. Absent! She's still heard nothing about it on TV, radio, or even on the internet. She checks her computer before she leaves the house; ABC News and local San Francisco Crime Watch. Nothing! There's a police station on Market Street, not too far from where she's meeting Rico later this afternoon. She'll drive over there instead of taking a streetcar. Park at Union Square. No. No. A streetcar would be better; less likely to be followed and watched. It's one o'clock; so I have plenty of time before I get over to the Hotel Metamorphosis. The station is about a 25 minute ride from my house and also not far from the Renaissance Hotel, where the scene played out. If she needs to take a policeman there to show him the restaurant, the actual table where she and Nick sat or the street below where the violence took place; they can easily walk over there.

Jessi jumps off the streetcar, and rushes into the Market Street police station. She asks the uniformed receptionist if she can please talk with an officer or detective on duty. "It's urgent. I have something important to tell him about a disturbing incident I recently witnessed."

"Okay Miss," the receptionist barely looks up from his paperwork. "What's this regarding?"

"Well, it's about a limousine I saw from a hotel window some days ago. An old man... something bad happened to him. He may have been shot. I know that he was definitely kidnapped!"

"Got it. Okay. You'll need to fill out this form first. There's a seat over there. Here's a pen for you. Please return it." He hands Jessi a two page form.

A woman approaches behind her. Judge Martina Wells has also just arrived at the Market Street police station. She's frantic about her father. Her eyes are red from crying and drinking all night. Regardless of the repercussions, she must come clean, and she must try her damndest to save her father's life. She has no faith in accomplishing that on her own and doesn't feel secure that this manipulator will actually release him even if she gets Vicente Rodriguez off the hook. Arguments end tomorrow morning; with a possible verdict in the afternoon or maybe the next day. She overhears the attractive woman in the police station talking to the receptionist. The story she told him sounded like it was about her father. Oh my God! This woman – she must be the witness to my father's kidnapping. She said he was shot! Is dad dead?

The judge then overhears the woman ask, "Can I get a copy of my completed form once I fill it out?"

The man shrugs his shoulders. "Yeh. It's possible. I'll make a copy for you."

"Excuse me, Miss. Excuse me."

On edge, petrified to be there in the first place, Jessi spins around. She's disoriented, half expecting to see an angry Latino man standing there, with a gun hidden in his jacket. Instead, it's a petite, well-dressed woman.

"Please, please may I speak with you?" The woman moves Jessi away from the reception area.

"Who are you? What do you want? I'm in the middle of something important. I'm sorry, I can't talk to you now." Jessi turns and starts moving away, headed for the bench where she can fill out the form, and get on with her deed; before she changes her mind.

Martina's eyes well up with tears. She touches Jessi's arm and talks softly so nobody else can hear her. "My name is Martina Wells. I am a judge for the San Francisco Superior Court. My father was kidnapped; abducted. It sounds like you saw this happen from a hotel window. I must speak with you privately."

Jessi stops dead in her tracks. She sees the distress in the woman's eyes; feels her pain. The judge resembles a small wounded animal, one that might walk into Jessi's veterinary practice.

"Let's not say another word until we're in a quiet place. Just follow me. I'm going to walk out of here, and down the street to the Hotel Metamorphosis. There's a bar in there where we can talk privately," she whispers. The judge listens carefully, and responds with a nod. She stuffs the form into her purse.

The judge follows her, but trails several feet behind; trying her best to camouflage any indication that they are together. She stops to gaze in a shop window, while Jessi proceeds further down the street. Martina can see Jessi make the turn at the end of the street into a hotel. As she moves past dozens of scurrying tourists, the stylish sign on the side of the building becomes visible: *Hotel Metamorphosis.* Martina eyes the Reception desk; then makes a left turn into a dimly lit, handsome art deco restaurant and bar. She sees the woman from the police station sitting there in a burgundy leather booth. A small lamp sits on her tiffany-style table, casting a shadowy light on the woman's face. Martina sits down across from the striking woman, noticing her long, flowing dark hair, and electric blue eyes. She can see the worry on her face and that her hands are nervously fidgeting.

"My name is Dr. Jessi Salazar. I'm a veterinarian here in San Francisco. Yes, I saw what happened to an elderly man who was dragged out of a black limousine by two thugs. It was a week ago. I was sitting in the Carrington Grace Restaurant at the Renaissance Hotel. I was alone, nobody there in the dining room but me at the time."

"Did you say he was shot?" Martina bites her lip; fearing Jessi's response.

Jessi nods her head. "But, I-I don't think he's dead." She cringes as she says the words. "I think maybe it was just a wound. I saw the elderly man was still moving. After the gunshot, the two men threw him into a red tow truck." She drops her head in her hands. "Oh my God! That was your father, then. I'm so sorry, Judge." She reaches for her hand, even though she can't control her own hands from trembling. Jessi tells the rest of the horrid tale, re-capping her birthday celebration. She describes the evening; how Nick was in the restroom when the limo and tow truck first drove up and how the whole scene unfolded from the window; before her eyes. She admits that she was half drunk and on pain killers, but she saw what she saw. And now, it's been confirmed by some crazy Latino man who is threatening the lives of herself and her family. She talks about Dr. Pepper, that he's gone, shot or horribly cut by that same deranged man. She's scared and felt that going to the police was the right thing to do, even if it places her in increased danger. She explains how the man came up behind her at Golden Gate Fields and that he's phoned her numerous times since then, reminding her that her life is on the line if she says one word.

"But, how can I be in any more danger than I am in already? That's what I thought this morning. I have some other bad things going on in my life. For me, this is the arsenic frosting on a badly burned cake."

Martina feels empathy for this young woman; having to witness such a brutal scene. She talks to Jessi about her father; how he's a multi-millionaire – a potential target for any kidnapper. "This is different. It has nothing to do with money. The abduction was all because of a murder trial I'm presiding over, and my father is now the choice collateral. This man demanded that I somehow successfully sway the jury, get acquittal for a Drug Cartel member who's committed a heartless murder. I've already compromised my ethics in the courtroom. But, like you, Dr. Salazar, I realized that I just can't live with myself. My strong moral compass has taken over. Whatever the risk, I've decided to go to the police. Damn it!" She bangs the table with her small fist. "I pray that he's still alive. I hope you're right! The gunshot resulted in a wound, maybe a serious one; but not in his death."

Jessi sees the distress in her eyes. She squeezes Martina's hand. "I think we need to go back to the police station together."

The judge nods. Jessi glances down at her watch to check the time. Rico should be here soon.

"Sorry Judge. Before I can go back to the police station, I must first meet someone in about 20 minutes. I promised I would be here. He's an old friend from long ago who has come from very far away to tell me something important."

"Of course, I'll come back here in a couple of hours. Would that work?" She looks at the clock on the wall. "It's 4:40 right now. How about if I return here at 6:30 tonight? That gives you almost two hours. Then, we can walk back to the station together; first collaborate on how to fill out the form and present it to the police. I've met the police chief once before, and I think he sits in that station. We can ask for him."

"Yes, that's a good plan. You know, you sound like a judge." Jessi smiles weakly, intending to lighten things up.

Martina stands, looks around the bar, and walks out.

Jessi feels a slightly better now that she has a partner; someone to support her through this process and someone she can equally support. She's thankful for the uncanny timing; them both coming to the station at exactly the same moment. The bar is filling up. Three businessmen take a table by the window. Another short stocky man with dark sunglasses sits down at a table close by. A young couple wanders in behind him; wearing clothes like they came straight from Kansas this morning, completely out of place in the San Francisco scene. The waiter approaches Jessi. "Hello Miss. I see you're alone now. I didn't want to disturb you ladies. It looked like you were deep in conversation. Would you like a drink or something to eat?" He hands her a menu.

"Y-yes, how about a sparkling water with lemon?" I'm waiting for another friend who will be here in a few minutes."

"You got it! Be back in a flash with that." Right behind the waiter stands a dark-haired, golden-skinned Rico. He looks fresh, his dimples deepening as he flashes his broad grin. The waiter excuses himself. "I'll be back to take your order, sir."

"Jessi. Look at you!" He gives her a brief embrace, not wanting to draw attention to the sensations he's feeling right now.

The short, stocky Julio turns his head to look at them. He had dutifully followed Jessi as she rode on the streetcar but then he lost track of her. He was in his old Honda Accord, and it had stalled along Market Street. He could see her long hair blowing out from the streetcar's window. He tried to re-start the engine. The streetcar took off for its next stop with him sitting there like a fool. He tried again, and got it re- started but a mega truck was honking at him to get out of the way, and turn the corner. He had no choice since he was in the turn lane. That's when he lost track her. For the last hour, he walked up and down Market Street searching for her; going in and out of shops, boutiques, restaurants and hotel lobbies. Then, he dipped into this trendy Hotel Metamorphosis, and there, tucked away in a booth; some young, good-looking Hispanic man staring into Dr. Salazar's eyes. She looks mighty fine, he thinks. She's a catch, with her long wavy, hair and glistening white teeth. A veterinarian, too. He watches her, has a little fantasy about touching her, feeling her skin, ripping her clothes off as she begs him to continue; then screams with pleasure as he enters her. Ahh, that would be heaven. I need a beer, he thinks.

The waiter approaches. Julio orders a Corona. He wishes Dr. Salazar had been the one stuffed in his stinky apartment's closet; instead of the dead, old man whom he just moved to the bathtub. But, he would want her alive, maybe kicking, squirming under his full weight; begging him for mercy. That would be even better than her wanting him. He sits there in his black leather jacket and his dark sunglasses. His hair is neatly tied back in a ponytail, similar to his brother's styling, except Julio stands 8 inches shorter, with a large, flat nose and a bad complexion. Rodrigo is tall, muscular, with small features and high cheek bones. He could be a model in magazines, if he put his mind to it; maybe invested in some professional full body photographs. Friends and family members had often recommended this to Rodrigo, but he would laugh away the idea. "I have bigger plans," he would say. He didn't have to worry about money. With his uncle as Cartel leader, as long as the brothers successfully did their jobs, they would always enjoy security, and the good life, when not on assignment.

Julio was beginning to tire of Rodrigo always being the one in charge. He considered himself just as smart as his brother. But with Rodrigo's good looks and charisma, he seemed to always end up in the driver's seat on Cartel plots and projects. I've had enough of that. I'm going to start calling the shots more often, he thinks as he listens and watches the vet, and her handsome man.

23

POIGNANT REUNION

"**G**od, you look like a shiny penny, Rico."
He blushes and responds with a return compliment.
"You look the same as when you were 13 years old in the jungle; except for the city wrapping and maybe you've, well…." He clears his throat. "Maybe, you've physically matured a little." They both crack up. "I guess you got rid of that jungle girl outfit. Your clothes, very San Francisco. Sí! Sí!" he says with approval. She's missed that smile all these years. They talk for the next half hour about their lives, how they've each evolved since their childhood days in the rainforest. Jessi tells him about her career as a veterinarian in the city; a busy, interesting and successful practice. Never the same from day to day. Different animals with diverse and specific needs come and see me. It's my dream job, Rico! I have many friends from a wide variety of species. I truly love my work.

"You are extraordinarily lucky, Jessi. Fortunate to be in the business of helping animals day in, day out." Rico shares the tales of his life. His studies were in architecture, obtaining the equivalent to a Master's Degree. He modestly describes the awards he's won in both Central and South America for his progressive work; now selected to design the tallest and most artistically modern new cultural center ever to be built in Panama City. In San Francisco for a global Architectural Summit, he's been invited to be the keynote speaker. It's all happening tomorrow at Moscone

Center. Jessi is impressed and proud of him; this jungle boy, now an extremely handsome man with a brilliant career.

Rico turns silent, and takes her hand. "I found out why you dropped me back in the jungle, Jess. It was the relationship between your father and my mother. I spent last Friday with your father." Jessi feels her body stiffen.

"So, my father told you this last week?"

"No, I found out about their affair just a week after you left for California. My mother broke down and told me. She could see how miserable I was; how I was holding your departure against myself. How I thought you just couldn't stand me. You wouldn't talk to me after our break up. That was two years before you left the jungle. I watched you everyday; from afar. Finally, my mother confessed one night as I moped about in my bedroom. She cried and cried; was very ashamed of what she did. Their tryst had been over since the day you found them. My mother and your father saw you standing there – just before you turned and ran away. Your father just didn't want to discuss it with you. He was afraid and so greatly embarrassed. I think he also told your mother about it well before she passed away, but I'm not absolutely sure of that."

Jessi swallows hard. It's a lot to take in. She wants to hug Rico for many reasons right now. She's missed him. She feels sad for the their lost close relationship. The potential of "forever together" had been there when they were so young. It was destroyed by a heavy hammer in just an instant. Maybe she should have confronted her father right after she observed the ugly scene. But she didn't. She couldn't.

Rico drops his head. "Mi mamá died two years ago. Her heart failed. I don't know. Maybe it was a broken heart. She passed away quietly in her sleep."

"I'm so sorry Rico. I don't blame her for what happened. It was my father I hated. What about *your* father? Where is he now?"

"My father was a drinker. Remember how he'd go off to the cities and sell his crafts. Most of the time, he was on an alcohol binge. He had an accident in Panama City on one of his trips, over 7 years ago. A car hit him while he absent-mindedly crossed the street when the light was red." His eyes fill with tears.

"Rico, you've had a tough time with family."

"There's more bad news, Jess."

"What?"

"It's your father. He's not well. He has diabetes. It's getting worse. It's become life threatening. He may not make it for much longer. I'm so sorry to tell you this. He looks frail, and he just found out that he needs to have his right foot amputated. The medications don't seem to be controlling the disease all that well."

Jessi closes her eyes. Her body goes limp. Hearing about her father takes her back to the rainforest. Back to when he carried her in his arms, tickling and teasing her. He'd take her out in his little outboard motor boat in the swamps of Panama; teach her everything about the rainforest. Have her spot animals, name the fauna and pick up insects of every color, shape and size. She'd write all about them in her water-logged journal; then go back and research them in books he gave her. She loved animals because of her father and that special love was reinforced when she befriended Rico at a very young age. They were both children of the jungle, learning and playing together; then falling in love.

"I figured out that you saw our parents making love on the very day we exchanged our promise rings."

"Yes, I did."

He suddenly spills out the two green and brown woven rings made of swamp weeds. They tumble onto the gray marbled table top. Rico holds the tree bark pouch in his hand.

Jessi is overwhelmed with happiness to see them there before her."

"They're still beautiful." She doesn't touch them, just gazes down at them, overwhelmed with happiness. "Maybe it was for the best, Rico."

"Why? What are you saying?"

"We both went on to great careers, fulfilling our lifetime goals. I know that my life would have been totally different if I didn't leave Panama when I did. Who knows? Maybe *you* wouldn't have become a famous architect."

He grins. "I'm not famous, Jessi." His dimples deepen again as he breaks into his spectacular smile. "But my English is good. Si? I studied for 5 years, spending a lot of time in Toronto, Canada on a 2 year long project."

"Your English is excellent. But then you did have a very knowledgeable childhood tutor."

"Yes, I had the best." He squeezes her hand.

Exhausted from the day, she's finding it difficult to stay focused when he's just thrown so much at her. Her day is a jumble rumbling around her mind; each element of it playing back to her: this morning, finding Stefan with Claudia and the flute player, Dierdre peering from the window, the police station, meeting Judge Wells; and now this afternoon seeing Rico after so many long years. She lays her head down on the table, her chin resting on her hands, up close to the two woven rings. She can smell the rainforest. Still preserved, as good as new, she thinks. When she lifts her head, tears are streaming down her face.

"Jessi, I didn't come here to upset you. Lo siento. Lo siento," he whispers, taking her hands again. "Should I go?"

"No. No. It's something else. Can I share it with you?"

"Yes. Please do, Jessi."

"But I don't want you to get involved. It's too dangerous. I just need someone I can talk to intimately without being guarded."

The waiter approaches again. "Can I get you something, sir?"

"N-no. Gracias. I mean, thank you. Maybe in a little while." The waiter is surprised, but nods and walks away.

"Please, tell me what's happening. Share anything you'd like. I'm in no rush tonight." He squeezes her hand.

Jessi discloses the details of what she saw from the hotel restaurant window. Rico listens intently. The man with the sunglasses perks up; having almost fallen asleep with the first part of their conversation. Now he hears her describe the abduction, his shooting of the old man. Fuck! That bitch! He wants to reach across and strangle her; shut her up. He resists, and downs his beer. It's his second beer since he got here; his sixth beer today. Jessi continues, now describing her dog's disappearance; the blood stains she found in her kitchen.

Rico longs to hold her, protect his childhood sweetheart. But he stays in his seat, listening, thinking back to the rainforest, still picturing Jessi as a young girl. Being with her, hearing her speak is more satisfying than any architectural achievement he's ever had. "How can I help you, Jess?"

"Help me? I don't know, Rico. I don't think you can do anything. You are helping me just by listening! I'm going to the police later this afternoon." She didn't tell him about Martina Wells; because she felt that to be respectful of the judge's privacy. She didn't want to expose her identity to anyone; not even to Rico.

Rico understands and agrees with her decision to get help from police. "Jessi, listen. I don't want our reunion to end so soon. How about if I meet you for dinner?" he suggests. It's only 6:20 now. We can meet at 8:00 at my hotel. I'm staying close by, just a few blocks away, at the Marriott Marquis. They have a really nice restaurant and I know how you like to eat." He laughs. "I want to see more of you before I get too absorbed with this conference tomorrow. Besides, I think you're going to need an old friend after you spend some time with the police." His dimpled smile steals the scene.

"You know me so well." She grins.

"Yes I do. Remember those contests we used to have – which one of us could eat the most mangos in ten minutes? You always won; every time, I think." They both burst out laughing.

"Yes, meeting you later would be ideal." Maybe you can see me home. I'm really scared that my cats are now in jeopardy."

He gathers the two rings and returns them to their pouch. "Can you do one thing for me, Jess?"

"Sure." She nods.

"Hold onto these for me." He hands her the pouch. "It's a memento of 'us'; the way we were together. It helped build the foundation for what we've become today; not just our careers; but who we are as people. Relationships are important." She nods and smiles as he stands up to leave.

"I'll see you at 8 o'clock at your hotel. Meet you in the front lobby." He bends down and kisses her on the forehead.

"Glad we re-connected. We still have something, Jess. It might be limited to a strong friendship, I don't know. Maybe it's much more; but whatever it is, our bond will never die." He leaves.

Jessi takes the rings out from the bark pouch. She holds them in her hand. Looking down at her hand, she gets distracted by the deep lifeline on her palm, pointed out by Nick just last night. It is a long line. She thinks about Nick, again how similar he is to Rico. Awaiting Martina's return she can't help but notice the stocky man wearing sunglasses suddenly rush out just as Rico exits. The afternoon crowd is emptying out; probably all going someplace else for dinner or maybe catch a movie; or do more shopping. In five minutes, Judge Wells should be here.

Julio follows the good-looking Hispanic man down the street. Damn, that Rodrigo! My bastard brother, always having me do the dirty work. I'm going to have to take care of business, again. Mierda! This time I'll take control, be the decision-maker.

24

MALICE ON MARKET

Rico exits the Hotel Metamorphosis into the late afternoon sunlight. The wind has picked up here in the city by the bay. There's a spring in his step; his heart sailing like a boat catching the wind on a beautiful ride into the sunset. Finally! Finally, he saw her again. *She's still my girl, my jungle girl. Something good will blossom from this reunion. I should have come to San Francisco much sooner to talk to her. We'll talk more time together in just a couple of hours. She's caught up in this insane quagmire. Once she gets this out of the way, I know she'll be open to considering "us" again as a couple.* He rushes back down Market Street in the direction of his hotel; almost forgetting that he'd promised his colleagues he'd meet them for a drink in the bar at 6:30. They're probably waiting for him. He'll excuse himself from dinner once he catches up with them. He'll tell them about the part two reunion now planned for tonight with his childhood sweetheart.

As he walks along Market Street, he remembers his mother's words to him, just after she confessed her indiscretion with Jessi's father. It was four months after Jessi had seen Denny and his mother, Carina, together; locked in their hungry embrace. It was just four months and one day after Jessi broke off the relationship with Rico. "My son," she cried. "I've done a bad thing. It may have cost you the one you love most. I've seen it in your eyes, Rico; how much you care for that girl. She has rejected you and you still suffer months later. It is true, no?" Rico had been trying to keep his emotions a secret; never mentioning what happened with Jessi. He kept to himself, spending hours in his room drawing sketches.

Rico nodded his head, hiding his wet eyes in his pillow; not wanting to admit even to his mother how hurt he had been. She turned him over, looked into his dark eyes, and tenderly stroked his forehead.

"I'm afraid I've ruined your future with Jessi." His mother gently placed her wet cheek against his. "I will never lay down with Jessi's father again. You have nothing to worry about there! But the pain in that girl's eyes when she found us told me that she will not only hate me forever; but she will also reject you. Lo siento," she whispered softly. "I made a mistake because I am so lonely for your father. I have no excuse, I know; but he's gone so much." Carlos, his father, was away again in Panama City. Carina sat at the foot of his bed. She had climbed the tree-limbed ladder to his bed, ready to make her sorry admission. Her feet dangled, as she sat by his side, still stroking her teenage son's hair. She began to weep in disgrace. He immediately forgave her. He loved his beautiful mother. He shared her shame, but he felt no anger. There was nothing he could do about Jessi. He respected the teenage girl too much to confront her, or ever talk to her about what happened.

His father had built him the tree house bedroom; that sat half way in the open air. Open to the trees, and to scads of howling monkeys who would jump from up high in the trees down to the ground every morning at about 4 a.m. His room was like a blended wonderland of home comforts and the open jungle. As a young boy, Rico loved the monkeys; was always amused by them. He told his father that he wished he could sleep with the monkeys. Carlos Mendez recognized the six year old boy's fascination with the howlers, and proceeded to construct a special tree house bedroom for him. Rico looked forward to climbing the ladder made of tree limbs up to his bed every night. It was his piece of heaven in the midst of a fascinating rainforest. His father was so gifted in woodworking and creating handicrafts from the fruits of nature: hammocks, vases, wood boxes, purses, chairs, beds, all kinds of furniture and art objects. Carlos would travel to the cities and sell everything he could.

Rico smiles to himself, as he strolls down this bustling San Francisco street thinking about his father, the master craftsman. His father had one overpowering weakness. It was alcohol. Each time he went to the city, he'd first sell his wares, take care of business for a few days and nights; without stopping his sales pitch. He'd barter and make deals. His goal was to sell everything he had with him, to retail shops, wholesale houses and even city market stalls. Then, he'd go on a shopping spree for his family, purchasing things he couldn't get in Boca del Toro. Lots of gifts for his wife and son. Before he left Panama City to go home, he'd go to some bar, drink all night, engaging in a 24 or sometimes a 48 hour binge. He just couldn't stop slugging down cheap whiskey. When drunk, he'd play poker and lose half of what was left of his precious profits. The picture of how his father probably died that night in Panama City flashes across Rico's mind. Drunk, crossing the street, late at night, his father was killed by a speeding car within a few seconds. A sad ending for a talented man.

But today, Rico wants to celebrate the reunion with the woman he never forgot. On top of the world, he stops off at a Ben and Jerry's ice cream store where he orders two scoops of mint chocolate chip topped with some crushed pecans, asking the clerk to please add a cherry. He's feeling so good. When he exits the Market Street store, ice cream cup in hand, a chubby Hispanic man with a buff bull dog body bumps right into him; head-on. It seems almost on purpose. Rico immediately reaches for the wallet he just put inside his jacket pocket. He had been told about this city's notorious professional pickpockets. His wallet is still there. He's now annoyed at the stubby man's inability to walk down the street without knocking into people. Some of the melted green ice cream had escaped his cup and during the collision, fell onto Rico's shirt. The man with the greasy ponytail and dark sunglasses stands very close to him, not backing off. Rico looks down at his face. There is no expression. Then he glances further down and sees the small black gun now pressed into his stomach. Shit! What the…He knee jerks, and kicks the man in the leg.

The man groans and falls to the ground. "Mierda!" He fumbles around, hurriedly putting his gun out of sight. Rico breaks into a run. The chase begins. Rico dodges into Macy's department store. He can lose him there. Looks like a huge place. "Who the hell is that guy? Why does he have a gun?" Sprinting through women's shoes and then through accessories, Rico springs out another door further down the street. Flying into Neiman-Marcus, he maneuvers through a variety of departments and then out yet another door. He runs back down to Market Street.

"Por Dios! Does this mongrel have anything to do with Jessi's story about the abduction?" Rico turns around. The man doesn't see him; but Rico spots *him*. Desperate to hide out somewhere for a while to ensure that he's lost him, he starts to panic. "Where the hell can I blend into a crowd?" A movie theatre marquis catches his eye. He races to the entrance and bypasses the ticket counter. Between movies, the kiosk is empty; no attendant on duty. He rushes into one of the several screening rooms. An animated film; some jungle story – colorful, giant animals and insects dance and sing before him. Kids are clustered in small groups throughout the screening room, some with parents and many without them. All of the viewers wear 3D plastic glasses. The place is maybe half full. Rico finds a quiet section at the front, off to the side – in the 3rd row from the screen; nobody around him for at least two rows. He sinks down into the cushioned seat, trying not to be noticed. His heart flip-flops in his chest. "Thank you God. I lost him now!" The kids laugh and shout as the singing continues; and a giant bird lays a golden egg which cracks open, hatching a goofy-looking miniature dinosaur. Some children toss popcorn in the air, screaming with delight.

Rico doesn't feel what happens next. He only hears the sound. Julio is careful to use his silencer but there is still that slight audible click of the trigger. The bullet hits his head in a fraction of a second. Seated behind him, Julio watches Rico slump down into the seat. Nobody notices. Their eyes are all glued to the magic of the big screen, fully engaged in their 3D experience.

Julio grins and thinks, you fool. Unfortunately, you were in the wrong place at the wrong time. Panama man, you came a little too close to the truth. You had to die. Now that bitch vet will never say another word, unless she wants to see the rest of her friends die. Rodrigo owes me for this one! I did what he said; his dirty work! I need to get out of here. I hate cartoons. He carefully separates the silencer from the gun and places both pieces back in his pocket. Julio had no idea that before Rico arrived at that hotel bar, Jessi Salazar had already met with Judge Martina Wells. Once his leather jacket is zipped, and his collar up around his neck, Julio Rodriguez, the man behind the dark sunglasses, slithers out of the movie theatre. Nobody notices him leave.

25

THREATS SHIFT MINDS

Martina sits in Union Square, half listening to the jazz band playing for the tourists. Another fifteen minutes, and she needs to walk back to the Hotel Metamorphosis to meet Jessi Salazar. She has an energy bar in her purse. Starved, she starts to nibble on it; but she can't eat or really do anything. The sensation she has is almost out of body, like she's floating above the scene she's in right now. Her shoulders are hunched down, her spirit broken. She's conflicted; having second thoughts about going to the police with Jessi Salazar. I must be stronger. Her mind shifts back and forth. What is the best path to follow to save her father? Sway the jury and basically commit a horrendous crime or go to the police and risk her father being killed by the Cartel? She breaks up the energy bar into small pieces with her fingers; imagining instead that she's smashing that blood-sucking scavenger into small crumbs; just like the crumbs she tosses to the pigeons here in Union Square. Her energy is spent. She can't even manage to shed another tear.

Rising from the stone seat, she walks closer to the five piece New Orleans band. Ahh, I love the saxophone. Her father used to play his sax when she was a little girl. She remembered her first day of school. Just a kindergartner, apprehensive about leaving home; getting on a school bus. She didn't want to go. She loved it at home; had her own nanny, Jasmine, whom she adored. Daddy had insisted that she get on the bus just like the other kids. He opted for her to attend public school. Her father and Jasmine escorted her to the yellow bus that morning. Her mother was still in bed and protesting her husband's decision not to send Martina to Harper, the elite private school, more appropriate for their echelon of society. Parker was dressed in his expensive suit and tie that day; but he was smiling and holding his saxophone. Right there, before she got on the bus, he played her a tune. It was his own rendition of "She'll Be Comin' Round The Mountain." Martina loved that song. He played it often for her on his sax while she'd sing. He'd wake her up early on Sunday mornings with a tray full of breakfast goodies and his saxophone in tow. He'd play all her favorite kiddie songs on request. He was standing at the bus stop that day when she returned home from her first day at school; his tie askew, and his work sleeves rolled up on that hot September afternoon. He snapped a photo as she stepped down from the bus, waving goodbye to the few kids left on board. "Time to celebrate. You made it! Not so bad, huh?" her father inquired. While their own private chef made pizza by hand as she watched in their sprawling granite and stainless steel kitchen, she told her father all about her first day of kindergarten. Her mother was gone again; this time at a hairdresser appointment.

Martina's phone rings out, interrupting her reverie. Oh my God, an unknown number.

"It's been too long. Where are you Judge? Are you preparing yourself for court tomorrow? I hope so!"

"I-I'm...Yes! I'm reading all the documents tonight. How is my father?"

"He's a little under the weather. You are fortunate that I honestly care about him."

"What's wrong with him?" Rodrigo had very carefully recorded her father's groans the first night after Julio had thrown him in the closet. "Now is a perfect time to play this for the fretting judge. He clicks the recording on. "Mar-Martina. Martina."

It's her father's voice." Is it really him? Let me talk to him. Please."

"No dice. I managed to get him some medication. I think he's got a throat infection; something like that. Anyway, I'm a hero. I got him some antibiotics. Don't ask me how."

"Please. Please. I need him back. He's sick? Oh please - don't hurt him; or make him worse than he already is."

"He's okay. Martina, are you being a worry wart?" He laughs his nasty laugh, the one that fills the phone with venom. I'll call you promptly as soon as court adjourns tomorrow. I hear the closing arguments may be happening before noon. Is that right?"

"Yes, maybe. I can't say for sure. There's not much more to present in the case that I'm aware of at this point. My father, how will I get him back if I manage to save Vicente from conviction?"

"Judge Wells, there is always one thing you can depend on me for. Do you know what that *thing* is?

"What?"

"I will give you information on next steps once I feel like it and when I'm ready to do that. And I'm not ready yet! Remember to honor your commitments to me, which includes your total silence. You know, I can hurt you too." Something jingles again in the background. Keys. It's his damn keys.

Dial tone. He's gone. She checks her watch; and runs down the block to Market Street. Streetcars and crowds of people are everywhere. She's already late meeting Jessi back at the hotel bar.

Rodrigo walks out of the ranch house; his cowboy boots heavy on the creaking porch boards. The sun is shining. It's hot down here in Salinas, probably in the high 90's. I'm roasting. He wipes his forehead with his red neckerchief. His great uncle rocks in the Spanish style chair. 89 years old and doesn't speak any English. "Rodrigo! Rodrigo! Qué pasa?" Rodrigo smiles, and moves to the rocker; hugging his frail head in his hands; then giving the old man an exaggerated kiss on his balding head.

"Bien. Bien." The Columbian cowboy turns and walks down the stairs towards the old corral where the boy watches the wildest of horses being trained. It's a black one named Giant. "Hey

Lance, are you ready to go back to the rodeo for tonight's show and fireworks?" The boy smiles, and nods eagerly.

Lance is having the time of his life. His mom's new friend is the coolest. He jumps up on the fence posts and waves to the beautiful black horse, who raises his legs, and fights to bolt from the Spanish cowboy trainer. Myrna beams at Rodrigo. Mmm, look at him, she thinks. So very fine a man; and he's mine. I really like those jeans on him. His cowboy shirt is unsnapped almost halfway down his chest. His muscles are well cut, smooth and his skin a nice light brown. He embraces Myrna; then places his hand on her lower back, slowly easing it down the back of her tight jeans. I want to pinch her ass, he thinks.

"Hey, you!" she giggles. She pulls away gently; while her body aches to just remain there and enjoy it. "That's not yours again until tonight." She speaks in a hushed tone, and glances at Lance, shooting him her warmest smile. "Rod, I'm a mom. Remember?"

"Sì. Sì. But for me, you're a sizzling hot cowgirl! Every man can see that!"

"I enjoyed last night, Rod. I didn't think it could get much better, but….Ayiyi." She shakes her hand in the air, as if a flame just scorched her. "Ouch!" They both laugh.

"Sí, I felt the same. Myrna, how about if you take one extra day and we return to San Francisco Monday night, instead of tomorrow? Can you do that?"

"Oh, I don't know. I-I." She pauses, considering his invitation for yet another night of bliss. That means two more solid nights with him. "Well, yes! Lance doesn't go back to school until Tuesday as Spring break ends with a teacher's training meeting or something like that on Monday. I guess I can call in, and take a day off. My boss is out of town for a week, anyway. He probably won't even notice."

"Sí Señorita! Case closed. I want to take you to another special place before we go home."

She gazes up at the 6'2' cowboy, now curious. "Well, what is it?"

"Shhh." He puts his fingers to her lips and circles her mouth; then whispers in her ear.

"No, no. It's a surprise. You like it when I surprise you? When I'm spontaneous?"

"Yes, I do. I certainly do." She puts her head on his arm, pulling him to her. Lance laughs and shouts with delight at the wild black horse. He waves his cowboy hat high in the air. He loved the rodeo today, and can't wait to return tonight to the bulls, the lassos and the hotdogs.

Rodrigo wonders why the hell Julio hasn't called with news about the vet; what she did today, who she saw. If she blabbed to anyone, she will receive her dear cousin Myrna and son back in big plastic bags. This time I won't let my victims get away like that sniveling little dog of hers managed to do.

26

THE CONVERSATION

She rushes into the Hotel Metamorphosis, frantic that she might be seen by someone like that deranged Cartel nemesis. I think his name is Rodrigo. I heard someone call him by that name twice now.

Sitting in the same booth she left only a couple of hours ago, is the Dr. Salazar. Flustered, Martina falls into the seat. Jessi starts to get up from the table, thinking they were both now leaving, together heading back to the police station. Martina leans over, grasping Jessi's arm. "Please, can we sit down and talk."

"Oh yes, that's right. We were going to strategize how to present all the details to the police."

"I-I've re-considered our plan. Please listen."

Jessi is confused but is eager to hear what the judge has to say. At least Jessi has connected with the one person who can completely understand this insane ordeal; someone who has a more brutal situation brewing – her father's life is on the line.

"The kidnapper just called me...the Latino man from the cartel. He will likely return my father, maybe even tomorrow. I'm worried. My father's got some kind of throat infection. That's what the man said on the phone. I can't risk it Dr. Salazar. I know I sound crazy but..." Her head drops down, and her hands rip through her curly brown hair. She looks up at Jessi. "I just can't chance it. I need to try to save my father. Although this Rodrigo guy is certainly a maniac, somehow I trust him on his promise to return my dad to me if I accomplish the task." Her hands now fold, and then unfold on the table top. "Sorry, I have this nervous habit when I'm stressed. A judge with such a nervous habit! Embarrassing! Dr Salazar, do you have a father that you love very much? Do you understand why I made this irrational decision, even though it will cost me my career?"

Jessi feels her heart flood with pain. "Yes, I have a father. He's in Panama. I realize now how much I really do love him. I can understand how you feel. You can't go to the police now, if you think it will dangerously risk your dad's life. But – but, what about the trial?" Martina nods. Jessi continues. "Of course, I'll be discreet. I won't utter a word, but I'm not sure if I trust that Rodrigo on anything. You know that his name is definitely Rodrigo?"

"Yes, I heard someone call him that name twice now."

"The sound of this depraved man's name sends Jessi into new heights of anxiety. Her phone buzzes. A text. Shit, it's Stefan. Thank God, it's not the diabolical Rodrigo. She reads it.

"Please understand. Claudia means nothing. I don't know why her friend was with her, too. They both surprised me at my house very early this morning. Trust me, I tried to throw them out. I beg you, Jess. Call me." Yeah, I bet you did, she thinks to herself.

She looks across at Martina who seems defeated, quickly debilitating before her eyes. "It's not him, is it? Is that Rodrigo? She can barely suppress her rage, as she slams her small fist down hard on the table.

"N-no. It's someone else I don't want to see ever again. Never mind – stupid personal stuff." Jessi shrugs her shoulders and quickly refocuses. "You better get home, Judge. I won't go to the police now that you told me your change of plans. No worries. I'll just wait to hear from you after the trial. You're exhausted. You need your rest before tomorrow."

Martina's watery eyes stare across at Jessi. Her tears drip down onto the granite table. "Thank you. I owe you so much, Dr. Salazar. I'll call you."

"I'll pray for you."

The small woman exits the restaurant; a hollow Judge Wells – stripped of her soul.

Oh God, another text. It's Stefan again.

"I want to talk to you, Jess. Can you meet me after tonight's symphony at 10:30? My place?" Jessi is incensed. She starts to shut off her phone, disgusted with his pathetic pleas. A third text follows. It reads: "You need me and I need you."

Yeh, like I need a stake through my heart. Her stomach tightens.

Another buzz. But this time, it's an email from Nick. "Jessi, I'm worried about you, on pins and needles. Let me know what happened at the police station. Did you meet with a detective?"

Warm feelings flow through her body. He's a true friend – regardless of whether there is any relationship for them in the future. He's a rock. I need to call him later. She asks the waiter for a drink, this time something stiffer than a sparkling water. "Gin martini, please." She finishes the cocktail. It's 7:30. I should start walking over to the Marriott. She takes out her compact and frowns into the small mirror. Oh my God, I need a makeover. I look totally washed out. She leaves a twenty dollar bill, and heads to the restroom to freshen up.

27

SALINAS SUNSET

Myrna walks into the family room at the Salinas ranch house. Lance sits on the beautiful patterned rug in front of the roaring stone fireplace, playing with a miniature set of cowboys, and old western plastic figures. The room is decorated in an authentic cowboy motif, complete with animal heads on the wall and a sweeping western landscape hanging over the fireplace. In the corner of the room, on a wooden pedestal is a stuffed rattlesnake attacking a stuffed squirrel. An engraved sign under it reads: Seeking Prey and Winning! Noticing it for the first time, a shiver runs down Myrna's back. She refocuses on her son who doesn't know she's standing there. Lance performs with passionate animation, hurdling a plastic stagecoach across the expensive Persian rug, facilitating a full action scenario where some mean cowboys are planning to storm the toy stagecoach and rob all the people on board. He plays it out – the fighting, the defeat of the bad guys; the 'good overcoming evil.' "Come on men, let's get 'em. Wipe out all those bad guys. Are your horses ready? Let's charge!"

Fully entertained, Myrna laughs and cheers when the good guys obliterate the bad guys. "Yay. That was fantastic, Lance. You could be a Hollywood director."

"Rod is so cool, mom, buying this cowboy set for me on the way here. I can't believe they had this in a gas station 7-Eleven store. Wow!" He stops his play and comes over to Myrna who sits on the stone hearth and looks into the fire. "Mom, when someone is a good guy, is he all good, through and through? Or, can he be bad, too?"

Myrna wants to give a balanced answer, not paint the whole world rosy and pink; but at the same time be uplifting to her son. "Well, it's true, people can be good on some things and maybe bad on some others. But if a person shoots for being good 100% of the time and achieves at least 95%, then that's very good. Why do you ask, Lance?"

"Um, well I was playing early this morning, and I heard Rod talking to someone on the phone. He was mostly speaking Spanish to someone but I thought he said Aunt Jessi's name. Then he said a bad word. The 'F' word. I think he was talking to some man named Cèsar or something like that. He kept saying yes Cèsar or no Cèsar. Rod sounded really mad at the man. I think he was saying a lot of curse words."

Lance zooms around the room. Myrna is stunned by Lance's interpretation of Rod's phone call. "I'm sure that Rod didn't see me. I was just looking around downstairs. This house is so big, like a castle. But I really did hear him say Aunt Jessi's name. And I thought he said 'bitch vet'. Does he know her? "

"Lance!"

"I know, mom, but that's what I heard Rod say on the phone. Bad, huh?"

Now, she understands Lance's earlier question about people being both good and bad.

She moves closer to her son and sits him down on the hearth next to her. "Hmm. Well, maybe he knows someone named Jessi. You know, Jessi could be a man's name too."

Lance nods his head, and moves back to playing with his cowboys and horses. He wears the cowboy hat also gifted to him by Rod. Myrna strokes the boy's back, as he plays. "Well, cowboy, you better put on a warmer shirt for tonight. I think it might be chilly at the rodeo after the sun goes down; and remember we're staying for the fireworks too. How about that new blue

Nike sweatshirt, the cool one you got from Aunt Jessi for your birthday? Wanna go put that on now, sport?"

"Okay mom." He leaves to go up to the guest room. Myrna scoops up the plastic cowboys and horses; putting them back in their red plastic box. She thinks about Rod. There is something about him that puts her on alert. She can't pinpoint it. But sometimes, she catches him pounding his fists together, like he's imagining punching someone hard. Looks like he's got an angry edge; just below the surface. Nobody's perfect. She doesn't feel frightened of him; not really. He's dreamy. But, there is something about him that seems unexplained. The Jessi thing that Lance heard from Rod must be a reference to some family member or friend. A child's imagination – a wondrous thing, she thinks.

She moves to the window, opening up the wooden blinds. She can see Rod standing there watching the horse being tamed by the ranch hand. Myrna closes her eyes, smiling to herself. She remembers how she felt when she laid there, her head on Rod's handsome chest, stroking his rock solid stomach while he ran his fingers up and down her arm, arousing her for a second time last night. Her Spanish cowboy! She was falling for him, more and more, despite her slight degree of uneasiness. Now, he's asked for even more time with her. Lance comes running back into the room, galloping over to Myrna.

"Hey mom, are we ready to go back to the rodeo now?"

"Sure, let's go ask Rod if it's time yet. Wow. Look outside at that beautiful cowboy sunset."

Rod comes into the house. "Myrna. I must talk to you. Is it okay if you go to the rodeo without me? Carlos will drive you there and pick you up. I just got called to a facilities emergency at my company's site. I need to drive to San Jose and take care of it. Some spill in the manufacturing area. I don't want you guys to miss the rodeo. I'll be back before morning; and we can have one more day here."

"But Rod…"

"Please mom, I want to go back to the rodeo tonight!" He pulls on her sweater. "They have rides too, and cotton candy."

"Okay Lance. We'll go." She smiles down at him; and then looks up at Rod; not sure whether she's making the right decision. The sun shines across her lover's face. His five o'clock shadow is past due and he's looking very sexy.

"I'll be back before 5 a.m." He kisses her, turns, and notices Myrna's cell phone sitting on the coffee table. He swiftly slips it into his pocket. She can't have that, he thinks. Oh no, no, no. Once outside the ranch house, he walks behind the house; takes out Myrna's cell phone and throws it on the ground. He crushes it with his heavy brown cowboy boot; smashing it into pieces. With his metal-rimmed boot, he pushes the pieces of plastic and metal all into one spot of red dirt. With both hands, he picks up a large gray stone and drops it onto the little chunks of broken cell phone. Destroyed and invisible now. He rushes away, getting into his SUV. He must get to San Francisco quickly; and do the deed. My little puppet Myrna won't suspect a thing! A dumb beauty with no clue that I will, in fact, be connecting with her cousin. And if the doctor doesn't cooperate, then I have more in store for Myrna, my little sweetheart.

28

THE MARRIOTT MARQUIS

Jessi rushes into the Marriott Marquis Hotel. It's 8:03 p.m. Whew! Not too bad; just three minutes behind. She hates being late for anything; whether it's an appointment with a patient or a date with a friend. Crowded and noisy, people are coming and going from the hotel. She scans the expansive, bustling lobby looking for Rico. Jessi thinks about her feelings for this friend who has suddenly appeared in the midst of the worst week of her life. Touching the pouch which holds the promise rings in her pocket, she realizes that she feels almost as if Rico is a brother to her; more than a romantic interest. Whatever their future, she craves to spend time with him; hear about his education, his career, his life in Panama City and also talk about her ailing father. Rico, a welcome oasis outside the nightmare of Stefan and the despicable Latino man who tortures her daily.

No sign of Rico at 8:35. She calls his cell phone. Straight to voicemail. She approaches the now empty reception desk area; and asks if she can phone Rico Mendez's room. The clerk hands Jessi the phone, punching the room number. She listens to the ring. No answer. She leaves a message on his hotel room voicemail. "Rico, your old pal Jessi is calling. I'm in the lobby; but haven't seen hide nor hair of my deep-dimpled jungle boyfriend. Where are you? Call me. You have my cell phone number; or just come and get me. You know that I'm hungry, as usual." Maybe he thinks I'm meeting him at the hotel restaurant. She thanks the clerk and walks over to the hostess station at the front of the restaurant. No sign of Rico. Jessi pokes her head in the elegantly decorated dining room, which features several rounded booths and beautiful lamps. She doesn't see him there. She decides to take a stool at the dark wooded bar connected to the restaurant. If he comes in, she'll see him. She tries his cell phone again but it goes to voicemail.

She takes a sip of the glass of red wine she just ordered. It hits the spot. Her mind wanders back to the jungle; her childhood with Rico. She recalls those carefree moments; both of them lying side by side in that rip-torn hammock, each chewing on a long, skinny marsh reed. She can see the birds swooping down as the two children pan the vibrant kaleidoscope of rainforest, fully engaged in their daily "First To Spot A Tree Sloth" game. Together, they would scan every inch of what their eyes could see as they competed to locate the slowest and most camou-flaged creature inhabiting the wet, humid rainforest - the sloth; the one jungle animal which seemed to have all the time in the world to go from point A to point B. There would inevitably be at least one sloth within their range of view. If Rico found the sloth first, he'd tickle and tease Jessi until the hammock would flip flop, tangling them up together like one big pretzel. If she found the sloth first, she'd push Rico out of the hammock onto the hard ground, announcing that she was Queen of the Jungle. She would demand that he immediately bow down to her, as she is the Exalted One. Everything in Jessi's life at that time was innocent and easy; up until that dreadful day when she came upon her father in the midst of committing adultery with Rico's mother.

Sitting in the Marriott bar, Jessi looks down at her watch; and finishes the last drop of red wine in the glass. Almost 9:00. Still no Rico. The bar is crowded now, people laughing, talking loud. She tries to text him. "So, are you standing up your best friend?" No return text.

She overhears a group of men right by her at the bar, busy telling animated stories. Several of them have Latino accents.

They're talking about architecture! They must be with the conference where Rico is a featured speaker tomorrow. One Latino man says, "Sí, the architecture even in this area on Market Street is striking. Me gusta. Sí! Sí!" He gives a toast to the group of five or six of them huddled together. It's a long shot but what the heck, she thinks.

"Excuse me. I'm sorry to interrupt; but by chance, do you know Rico Mendez? The corpulent man quickly speaks up. "Do we know him?" He laughs heartily. "Sí, we all work with him in Panama. Even these two Americanos here. The hombre is amazing to watch. Creating, inventing fabulous designs and always with common sense in terms of the business. Very talented; gifted. We love him!" He laughs again.

One of the Americans speaks up. "He will represent our firm at the conference tomorrow. We will all be stars after that!"

A Latino man adds his opinion. "Sí. Rico will make our country famous. We are proud of him. Here's to Rico!" He raises his glass and they all toast in unison. "Salud! Salud!" They are merry, boisterous; and all somewhat drunk. The whole bar, now full of people, look at the elated Latino dominated group. The six of them clink glasses and yell as if at a soccer match. Jessi can't help but laugh along with them.

The tall American in the group speaks out, just after taking another gulp of his beer. "I agree. Here's to Rico. That guy is on fire!" He looks into Jessi's eyes. "Do you know him well?"

She smiles. "Yes, I grew up with him in Panama."

The group goes silent; now taking a closer look at her as if they somehow know all about her. Several of them grin at each other, a couple of them nodding their heads and the rest of them exchanging another sideline toast. The way they look at her makes her feel like she's wearing a low cut evening gown and maybe four inch heels; or maybe she's just naked altogether.

"So, you must be Jessi, 'the jungle girl.' Jessi, is that your name?" the Latino with longer hair asks.

"Yes, I'm Jessi Salazar."

"Ahh, we are all happy to meet you," the oldest Latino man adds.

Once the laughter and secretive glances wind down, Jessi asks, "Have any of you seen Rico in the last hour or so? I was supposed to meet him here over an hour ago. Actually, we planned to meet in the lobby at 8 o'clock for dinner in the hotel restaurant."

"He was supposed to have drinks with us right here about two hours ago," one of the two Americans comments. "He didn't absolutely commit, but sounded like he was going to show. Never arrived. We're still waiting for him."

Jessi's stomach begins to cramp.

The stouter Latino man starts to show some more serious concern. "No. No. It's not like Rico to not show up. He's always on time. If he says he'll be there, he's there."

"Let me buzz him," the taller American says. He takes out his cell phone, punches in the number; expecting no delay in pick up on the other end. He holds up the phone so they can all hear Rico's voicemail greeting. "Hmm, that's strange. Rico is the best one I know at answering his phone even when he's in an important client meeting. No answer, Ms. Salazar."

She needs to escape so they don't see her panicking. He didn't show for his friends and he didn't show for the girl he gave his promise ring to so many years ago. It's not like him. I know that, and so do his colleagues. "I'm so sorry; but I must go. When you do see him, here's my card with my phone number. Please have him call me as soon as possible; or one of you please phone me and let me know he's okay. I know it's silly, but I'm a bit worried about him." Jessi is careful not to exaggerate her concern. She doesn't want to alarm them. She thanks them for their time and wishes them a good conference for the rest of the week. Dashing into the lobby, she takes one more look; then runs out through the hotel entrance into the dark, windy night.

29

ONE PAYBACK AT A TIME

On the streetcar home, Jessi thinks about her cousin and nephew. She hasn't heard from them. Myrna promised to phone her on Sunday evening when she returned from Salinas. Where is she? Why hasn't she called? I know that she's immersed in love and completely distracted. I've been there, done that; and fully understand. At least I don't have to worry about Myrna being here, vulnerable to these crazy Cartel people. She double checks her phone messages. Nothing from Myrna. Nothing from Rico. Jessi stares out at the dark streets still full of tourists and people out for late night activities. San Francisco, it never sleeps. She opens her purse to get her keys out. Her key ring has a small photo of Myrna and Lance in Disneyland last year. She looks at it fondly, thinking about Myrna now in love. Then it hits her as if she is suddenly shot between the eyes with a piercing arrow. Shit! Rod. Rod. Myrna's new boyfriend. Is he really Rodrigo? The puzzle pieces start to come together in her now mangled mind. Are Myrna and Lance both being held by that despicable psycho? Oh God. He seduced her to get to me. Jessi can't manage to swallow. He knew I would realize sooner or later; and get the message. Those keys, that chain jingling when I was on the phone with Rodrigo. I noticed it again on the phone with Myrna. Shit! Jittery, she almost falls, as she steps off the streetcar.

Running home in the dark, she speeds across the street. She glances to her left and then to her right. An old man walks past her in the opposite direction. It's....it's the blind Asian man, tapping his cane on the sidewalk in the dark. It's the same man who she bumped into at Starbucks, and who looked into her eyes and said, "Remain calm, dear girl. You will come through everything." Afraid to frighten the man who now passes right by her, she looks over at him. What's he doing out so late? He slows down and raises his head as if looking in her direction. Even in the dark, she can see his smile. He nods and continues walking on past her. She can still hear his cane hitting the pavement as he gets further and further away. Jessi feels a sense of peace wash over her. Ridiculous, especially after the dismal realization that her cousin may be in the custody of a heartless killer. But she can't deny this surprise moment of pure serenity.

She starts running again. Almost home. She remembers that she left her two cats outside the house. She turns the key in the front door lock. "Shit!" Someone just came up behind her.

"Jess. I'm...." She jumps.

"Stefan! Oh God. What are you doing here?" He wears his tux, bow tie, now loosened; and a white satin scarf hangs around his neck. She wants to grab it and strangle him. He squeezes his way inside her house and closes the front door behind him.

"I need to talk to you Jess. Claudia....honestly, she means nothing. She showed up unannounced with that young flute player in tow last night. I was helpless; practically asleep. I mean Jess, my mother was actually upstairs the whole time."

"You sleazebag. They obviously stayed all night with you. I can only imagine."

He moves to her, runs his hand through her hair, and reaches down under her blouse. "Please, I can make amends. Let me just..."

She pushes his hand out from under her clothes. "You're crazy! My best friend from Panama is here in San Francisco; and he's in bad trouble. I think he's hurt. It may be worse." She breaks down in tears.

Stefan tries to soothe her, stroking her arm. "You mean Rico, that unsophisticated, insignificant jungle boy from Panama.

Forget about him. You have a much more interesting man standing right here in front of you," he whispers. He tries putting his hand under her blouse a second time. "Jess. Jess. I can help you relax."

She knees him in the groin; with all her gusto. He doubles over in pain, almost falling to the floor. Jessi runs into the kitchen and picks up the biggest iron pot she can find. She runs out and sees Stefan still crumpled up, trying to sit up against the wall near the grandfather clock. "Jess, what are you doing? Trying to injure me? Are you losing your mind?"

"Yes, I've lost my mind!" she yells. "See this spaghetti pot? If you don't get out of here in two seconds, I'm planning to head on charge at you and knock you unconscious or worse."

"But Jess, I'm in love with you. Are you blinded by jealousy? Please." He tries to get up.

"The only one around here who is blind is you, Stefan. If you don't get out of here on the count of three, then I may have to use this as well." She raises up a kitchen carving knife in her other hand. "Remember the three blind mice? But rest assured, it won't be your head that gets whacked off!" She gestures to his groin. Her anger erupts like a spewing volcano.

"Do I have your undivided attention now, Mr. Bon Jovi of the Symphony?" She moves towards him with the knife. He backs up to the front door, shaking in his shoes, almost unable to talk or walk. He falters and trips. She keeps coming, the pot also still in hand. She drops the knife on the floor, rushes to the door, before he gets there; and opens it. She signals for him to get the hell out, holding up the heavy pot. "Narcissist!"

Stefan takes the hint, and runs down the driveway in fear of this woman gone wild. He disappears, his long white scarf blowing in the wind. He's gone, into the foggy San Francisco night.

Exhausted, she slams the door, carefully locking it behind her. Jessi slides down to the floor, her back up against the closed door, dropping the heavy pot. It crashes with a thud. That pig of a man! That will never happen again! He was the ventriloquist and I was the dummy! Breaking into uncontrollable sobs, she's scared to death. Rodrigo, he'll be here tonight. He'll come for me now. He must have Rico. But if Rodrigo's with Myrna and Lance, how did he get Rico? She re-plays the day in her mind. Oh God. That man…that man in the bar at The Hotel Metamorphosis. The one with the sunglasses. I noticed that he gave me a strange look. Maybe that's the other masked man that I saw from the restaurant window. Damn! I don't know. Her mind jumps from one bad thing to another. What happened to Rico? Where is he? What the hell do I do now? Is this all part of a fateful plan, punishing me for hating my dying father?

Creature and Pandora prance back into the room as if it's just another ordinary evening at home; meowing and jumping across Jessi's weary outstretched legs. She sits there, motionless. She reaches out to embrace them. Thank God they're unharmed. He hasn't come back for them yet. Damn, how did they get back into the house? I let them both out before I left. She gets up and checks everywhere for an open window or door, petrified that the killer might be in the house. Either Rodrigo or his partner. She can't figure it out. Picking up the carving knife from the floor, she holds it out as her weapon. That's when she fully realizes how she almost lost her mind with Stefan. She could have killed him. He has no idea how close she came to it. Her mind shifts. Maybe the cats came in through the front door when Stefan entered. Her mind leaps and then sidesteps from rational brain to nervous wreck, and then back again. The grandfather clock strikes 11. I can't sleep here alone. I won't make it through the night. She picks up her cell phone, and phones Nick. He answers on the first ring.

30

THE ULTIMATUM

"I thought something happened to you. I've been calling you. Jessi, I was a little frantic."

"No, I'm still kicking and screaming; and causing trouble," attempting a slight degree of levity. The knife she held on Stefan flashes through her mind. "You've been calling me? I have no messages." She looks at her phone. "Damn! I'm sorry Nick. I've been so freaked out for the last few hours. I-I thought I had no messages. I was looking at my text icon instead of my phone icon."

"I didn't text you Jessi. I thought maybe someone else might look at your phone and see the text; and you might not want that."

"Someone else? What do you mean?"

"Well, I saw you this afternoon. I-I'm sorry. I was walk-ing down Market Street and I saw you at that bar at the Hotel Metamorphosis. I peeked in the window and there you were. I stayed a little longer than I should have. You must have been on a date. Some good-looking guy was sitting with you in the booth; and reaching across the table, holding your hand. It appeared to be a serious lunch date." He pauses, then adds, "I'm sorry. I don't mean to pry."

"Th-that was Rico from Panama. He's in town for a conference."

"Oh. Uh. I see. I called you a couple of hours later; just to say hi. That guy seemed really interested in you. I don't quite understand, but I started to get this weird sense that something was wrong for you. I guess you're fine. But I'm glad you called tonight. Sorry, I was a voyeur for a few minutes while you were catching up with Rico."

His warm voice gives her comfort.

"Nick. I-I…." She begins to cry. Everything from today comes rushing in, consuming her like a firestorm. "Nick, something terrible has happened. Not only is Dr. Pepper still missing, but …" Her voice cracks. She's in panic mode.

"Jessi, what's going on?"

"I'm afraid for someone's life. Not just for one person but for three people, including my cousin Myrna and her son." He hopes she's exaggerating; perhaps imagining the worst. She kicks ass in the brains department, so there must be some real substance to her fears.

"Jessi, I can be at your place in 15 minutes. Please accept my support."

"Yes, come over. I need you." She goes silent, not quite sure what to say. "Look Nick, I want to apologize for how I've been acting with you lately. I've been lost in a fog." She just wants to see him, feel his arms around her.

"I don't need any enticement. I'll be there in three minutes. Bye, Jessi. I don't know whose lives are in jeopardy; but we'll think of something together." He hangs up.

Thirsty. I need some water. She goes to the kitchen, takes a clean glass and pushes the filtered water spigot on the fridge. Her hands tremble. Water spritzes out everywhere, all over the wood floor. She doesn't care. Her life is falling apart. She tries to call Myrna again; but no luck. The call automatically goes to voicemail. Conflicted, she considers leaving a message; then decides to hang up. She stares at the picture magnets of Myrna and her son, and at Lance's pre-school painting; all posted on her fridge. Her cell phone rings. Unknown number. It could be the Judge Wells. Anyone but please not him! She stares down at the buzzing phone as if she can somehow cosmically figure out who is calling without actually answering the damn thing; but knows she has no choice but to take the call.

"Yes?" she says meekly.

The sound of his voice stabs her in the heart. Probably a killer, at the very least – a kidnapper. She fears the worst is about to come out of his mouth.

"Don't move; breathe, or even say a word, until I finish. Just listen to me. Listen good senorita. Comprendes? Your cousin....I guess you finally figured it out!"

His voice spills out in a very low register and aggressive force, like a bulldozer; its full metal weight crushing the life out of her. She drops the glass of water which smashes to the tile surface and breaks into a dozen shards, the ice splattering and rolling across the kitchen floor in various directions. When he said the word cousin, it made her sick, nauseous. Oh God. He's got Myrna and Lance in captivity. She wants to cut his throat with the large sharp piece of glass she sees on the floor by the dishwasher. She'd gladly risk her life to see his ended. Regardless, she tries to obey his command not to interrupt until he's finished.

She can't take it any more. "Fuck you!" she screams into the phone.

"Now, now. Anger won't get you anywhere, Dr. Salazar. I thought you were a professional. You're not acting like one!" He laughs. "Ahh! You are just being a comedienne. Myrna, she's so sexy and flexible too. Ooooh. A very good screw! Muy buena! They will both be dead. Hear me?" He raises his voice. "Dead, if you make one more move to the police or talk with that judge again before the trial ends. Actually, Little Miss animal lover, if you ever contact the judge – even if I kindly return Myrna and little Lance, I will come back for them. Cut their heads off!"

"You have them?"

"They are my hostages; although they don't quite know that yet." He laughs, sneering into the phone. She hears noise in the background; sounds like a loudspeaker at an event. Damn it, where are they? Salinas? That's what Myrna said.

"I'm going to kill both of them unless I have some proof that your mouth will be kept closed; not like today when it was dangerously spilling out some fairy tale. We had the Judge Wells shut you down. She knows better. Her father's life is on the line; just like you with your cousin and little nephew. So, I need proof!"

She pleads. "What proof? How can I give you proof? Just don't hurt them. I won't say a word."

"There's only one action you can do to save them. If you don't comply, you should start the funeral arrangements – a shapely casket for Myrna and a young child's casket for Lancelot."

"No. No. What can I do? What?"

Nick knocks on the door. She can't move; afraid Rodrigo will hear the door close behind Nick if she opens it. She stays in the kitchen. He goes to the back door. She turns on the back porch light and peers through the glass panels; making eye contact with Nick. She points to the phone and points down to the doorknob. Jessi puts her fingers to her lips to signal him to quietly enter. She moves into the living room so Nick can enter from the kitchen's back door without Rodrigo hearing someone else in her house. Nick quietly crosses the room to Jessi. She dares not put it on speaker phone. Nick can hear the Latino man say his next words. He just can't believe the horrid demand being made. Jessi thinks that only she can hear Rodrigo's commands. It's better for Nick to stay in the dark as much as possible. It will protect him, at least to some degree.

"If you want to see that little boy and his madre breathing again, you must eliminate Judge Martina Wells." The unbelievable words spew out, raging in her ears; snapping like hungry sharks inside her head. Nick sees Jessi physically weaken and almost collapse. Jessi is sure that Nick can't hear the man, but he's catching every word, every savage and incorrigible syllable – everything she hears.

Rodrigo continues. "Yes, you'll need to do this little, tiny favor if you want to save your dear family. My little endangered witness! I have the weapon all ready for you to use. It will be easy!

The action will take place tomorrow night at exactly midnight. It will be after the trial is over. You only need to press a white switch just outside her residence, and the rest will be done. 659 Ashburn Street, Nob Hill. Write it down. Immediately! Repeat the address to me as you write it."

"But…"

"Do it! Write it down now or I hang up and they're both dead within ten minutes."

She grabs some paper from her refrigerator pad; and the pen hanging right beside it. She writes down the address. "What… what is it again?" she asks, having truly forgotten the numbers in her frenzy.

"659 Ashburn. Nob Hill. A blue Victorian. Repeat it!"

"659 Ashburn. Nob Hill. A blue Victorian." She's nervous and thinks maybe Rodrigo can hear Nick; although he's trying his best to be absolutely still. Nick pretends he doesn't understand what she's doing or what the man is requesting. He doesn't want Jessi to know that he's hearing every instruction being given. He can recall his mother saying, "Nicky, you amaze me. You can hear a spider weaving her web if you cared to do that. Where did you get such incredible auditory ability? I wish I had half of it."

Rodrigo clears his throat. He opens the door to the San Francisco apartment, his cell phone in hand; still enjoying his phone dialogue with the lovely Dr. Salazar. He opens the door and sees Julio, who's sitting at the kitchen table, drinking a beer. Rodrigo continues his precise instructions to Jessi. "The white switch will be on the ground just outside the judge's residence, just at the end of the path, on the right side. A little red flag will be sticking up in the dirt by the white switch. Press hard on the switch, and get out of the way. There will be quite an explosion inside the house." Jessi cringes. Nick does the same, but with no noticeable physical reaction. "We will hook up the bomb tomorrow night before 11:30 p.m. A remarkable work of art. You'll see. At exactly midnight, you must be there and click the switch. Again, the switch will be obvious. For tonight, just relax and enjoy your cats. Meow!" Nick moves away pretending he still can't hear what the man on the phone is saying.

In disbelief, she tries to reason with Rodrigo one more time. "B-but- but I …I would…"

"Bitch vet! You will do exactly what I ask to save what's left of your pathetic little family. If you fail, there will be no more visits to your office from Myrna or little Lance. Never again. I will hang them both from a tree here at the ranch. I have a very nice spot!" His sinister laugh. "And tell me doctor, who does the black eye make-up for your attractive young veterinary assistant? She's so… how you say – gothic?"

Jessi gasps. He knows everything, even about Sarah. Oh my God!

"If you succeed, and the explosion goes off as I've instructed you, then your Cousin and her son will be deposited on their doorstep sometime early the next morning. Are we clear? Please confirm to me with a yes!" His obnoxious evil laughter fills the air space.

"Y-yes. I am clear." Click. Dial tone.

She notices Dr. Pepper's white ceramic dog food bowl; decorated with the little blue dog bones around the rim, and his matching water bowl sitting there on the kitchen floor. She can hear his tiny Yorkie nipping at the water, and his loud crunching of the Purina Dog Chow. Often, he'd pause, and look around to make sure Jessi was close by. He didn't like to eat alone nor when the cats were hanging around. He wanted her to be there. He was finicky and she loved that about her dog. His image disappears as Jessi refocuses on Nick. Tears well up in her eyes. She misses her spunky dog and his cocky little personality.

"What's going on, Jessi?" Nick leads her to the living room and helps her sit down on the sofa.

In the one bedroom San Francisco apartment, Rodrigo sits down at the table with his brother. "Julio, get me a cerveza. Ándale!"

The San Francisco apartment is hot. The smell is putrid. Julio bends back on his chair, almost crashing to the floor, and stretches his arm to reach into the fridge for another can of beer. He throws it at Rodrigo, who catches it with panache. "I'm good, what can I say?" Julio takes the opportunity to brag, a rare chance in the company of his brother. Rodrigo flips open the can with his teeth. So, tell me about your day? What happened with that Rico guy."

Julio laughs and with animation, describes how he overheard the bitch vet telling a South American hombre all about them; everything she saw from the restaurant window. Every detail and even your name, Rodrigo. She had figured it out from the judge like you knew she would eventually do. This Rico guy just showed up out of the blue and she spilled it to him, the whole story. Like you said man, there was only one thing to do; get rid of him. Who was he, anyway?"

Rodrigo plays with his noisy key chain, slapping it back and forth on the table top as he chugs down his beer; seeing how many marks and cuts he can inflict on the table. Like most things in his life, he doesn't care about the table. He wants to see it beat up and bruised.

"Hey Rodrigo, I heard her mention that Rico was from Panama. They grew up together or something like that. He just showed up in town and called her. Bad timing! Seriously, he has a poor choice of friends. If she didn't squawk that hombre, I wouldn't have touched him. Sí. They looked like more than friends; handholding and smiling together over something inside a bag of some sort. I finished him off in a movie theatre filled with kids." Julio takes his gun out of his pocket and mimes exactly how he shot Rico in the back of the head. "Not one kid in the theatre had any suspicion of what went down. I was in and out of there within five minutes."

"No prints, right? Nothing?"

"Right."

"Okay, let's get moving. We've got a lot to get done tonight, mi hermano. First, we need to dump the old man's body. I know just the place on the edge of the city. We can take him in the truck. But before we get that rigged up, we need to assemble the bomb for the judge's house; ready for tomorrow after the trial. I already spoke to the vet, and got her to agree to flip the white switch tomorrow night, after we set the whole thing up before her arrival at midnight.."

"How did you get her to agree?"

"Well," Rodrigo goes on. "The pawns are the cousin Myrna, a nice piece of ass, by the way, and her five year old son. They are my hostages." Julio reacts with a puzzled expression..

"It's all under the champion's control. They don't even know they're hostages right now. They are at the rodeo tonight. I need to be back there before 5 am. So let's get going on making the house bomb. You got the stuff?"

"Yeh, I got all of it." He kicks a cardboard carton under the kitchen table, shoving it only partially out the other side. "Agh, that box is heavy." Kneeling down, he pulls the box out with his hands.

"Bueno. Put it all on the table. I have my checklist. Let's see if everything we need is here." The two brothers spend the next three hours constructing the perfect homemade bomb. They set up a mock white switch, exactly the same design as the one they will place in the judge's house on Nob Hill, and the same white operating switch to be hidden at the side of the path. "And Julio, it's good that it will be Dr. Jessi Salazar flipping the switch, not the Velasquez brothers. We want to share the fun! Sí?" They both laugh. "She saves the useless lives of animals and also ends live of other animals, everyday in her job. I think it's called euthanasia. The judge is just one more animal sitting in her cage that must be taken down. Our own version of euthanasia." He can't help but laugh again. "And the doc is just the one to do it! And if not, well the silver lining is I get to rape and kill her sweet cousin Myrna. I may leave the elimination of the young boy to you, Julio." His brother reacts by rolling his eyes and gathers the parts to begin bomb construction, while Rodrigo whistles the tune 'Raindrops Keep Falling On My Head.'

Julio teases Rodrigo. "You fancy yourself as someone like Butch Cassidy, the famous cowboy?"

"Sí, I do; and you, mi hermano, are just like the Sundance Kid?"

"So, I'm the good looking one then, eh?" Julio appreciates the unexpected compliment from his older brother.

"If you call that mess on your face good-looking?" Rodrigo guffaws with laughter. "Don't be an imbecile!" He drags Julio over to the mirror to make him look at his face. "You like this mug?" He pushes Julio's face up against the mirror and then pulls it back. "Oh, Grandma would be disappointed at *this* little baby grandson – sinfully ugly Julio. Okay, now let's look at this one instead." Rodrigo poses into the mirror. He pushes Julio out of the way, and smacks him in the head; commanding him to pay attention. "Is this an improvement, in terms of better looking? Eh ? Rodrigo flashes his best star quality smile, and poses like a cover model from GQ magazine. What is your opinion, Julio? Me or you? Who is much, *much* better-looking?"

Rodrigo, always trying to crap all over Julio's ego. "Stupid game, brother. I'm not playing. Let's get this bomb constructed."

"Okay, you have a decent idea, for a change. Seriously, we'll need to get out of town headed back to Cartagena right after this goes down tomorrow night. Once the verdict is delivered, and we've eliminated that tight-assed judge and her old man; it's time for us to flee. Uncle Carlos already gave me the tickets. We leave on the 5 a.m. flight out of San Francisco. We'll do the set up job between 11 and midnight; and be done. Then stay around to make sure that the doc does the rest; pressing down on that switch."

"Wait a minute. If we leave, right after that, what about the cousin and the boy? The logistics, Rodrigo? Eh?"

"That part is just a hoax. I will bring both Myrna and Lance back to their home about 10 o'clock tomorrow night; then meet you before 10:30 so we can drive over to the judge's house, set the bomb and prepare the switch. I've smashed Myrna's cell phone into little bits. She probably won't even realize that it's gone until late tomorrow night. Don't worry. I will keep her occupied. You know what I mean?" He makes a crude gesture with his fist.

Julio raises his eyebrows, and nods.

"Sí," Rodrigo continues; thrashing his key chain on the beat up table. "I also pulled the wires on her house phone. It will not work again until the phone company comes out to repair it; which would only happen at the earliest, after we're out of here. You know my tricks! Before Myrna ever gets to her sweet cousin, the doc will have pushed the white switch. I doubt she'll be talking about it to anyone."

Two hours later, they had a working bomb, strong enough to blow up Martina Well's small mansion. After dumping the bag occupied by the old man, into their tow truck, they hauled the bag to Cement Depot just outside of Burlingame, and pulled in a favor owed to their family. Within 25 minutes, Parker Wells was buried in cold, gray cement under an 'under construction' high rise office building. All in a Cartel member's good night's work.

31

PRETENSE, PANIC AND A PLAN OF ACTION

Nick sits on the sofa with Jessi, and holds her close. "I didn't really hear much of what that guy was saying on the other end, but I could see how much pain you were in."

"I can't tell you. It would put you in too much jeopardy. I think Rico is dead. Oh, I don't know. I just don't know."

"Jessi, I want you to rest." After leading her into her bedroom, he gently lays her down on the antique bed. He takes off her shoes and removes her thick black sweater; placing it on the brown suede Laz-Z-Boy chair by the window. He slips the blanket up over her body. She's trembling. "There you go. I can come back early in the morning. It's Monday, but I'm not in a staff meeting until about 11. I can check on you first."

She reaches up for him. "Nick, please. Can you stay with me tonight? I want to feel your arms around me. Is that okay?"

He lays down beside her, strokes her hair and embraces her. A streetlight shines through the window. He can see her eyes close, her long lashes glistening, still wet with tears. With her turned up nose, she still looks so young, so innocent; like a teenager at 40 years old. He adores her. She curls up in her usual sleeping position. Her mind wanders but she wants to escape in her dreams; shut out the world. She dozes off in his arms.

Nick can't sleep. He struggles to figure out how in the world to help Jessi. Would she really push that white switch and kill the judge? Could she commit murder to save her cousin and nephew? It doesn't seem possible, but he knows that she would probably sacrifice her own life to protect them. I know she won't go to the police if she fears that it could mean the end for Myrna and Lance. I need to make sure I don't put them in further jeopardy by taking some nitwit, knee-jerk action.

A shiver runs through his body. He understands that she doesn't want him to know what that Latino man said to her on the phone tonight; how he gave his precise instructions on exactly what to do, including when she should arrive tomorrow night, at 659 Ashburn on Nob Hill. He remembers every word the man uttered. I need to get there to that address before she's supposed to arrive and push that switch. A variety of potential plans fly through his brain. He mentally calculates the probability of each scenario's success. How would he potentially prepare for each scenario? Feeling almost hopeless, he finally falls asleep; his arms around the woman he loves.

She opens her eyes at 8:10 in the morning. Nick is sitting in the chair, his reading glasses on, looking down at his cell phone, and sipping coffee. He resembles a sheepdog, with his hair flopped down, falling over his eyes. Then, glancing at her clock, she yells out. "Oh my God. Shit! I overslept. Damn it!"

Nick moves to the bed. "Well, I'm not sure if you deserve this or not, Ms. Potty Mouth, but I did make you some breakfast." He hands her a filled coffee cup, and a slice of toasted rye bread. "Good timing!"

Jessi quickly takes two bites of the toast. Rye is her favorite. "Oh, thank you. Perfect! Thanks. Lots of nasty butter too. "That is good! Nick, sorry, but I need to get going. I have Herbie the cat at 10:30; just a 2 year old, and already with a serious kidney problem. Maybe I'm okay with time. She slows down a bit; then quickly resumes her frenzy, gulping down the rest of the coffee. "But I need to review a ton of files. I'm back to back all day today until 5:00. Lots of older dogs. All kinds of health issues. I need to get into the shower."

"Well, I guess that's my signal to get the hell out of Dodge. Okay. I got it. I think I'll stop at home, and take a shower too. Man, do I need it, eh?"

Jessi looks across the room, out the open window. The weather looks bleak, cloudy; looks like a light drizzle. She seems a thousand miles away, he thinks. He can sense that she's focused on tonight, the actions she must take to save Myrna and Lance.

"Nick, did it rain last night?"

"Yes, I listened to it for more than an hour. I think it was about 2 or maybe 3 in the morning. Came down fast, and heavy. I guess I didn't sleep much." She slides off the bed, and stands in front of him. Pushing his hair out of his tired eyes, she realizes what a rough night he's had too.

"I think you need a haircut. Hmm? Nick, you're such a caring man. You know that?"

"So, I've been told. "Maybe a haircut is past due. I agree. Okay, my sweet, I'll be back here at 6 o'clock this evening."

"N-no. Listen Nick, I need some time to think things through by myself. I don't want you to be involved in all this. Please understand."

"What I understand is that you're going to require some dinner. How about if I bring over take-out Chinese? Some Peking duck, and pork fried rice? The worst thing we could possibly eat, and we both love it! Admit it! Anyway, when's the last time you ate something?"

She waves the rye toast in his face, mocking him. "Let's see, when is the last time I ate something? Hello? Some toast right here in my hand! It's moving into my mouth." She takes another bite of the toast, and flashes her signature sarcastic "got you back" grin.

"Very funny, Ms. Sassy Pants! You know what I mean, when's the last time you had a real meal? Come on Jessi, let's get together tonight. I want to be sure you're okay."

"Only if you promise to leave here by 8:30 the latest; after we eat, and you're satisfied that I'm fine. Seriously Nick, I need to process everything – alone!" What she'll really want, he thinks, is to mentally adjust to how she's going to push that death switch. How can she possibly commit murder even if it avoids another two murders? She must protect Myrna and Lance.

Pandora and Creature wander into the bedroom, jump up on the bed, and begin their harmonious meow concert. "Yes. Yes, some tuna in a can coming right up," Jessi attempts to lighten up from her macabre thoughts. But when she looks over at her two felines, all she can think of is her third pet; in the clutches of that lunatic who shot him or stabbed him.

Nick kisses her on the forehead, and glances over at the cats. "Love you guys. And you too, Ms. Sassy Pants."

Is it because of the intensity of her situation, or something else? She wants to hear Nick say those words. She yearns for him to love her. It's the first time she's had these feelings for him. But not now. She doesn't want to encourage the expression of his love today. The worst timing possible; just when she's become a citizen of the 'walking dead' community. Her heart and soul have been ripped out. She knows she'll probably go to prison for a long time after tonight is over.

"You're going to lock the door behind me before you jump in the shower. Right? For some strange reason, I want you to be safe!" He smiles, teasing her, then touches her face, his palm resting tenderly on her flushed cheek. She nods in agreement. At the door, she looks up at the 6 foot tall, disheveled Nick Daniels. Standing on her barefoot tiptoes, she reaches up and gives him a long, soft kiss good-bye.

He leaves, sliding into his white Volvo, content that finally Jessi seems to feel something beyond friendship. Her kiss good-bye opened a new door of hope! Finally. Regardless, he is on a mission to save the woman he loves from ruining her life forever. He has the urge to jump out of his car, race back into Jessi's house, and disclose that he heard every word that man said on the phone last night. He's got to think of something to save her from hurling herself into a ring of burning fire. But he doesn't leave the Volvo, and go back to Jessi. He'll figure out this puzzle, like he does every day in his complex engineering work. He's a Stanford MSEE grad – Phi Beta Kappa.

Nick drives home but doesn't get ready for work, Instead, he calls in sick. He needs the day to decide how to proceed; determine the optimal pathway for action. Will it be Plan A, B or C?

Out there on Presidio beach, hiding in the bushes is a frail, badly injured seven pound Yorkshire Terrier. Dr. Pepper finds a puddle, lapping up all the water he can. His little body, bloodied, his long dark brown hair knotted and matted, his side bleeding. Despite his dismal condition, he was still able to flee, even with a bullet inside him. He's worn out, ready to give up the fight. He lays down between two bushes, just steps away from the sandy beach. Frightened and lost, he waits to die. His wounds have defeated him.

32

MARTINA WELLS: THE SCENE OF HER CRIME

Martina enters the courtroom with trepidation. The uneth-ical crime she's about to commit will most likely go down in history, if discovered. Swinging the case; disgraceful behavior for a judge. The first two hours of the defense's witnesses in-clude the coroner repeating the cause of the jewelry store sales-clerk's death to be a gunshot wound. The defense then painfully highlighting that the wound was not the actual cause of death. Their defense claimed that the Asian clerk actually had a heart murmur which was getting worse by the day, as diagnosed by the family doctor she saw faithfully each month. The inept defense attorney had the woman's doctor take the stand. Dr. Perdue re-luctantly admitted that the girl was suffering from a life-threat-ening congenital heart condition and he was monitoring it care-fully. However, he honestly didn't think that this was a cause of her death; although the gunshot wound could possibly have trig-gered her heart to fail in the end. Still, it seemed like a weak defense tactic since the murder weapon, the pistol was found out back; thrown on the ground by the killer. But the third hour of Monday morning's testimonies is where Judge Martina Wells torpedoes the trial.

The defense calls the two police officers who arrived at the scene of the crime. First, female Officer, Terri Bradley, whom the alleged killer took a bite out of when she bent down to talk to the injured Vicente at the scene, just after he tripped over the cleaning woman's cart which was packed with her bucket, mop and other paraphernalia. The male police officer, Tim Malachek, thought Officer Bradley read Rodriquez his rights but couldn't quite pinpoint whether that was before or after the perp took a bite out of Officer Bradley's arm. He ended his testimony with "she must have read them!" The judge stopped the action playing out before her. It was her opportunity to interject. She addressed the prosecutor. "Mr. Dunlop, can you hand me the police report?"

"Um, y-yes Your Honor. But, can you please give us five minutes to review the report, and then respond?"

"Mr. Dunlop, I guess we have nothing to do here today except wait for you, the prosecution, to review the report right here in the courtroom. Is that right?" Snickers erupt from the spectators. "Please, hand *me* the police report. I'd like to review it and then advise on this discussion regarding Miranda rights being properly read to the defendant at the scene of the crime."

Max Dunlop and the DA, Sanjay Dalla, exchange some words in hushed tones. The keeper of the evidence rustles through the paperwork sitting on the evidence table. He finally pulls out a document, the original Police Report!" He holds it up. The jury members look interested; trading raised eyebrows, and curious glances. Max Dunlop grabs the document, and goes to read it, back at the prosecution's table.

The judge clears her throat. "Mr. Daniels, perhaps you didn't hear me correctly. It's me, the judge in this case, who wants to read the Police Report." Some members of the jury and several observers laugh at the judge's continued sarcasm. Max Dunlop approaches the bench and hands it to her, visibly shaken. She takes about three minutes to read through it. She sees that there is no check mark on the Miranda Rights box, and there is no text in the report itself that refers to when Miranda Rights were read to the suspect during the span of the incident. She keeps reading, praying that nothing on Miranda will be there. Thank God. Something tangible to hang my hat on here.

That lucky bastard murderer!" She looks over at the accused. He slithers in his chair, like a snake.

Martina looks up from the document. People are busy talking in the courtroom; lots of murmuring, verbal speculation on what will happen next. She bangs the gavel twice. Then, a third time to quiet the crowd. All talking ceases. "Ladies and gentlemen. We will now take a 15 minute recess and be back here at 10:45, when I will address the court. I'd like to see the prosecution attorney, the defense attorney, and the DA in chambers during this recess. If the three of you can join me immediately. Court is adjourned until 10:45." She bangs the gavel twice and rises.

Her legs almost buckle under her as she steps down from her judge's chair. She can feel the heat of Sanjay Dalla's breath on her neck, as he comes up right behind her. His anger, his wrath, climbing as he walks through her office door, and then slams his notebook down on her desk. He attempts to gather himself, not wanting to appear too agitated in front of Max Dunlop, the prosecutor who directly reports to him. The pathetic-looking defense attorney, Gregory Harris, trails behind.

"Sit down gentlemen," she gestures to them.

"I have reviewed this Police Report. There is unbelievably no mention of Miranda rights having been read to the alleged murderer and thief. The female police officer is clearly confused, based on her testimony, not recalling if she even read them to Mr. Rodriguez. The male officer also seems to be in a muddle, based on his hesitant testimony this morning."

Sanjay is now incensed. "Let me see that." He stands up, trying to take the document out of Martina's hands. She lets him take it from her. He desperately searches for any Miranda reference. Nothing! "That's impossible." He throws the document down on the desk with disgust. "Shit!" He can't help himself. He makes drilled eye contact with Martina, with the woman that he was considering romancing at one point. There had been an undeniable attraction between them. He was waiting for an opportune time between trials, to ask her out to dinner. It wasn't exactly kosher for them to date; but he was thinking of going back into private practice, anyway. There would ultimately then be no conflict of interest. Martina glares at Sanjay, her eyes commanding him to be seated again; not to demonstrate one iota of physically threatening body language in judge's chambers. Sanjay weakens, falling back into the brown leather chair. The defense attorney can't help but grin. Max Dunlop, the prosecutor, holds his head in his hands, feeling a harsh migraine coming on strong; something he deals with when under stress at work. He knows that Sanjay will blame the whole thing on him in the end, even though right now, he's angrier than a hungry pit bull.

She straightens up in her chair. "Let me be blunt. I'll have to rule a mistrial which translates to acquittal for the defendant. She looks over at the relieved defense attorney, who can't seem to quite comprehend his accidental good fortune. She tilts her head, and peers directly at Sanjay Dalla who locks eyes with her. He tries to reason with her. "You can't do this Judge Wells. It's not the right kind of justice. You know that."

Martina doesn't back down, just keeps her determined eyes on him. She's steadfast at this point; maintaining her unyielding façade, but secretly crumbling inside. Her ethics are about to take a swan dive into hell. Sanjay looks at the miserable prosecutor. "Dunlop, you moron. How could you not check and double check for Miranda rights on the fucking Police Report?" He wants to ring his neck. "Now, we all look like idiots in my DA's office."

Martina takes back control. "That's enough. Let's all get back to the courtroom," she directs.

"Wait," Sanjay insists. "Judge, I'd like to talk to you in private for a few minutes."

"That's not necessary at this point, Mr. Dalla. And I probably don't need to say this but I'd like to remind you of the importance of your professional composure in the courtroom. As DA, you represent San Francisco and the whole police community of this great city. Please, show some leadership and decorum." He gets up and storms out of her office. Max Dunlop follows him, embarrassed by the events of the last hour.

When back in the courtroom, Martina avoids eye contact with Sanjay. She proceeds to masterfully coach the jury on the strict requirement of Miranda rights being read when anyone is placed under arrest; about the impossibility of conviction when Miranda is not documented on the Police Report. "Additionally, the officers on the stand today did not quite recall if, and when Miranda was read to the accused, before he was taken into custody." She is commanding, articulate and convincing. The jury members listen carefully to her every word. She is their 'God' in the courtroom. Several of them nod as she speaks, and then again, almost in unison, when she finishes.

"Since Miranda has been violated in this case, I declare this a mistrial. I am acquitting the accused, Vicente Rodriguez. All charges are hereby dropped; both for murder and for felony robbery." The courtroom erupts in conversation and then chaos. Yelling. Shouting. Oohs and ahhs. Cameras flash.

Martina bangs the gavel multiple times to quiet the crowd. "Mr. Rodriguez," she says loudly. "You are free to go once you collect your possessions from the jail clerk. Your attorney will direct you in your release process." The jailer shrugs his shoulders and retreats to the sidelines, no longer needing to guard the alleged killer. Vicente smirks as the victim's parents scream out in terror, the mother of the murdered woman falling to the floor, sobbing. The grandmother of the victim tries to help her grief-stricken daughter. The old woman bends down, hugging and rocking her daughter; but at the same time gazing up at the judge with her dark, swollen, pleading eyes. She hadn't stopped crying since the day of her young granddaughter's death.

All Martina can see in front of her now is her father's blue-gray eyes, silently thanking his daughter for saving his life. She's accomplished the impossible. She bolts out of the courtroom, throws off her robes and sits down awaiting Rodrigo's call; awaiting his instructions on where she can pick up her ailing father. The news should be out on the streets in just a few minutes. An hour goes by; no call. Martina is frantic, furious and worried.

33

WORK: TEMPORARY FIX

Jessi arrives at her veterinary office; hair still damp from the shower. More important things to focus on than the way she looks. She had dabbed on some blush, and splashed on some apple scented after-bath spray. Sarah, dressed in new black garb is also prompt today; organized with the patient files ready for Jessi's review before any of the animals arrive. After two appointments, Sarah announces that there is a special someone to see Jessi. She's requested just five minutes of her time. She shrugs, and confirms that Jessi has 30 minutes until the next appointment; an unplanned rest period, since she finished early with the first two patients.

"Okay, I hope it's not one of those pestering salespeople from some drug company, selling their wares."

"Hmm. I think she might be a little old for that. But who knows? Maybe." Sarah leaves, and comes back with a special guest behind her.

"Dierdre? Um, please come in." Sarah departs. Jessi closes the door behind them.

"Dierdre, I don't really have time to…"

"I know dear. I know. Believe me, I'm not here to defend Stefan. Forget about him! You're too good for my arrogant grandson. I understand. A lost cause. He doesn't deserve you! Talented in so many wonderful ways, highly gifted. But he has no sense of right and wrong; and unfortunately lacks loyalty – especially in his romantic relationships. Yes, yes, he can love passionately but the love seems to only center around himself. I just happened to be in the wrong place. I fell asleep in the guest room upstairs and slept through much of the night." She rolls her eyes. "But I can't say that I didn't hear snippets of their activity downstairs. Honestly, I don't know what's wrong with him. He has no morals; no boundaries when it comes to sex." She drops her head, sorry to have said anything like this to Jessi. "Anyway, that's not why I'm here."

"Dierdre. It's not your fault. I take full responsibility. I've been a fool with Stefan – again!"

"Let me change the subject, Jessi. There's something more important that I want to talk to you about. I want you, as a highly respected local veterinarian, to be our spokesperson to announce a huge gift to be given on behalf of the San Francisco Animal Lovers Society; an organization for which I am chairperson. We are an elite group of business owners and philanthropists who strive to support animal research. We work in conjunction with the Audubon Society. As our spokesperson, we'd like you to present the funds each year to the selected recipients. We'd also like your counsel and vote on where we might target the monies each year. In short, we want you on our Board as well as being the keynote speaker at our next conference. We hope your topic will reflect what we owe to the non-human creatures that walk and fly this world. They are the foundation for all of us. We came from them! I know you're heavily involved in the animal research going on at San Francisco State University. Please, Jessi. Please say yes."

"Dierdre. I'm not too sure about this."

"Understood, my dear. I'd like you to come to our Society's board meeting tonight and meet the five board members. We will be having duck a l'orange, your favorite. She grins. "I'm so sorry for the late notice. I tried to reach you a few times, but I was too embarrassed after what happened." Her electric smile and sparkling blue eyes captivate Jessi.

"Dierdre, I'm flattered. But I'm off limits for the next three weeks or so with many personal matters." Her eyes well up with tears.

Dierdre moves to comfort Jessi. "I'm so sorry dear. Can I help?"

"N-no. It's really personal I'm afraid. Hope you understand."

"Well, alright, it's not a problem. I can wait three weeks. We'll set a date then for lunch. I'll email you a proposed date. The topic of Stefan will be off limits. No worries about that. Stefan will never appear at any of our events."

"Yes, Dierdre. That would be the end of any relationship between you and me, whether you are an animal lover or not."

"I loved you Jessi, like my own granddaughter. I still do. You partnering with my grandson would have been nice for me, but regardless, I am your friend." She laughs nervously. "Dear, I don't have much longer to spend on this Earth but I want to be in contact with you until the end. I'm afraid I'm stuck with Stefan as my grandson." She shrugs her petite shoulders, then opens the door, and waves a brief good-bye. Jessi stands there, immobile, nodding her head; appreciating Dierdre's professional confidence in her but wondering if she even wants to continue any connection at all to Stefan's family.

Sarah enters the exam room, looking immaculately stylish in black today, a vet's assistant fashion statement. She floats in, singing Old McDonald Had A Farm. "So, she didn't bring her pet today? Did she leave him or her at Nieman Marcus perhaps? Holy crap, did you see that old lady's jewelry? Huge diamonds. Expensive gems everywhere."

"Yeh, that woman could have been my grandmother in another life. Anyway…" she sighs, "let's see to our next patient."

"Doc – you've certainly been in some funk lately. I feel a vacation coming on for you." Sarah is hopeful for this, as she'd like to go to L.A. for the Star Trek Convention next week.

"Hmmm. Maybe soon. I might be going on an undesirable vacation for a very long time."

"Huh? What do you mean?"

"N-nothing Sarah. Just a little humor finally popped out of me, I guess. Who's next?"

"We have a rabbit named Nibbles. Well, I squeezed him into the schedule. He's so cute! He's not eating and hasn't pooped for the last five days."

"Okay. Let's see what we can do for him."

Sarah leaves to retrieve Nibbles. Jessi glances over at the sink where her exam instruments are ready, laid out by Sarah for the next patient. Her eyes land on the wood-framed photograph hanging on the wall. It's Jessi, about two years ago, surrounded by her three pets; now only two left. Dr. Pepper is gone and I need to accept that, she thinks to herself. It's hard to treat animals all day long when I wasn't able to help my own pet in his last desperate hours of need. Sarah walks in holding the emaciated little white rabbit.

34

BURIED IN CEMENT, NOT MADE OF IRON

Martina waits in her office for more than three hours after the aborted trial is over. Still no call from Rodrigo. What the hell is he doing, jerking her around? She checks her messages for the third time since she left the courtoom. First, her cell phone. Not one message. Then she checks her office voicemail, just in case. Three business voicemails regarding her judicial decision earlier today. Two of them applauding her holding up the violation of Miranda in the faces of the DA and the prosecuting attorney. Good work! Fine job! A third call from another judge wondering why she even highlighted Miranda as the presiding judge, when the accused was so obviously guilty of murder; caught at the scene of the crime just outside the back door of the jewelry store. The accused even had all the stolen jewelry in his pocket. It was Judge Maury Snyder, asking Martina to give him a call about it. He respected her decision, but just wanted to understand more.

In San Francisco, judges stay on top of the various trial rulings and outcomes, especially when the judge is influencing the jury referencing previous court decisions; and in this case making the provocative call to drop all of the charges against the defendant. Judge Snyder ended his voicemail with a slight chuckle and a final statement: "I bet that DA, Sanjay Dalla, is now out for your blood, probably piping mad at your unpopular ruling."

She doesn't want to talk to her colleagues about today. She's compromised her ethics to save her only living relative. "Where is my father? Where's the kidnapper's call? Damn it!" She stares hopelessly out the window. It's a bleak day in San Francisco; windy, foggy and cold at almost 4 o'clock on a Monday afternoon. She turns out the lights and leaves her office, sneaking past Leon, her legal assistant. He's busy filing, his back to her, as she walks by. She doesn't want to have to explain why she's leaving early, why she can barely speak or have any kind of an engaging conversation. She can't concentrate; can't focus on anything but her father.

At home on Nob Hill, her distress increases. She opens a bottle of Irish whiskey and sits down at her mahogany dining room table. She starts drinking; still on edge. Her ethical code which she lives by in both her work and her life in general, has been compromised.

She's basically destroyed herself professionally. How can she ever preside over a courtroom again? Not after what she did. Once she gets her father back, she will have to resign her position. Even if not forced out, she is compelled to remove herself from the bench, and probably from the legal world altogether.

At 44 years old, she never married, and will never have children. The legal profession was her entire life. She had been an upstanding contributor to the community, volunteering on weekends; also taking a evening course at SFSU to upgrade her youth counseling skills. She wanted to help juveniles who were in trouble, who lost their way. Dedicate herself to helping them get back on track, possibly encourage some of them to enter the legal field; inspire them to help change the world - preserve the justice system. That was all over now. Her life was ruined; in shambles. It doesn't matter. I would sacrifice anything to get my father back.

She takes the last sip of her second whiskey. It burns her throat. Just as she begins to pour a third glass, her cell phone rings out. Shaking, Martina almost drops the bottle of whiskey, just managing to put it back down on the table.

"Are you ready to have your precious father returned?"

It's him. That gangster. Rodrigo. "Why didn't you call me as soon as I dismissed the trial early today? That's what you promised. I was worried sick that you lied about returning my father at all. How is he? When can I…"

"Shut up and listen to me. You made it happen. Muy bueno, Judge Wells. We will release your father tomorrow at high noon, at the Union Square parking garage, just opposite Macy's. He will be there on the 2nd level of the garage, right by the elevator. He's doing much better today. No fever. The antibiotics seems to be working well. He was smiling at me about an hour ago. The old man is made of iron. Just like you!"

"Can't I pick him up from you tonight? You got what you wanted, didn't you? Please, I can meet you anywhere you say."

"No. Tomorrow at noon. Did you forget that I make the rules? Comprendes? You don't want me to change my mind? Do you?" He laughs because he knows that he and Julio will be on a flight to Cartagena by 5 a.m. tomorrow morning. She has no idea that her dear padre is dead and buried in cement. Rodrigo doesn't want to deal with the judge's grief tonight. She might go nuts and try to go to the police again. And by 2 a.m. or sooner, she, herself, will be blown up, into very tiny pieces of flesh and bone. Dr. Salazar will be pressing the switch. Life could not be sweeter!

He wants to rush off the phone now and be done with this used up judge. Myrna is waiting for him in the bedroom upstairs. Lance is taking a nap, tired out from riding the now tamed horse in the paddock. Rodrigo rode for an hour with the boy behind him, as Lance waved his cowboy hat in the air. Ha. Ha.

I'm such a good actor! The boy loves me. Rodrigo plans to screw Myrna just one more time before he returns her home tonight, before he hooks up with Julio and together they prepare the lethal bomb on Nob Hill. He's confident that the woman waiting for him upstairs is eagerly anticipating him slipping into her. He will show her a good time provided she complies with his parting sexual requests. First, he will tell her how much he's looking forward to growing their relationship. Then, she will do anything for him. Desperate bitch! What a party for me! He smacks his lips thinking about her. Once they fuck, he will to get them on the road back to San Francisco. He has a busy night planned!

"Mañana, Judge. Be at the parking garage at Union Square. Noon. By the way, your father will be dressed in a navy blue sweatshirt and sweatpants. You'll recognize him though. He's your father after all!" Rodrigo laughs one more time before he hangs up; jingling his key chains.

Martina holds the phone in her hand; now a dial tone buzzing in her ear. She bangs the phone down on the table. That bastard!" She's eager for tomorrow to come; but at the same time depressed and disappointed that she won't see her dad tonight. That's what she hoped. That's what she understood would happen. Is it true, that her father was smiling at the kidnapper an hour ago? She was trying to imagine, Parker Wells, grinning back at his kidnapper. That would not be like her dad. He'd be rip-roaring angry; wanting to wring the kidnapper's neck, and not keeping it a secret. Almost drunk and exasperated, she lays her head down on the polished table top.

35

THE OFFICE BECKONS

Nick spends his morning considering what he needs for his incredible feat coming up in a matter of hours. At home, he makes decisions about what things to stuff into his black exercise bag. First, he removes a bunch of gym clothes which smell rank. He takes an initial whiff as he unzips the bag. Oh, that's lethal! He hasn't cleaned it out since the last time he dragged himself to the gym, and that was about three months ago.

He goes from room to room collecting his gear, his brain in a fog. *How am I going to deal with an experienced terrorist? And since he used the word "we" on the phone, that leads me to believe there are at least two thugs showing up tonight to plant that bomb. I don't know what I'm doing, but I'm steamed up; committed to the best defensive action I can possibly muster. I can't have the woman I love destroy her own life, and our potential life together.*

His cell phone plays the funeral dirge, the ringtone he's dedicated to his boss, Bruce Whittaker. Damn! *He must have noticed that I wasn't in the office this morning. I left his assistant a message; but she probably didn't get it to him. It's already past 10:30.*

"Nick Daniels," he answers, seeking to sound just a little weak.

"Nick. Bruce here." His voice sounds stressed. "We're in trouble, Nick!"

No kidding, Nick thinks. *This guy doesn't know half of what I'm dealing with today. He's got a multi-million dollar project on the line. Me, I've got lives here on the chopping block.*

Bruce continues. "Cynthia just called from the CEO's office. He wants us to meet with him at 2 p.m. today, to explain the design engineering costs and timeline for the Endeavor project. Do you have that data handy and in power point format? Are you here on site?"

Of course, Nick thinks, the one day I'm not at work at 7 a.m., starting up my typical 12 hour day, something's up! "Good news, Bruce. I can have a summary presentation to you in, let's say 45 minutes, outlining the hardware, software and consulting costs for Endeavor; all broken down in an easy to decipher spreadsheet. The unfortunate news is that I woke up this morning with this ridiculous toothache. God, it's excruciating!" He feigns pain. "Geez! I managed to get a dentist appointment but not until 2:45 this afternoon. So no, I'm not on site. Crap, this pain is a doozy!"

Silence from Bruce. Then, some throat clearing. "Okay Nick. I trust you can pull this together but I wish you were on site. Is there any way you can get in here?"

"Hmm. Sorry, no way. I could barely shower and shave, let alone drive. I just fell back into my bed and called the dentist. I couldn't fight it anymore. After some serious moaning, the dental receptionist caved, and squeezed me into the schedule. His office is only 3 blocks from my house, so I can walk it."

More dead silence on the phone from Bruce. Nick can feel his frustration oozing out. His nostrils are probably flaring, and he usually makes this kind of weird breathing noise when he's stressed out. It almost sounds like someone taking their last breath; but it's only Bruce, hyperventilating. Yech. There it is now!

Nick reassures him. "Bruce, you know you can count on me to provide you with accurate and complete budget data you need. And on the timeline, I can give you a work breakdown structure that sings with project phases and specific task details, including estimated time frames and critical path info. The whole thing can be in your inbox in less than an hour."

"That does sound good. Just what the doctor ordered." He laughs and snorts into the phone. "Sorry for that bad pun, Nick."

I think I might gag, Nick noodles to himself. We, engineering types; we're sometimes, like, from some other planet. That's what "us" nerds must seem like to normal people. Aliens! "Heh. Heh. That's funny, Bruce." He lies to his boss for the second time today.

Bruce gets dead serious. "Can you be on the phone at 2 p.m. with me and the CEO?" He gently nudges, hoping for a 'yes' answer from Nick. "Cynthia can conference you in with us, before you're called into the dentist's office. Nick, I can't really do this without you; at least have you on the phone. Know what I mean?"

Ouch. That "know what I mean" stings Nick's ears.

"Uh...."

"Look, you know what a maniac Ralph is, and he's on the warpath this month; trying to cut expenses any way he can. The Board is out for his blood this quarter. Your project Endeavor is the future of this company; but of course, we need to continuously back it up and defend it."

"I understand. Not a problem. I'll email you the draft in about 45 minutes."

"You're the man, Nick. Make sure it's got solid legs, okay? Lots of concrete detail, and anticipate those tough questions."

It takes him 46 minutes to construct and organize his data into a robust, yet very organized fifteen slide presentation. He emails it to Bruce, writing: "One minute over ETA. Hope this works for you! Let me know. If you can get back to me in the next 15 minutes with your feedback, great!" He fumbles, hits "send" but forgets the important attachment. Shit! Bruce is going to fry him. He hates himself when he does something nincompoop like that. He quickly writes a second email, successfully attaching the document. "Sorry. Here you go Bruce; this time *with* the Power Point presentation. My bad."

Okay, that's done, he thinks to himself. Now, what the hell *is* my plan for eliminating Jessi's nightmare?

Nick arrives at Jessi's house at 6:30. It's strangely humid in the city tonight. Managing to gobble down her half of the Chinese food in record time, she sits on the sofa, nervous energy exuding from the core of her being. He pretends total ignorance as to why she is so stir crazy, but he knows it well because he feels the same degree of high anxiety. Jessi insists that although she appreciates Nick's care and affection, she needs to have time alone.

As soon as dinner is over, she walks him to the door, and kisses him affectionately. Ahh, she would love for him to stay; but she needs to prepare for this heinous mission on her own, without throwing him a clue. "I'll call you tomorrow Nick. I'd like to explain a few things to you. Nick, I appreciate everything you do for me."

"Jessi, I'll need to make confessions myself; some that may be hard for you to swallow. Tell you what - we'll have a sharing fest tomorrow." He laughs and tenderly kisses her good-bye. Just as she closes the door, her cell phone rings. Shit! Unknown caller. Oh God! He's probably reminding me to push that god damn white switch. She answers with reluctance. But it's not Rodrigo. It's a man's voice she's never heard before.

"Dr. Jessi Salazar?" He sounds formal and serious.

"Y-yes." Her voice chokes up. She doesn't want to hear it.

"Ms. Salazar, Detective Bob Downey here from the San Francisco Police Department. I'm very sorry to ask you this question, but I must. Do you know a Mr. Rico Mendez?"

She freezes, then manages a timid response. "Um, yes. He's a friend from Panama. Why? What's happened? I've been calling him all night and all day."

"I'm sorry Dr. Salazar; but he's been killed."

She collapses like a rag doll on the wood floor at the foot of the staircase just inside the front door. The room spins around her. Her head pounds.

"What?" her voice responds in a ghost-like, raspy tone.

"We found your business card in his jacket pocket. That's why I'm calling. Sorry to ask this, but when was the last time you saw him?"

"Yesterday, about 5 p.m. We met for a drink."

"Yes. I understand. Actually, his business colleague explained that you saw him earlier in the afternoon, and that you were wondering where he was when he didn't show up to meet you for dinner at the hotel restaurant. It appears that he's been murdered, and we need to gather as much information as possible for the investigation."

Her heart is crushed. She can't respond.

"Again, I'm very sorry Dr. Salazar. We need you to identify his body since you are the closest person in town to a relative? If you're willing, can you come to the Market Street police station tomorrow morning? Do you know where that is? I can escort you to the morgue for the identification process."

She can't focus. Tears flood her eyelids, dripping down into her mouth. She screams out inside. No. No. Her chasm of grief has no end. She's in a deep well and she's lost hold of the rope which can save her, and take her to the surface. She's falling. Falling.

"Please. I'm sorry Detective. It-It's just such a shock. I-I....Yes, I'll be there."

"May I ask? Does he have any relatives in California or anywhere? Do you have a phone number in Panama for his mother or father; or spouse?"

"No. I-I'm afraid not. He's not married. His parents have passed away. I don't know of any other relatives. I only knew his parents many years ago in Panama. I'm-I'm…"

"It's okay, Dr. Salazar. I understand. Please ask for me, Detective Bob Downey, in the morning. Is 9 a.m. okay for you?"

"Y-yes." He hangs up. She can't move from the floor; but she needs to prepare herself for 659 Ashburn. White switch! If she doesn't push that switch, and set off the explosion; Myrna and Lance will end up dead, too. These people have no morals. No limits. Heartless killers. Bottom feeders.

36

CAN GENIUS TRUMP CARTEL?

A black SUV, head lights turned off, pulls up just a half block away from 659 Ashburn. Nick hides in the dark, at the side of the judge's house; out of sight. He can see Martina sitting in her dimly lit dining room; her head down on the table. One empty glass, and a more than half-finished bottle of some kind of liquor in front of her. He turns his head the other way to the paved pathway leading up to the house, subtly illuminated with tiny outdoor lights.

A tall, muscular man jumps out from the SUV's passenger side and then a second, short, stocky man hops out from the driver's side. They both carry large, heavy-looking back packs. The taller one carries a toolbox in his left hand. They carefully place their loads on the ground, on the surface of the grassy area, and kneel down beside each other at the end of the path-way, closest to the street. They are both dressed in black; hooded sweatshirts and knit caps. They whisper to each other. One of the men takes a metal object from his pack. The other one puts some tools on the grass just next to him.

Here he is at the house of Judge Wells, squatted in the dirt behind some bushes, watching two devils from the depths of hell making preparations for murder. Dangerous quarters! Nick's thin navy blue jacket is damp from sweat. It's not even 60 degrees out here tonight, and he's wet like he's been hiking all day in the tropics. Mentally and emotionally exhausted, he spent the majority of the afternoon on the phone with Bruce, his boss, and Ralph, his CEO; except for the 45 minutes he was supposed to be under the care of his dentist. During that brief oasis of time, he hustled; assembling his 'save the world' kit. He didn't really know what to put in his back pack. He took a stab at preparing a checklist of what things might be useful for combating vicious thugs in the middle of the night. He wandered through his house, going from room to room and willy-nilly, gathered an array of disparate objects: a pair of pliers, some electrical wire, a long rope, several zip ties, scotch tape, a swiss army knife, two silk handkerchiefs, a fold up shovel, his sharpest kitchen knife and two ibuprofen from the medicine cabinet. He gulped down some water and swallowed the two pills. He successfully managed to save his precious Endeavor engineering project today despite an impending headache, but could he save Jessi and the judge tonight? How the hell would he do it?

Nick watches, and waits in the dark outside the judge's house; trying to be quiet, taking measured breaths. He cannot be discovered. He's in close enough proximity to these hoodlums, so that he can make out most of the dialogue between them. Sounds like the taller one is Rodrigo, just like he thought he heard Jessi mention; and the shorter, hefty one, is called Julio. They are the consummate "Mutt and Jeff" combination; direct physical opposites. He can hear them discussing the assembly of the switch, and the bomb; Rodrigo shooting orders to Julio. Nick's cell phone vibrates. Damn! He can't look at it now. He turns the phone to the off position, careful not to shine any hint of light. The short guy seemed to look up when the phone was vibrating. Oh shit! Now, he's standing up, looking around. Nick crouches deeper into the bushes, trying not to rustle them.

Julio whispers. "Ahh, it's probably a dog. Nothing else." He bends back down next to Rodrigo, and resumes his work.

"Come on, Julio. Concentrate. Get the wires set up right. Don't mess it up. Vámonos!"

Nick's college wrestling probably won't help him with these two experienced thugs. He wants to jump them now. But he can't seem to engage his body. Sitting in the bushes staring at his tools, his eyes jump from the two misfits back to his laid out tools and paraphernalia, then darts back to the two men. He repeats this process; his nerves hurtling out of control. The voices of the two men reduce to a bare whisper. They huddle closely together. He's unable to make out their words. But he can see them through the branches, both working feverishly on their device. What's going to stop them?

Nick doesn't have a gun. He thought of buying a pistol awhile back, and then threw out the idea because basically he hates guns, and has even been active in demonstrations to stop gun violence. He doesn't want to stab them, and honestly would probably stab one, and then the other would turn and stab or shoot him. He can't call the police, and now is not the time, anyway.

Rodrigo stops his activity; packing up his bag. When he speaks now, Nick can hear him. "The switch is ready. Just needs hooking up. Julio, are you finished? Come on. It's getting late. The bitch will be here in less than 45 minutes. We need to get this over with. "Fuckin' hell. Hurry!"

Julio looks up at Rodrigo. "I'm almost finished. Mierda, my knees are killing me. Dios mío." He changes the subject. "It's a good thing the old man is dead, buried beneath eight feet of cement. He deserved it. We don't want the judge or her old fart father alive to talk. One down and one to go! Sí?" They both grin.

Oh God. Nick almost shrieks. The judge's father is dead. That's what he just heard. These freaks seem to kill without hesitation. It doesn't sound good for Jessi's friend, Rico.

"Good fucking riddance," Rodrigo nonchalantly professes. "Bastard. But Julio, you're still an idiot for shooting him. If you weren't my kid brother, I'd kick in your cabeza. You made a big mistake. What an ass you are!"

"What about the doctor's cousin and the kid? Where are they? Did you kill them?"

Rodrigo shrugs his shoulders. "No. I softened on them. They didn't know what was going on anyway. Nothing. And Myrna was such a good lay. I just wanted to scare the shit out of Jessi Salazar. It worked; shocked the crap out of her when she heard her dear cousin was in danger. Remember, I destroyed Myrna's cell phone at the ranch, and cut her land line at home. Then, I walked away with her laptop in my bag.

"So, the doc will push this switch, thinking she will be saving them."

"Sí. Ándale! Stop the chit-chat, Julio. Finish the job!"

"Mierda. I can't get this." Julio twists his wrench. Nick can see him dripping with sweat, lit up by the pathway lighting, like a freakish-looking jack-o-lantern.

"Are you sweating when it's cold out here? You're a pig!" Rodrigo makes fun of Julio.

"Ahhh. I think I got it." Julio grunts, relieved that he completed his task.

"Make sure the fucking switch is in the off position for now. No screw-ups, Julio!"

"We need to lift the device and get it into the house," Rodrigo orders. "Wait here. I'll go check the side window near her kitchen. I can jiggle the window and get this inside. I disabled her alarm the other night, before I left for Salinas."

"You didn't tell me that, Rodrigo."

"Tell you? Are you my fucking wife or something? Stay here. I'll be right back."

Rodrigo limberly rises from his kneeling position, his eyes glued to Julio, who works hurriedly, adding the final touches to the device. Rodrigo moves to the other side of the house."

Thank you God, Nick thinks. Damn! When am I going to make my move? And what is my move, anyway? How can I stop them?

Rodrigo returns to Julio's side. "The window is screwed up. It's broken, won't open. Some responsible judge. She doesn't even take care of her own house. I can see her through the window, her head down on the fucking dining table. Looks passed out." He winces. "You know what – let's just put the bomb on her porch. It's packed with power. When it blows, the entire house will explode. Come on, we'll lean it by the front door." Put the mat half way over it.

"Perfecto."

"Let's go. On 3, lift it with me."

'Uno, dos, tres!" Together, they lift the heavy device from the ground. Still hunched down, they move carefully in unison to Martina's porch. They place it down near the front door. Rodrigo takes the door mat and lays it over the black box bomb. The brothers make eye contact, and without any words, they both step lightly back to the white switch. Rodrigo does something with the switch. Then, both stand up, their backs to Nick who remains veiled in the bushes. He can't quite make out what the two men are doing right now. He waits.

Finally, the men talk more about the switch and the explosive. "Okay, ready to blow," Rodrigo whispers. "Let's go."

Shit! Nick reacts. I better act now. They're leaving.

He decides to spring into action. What the hell! It's my last chance. He eyes all his tools laid out on the ground. He grabs the zip ties, shoving them in his jeans pocket, picks up the large metal shovel, sticks the knife in his jacket pocket, and stuffs the two handkerchiefs in his back pocket. He raises the shovel high in the air, holding it with both hands like a baseball bat. And with all the energy, he charges the two thugs. They are caught off guard, startled. With surprising precision, he smacks them both hard in the back of the legs with his shovel. First Rodrigo, then Julio. Rodrigo attempts to pull something from his pocket. Nick smacks him hard two more times; then goes back to whacking Julio with the shovel. Breathe! Breathe! Man, I've still got some strength left in these wrestling hands. My adrenalin is in super action hero mode – flight/fight responses fully firing!

He shifts back once more to Rodrigo, and gives him two more head-on whacks to his upper back area. Some blood drizzles from his head. The two Latino men are both helpless on the ground. Rodrigo moves. Whack! Ahh, now both of them out cold! Good. Suddenly, Nick feels frightened, jangled by his own wrath. *God help me. I've turned into a maniac!* He flips the zip-ties out of his pocket, throwing them on to the hard cement pathway. He zip-ties their hands; then does the same to their ankles. He quickly gags each of them with the handkerchiefs. Julio is coming around and lets out a groan. *Damn!* Nick conks him in the face with the shovel. His cheek opens up; blood spurting out. *Okay, next step. What the hell do I do now? No time to think Nicky boy, just do!*

He drags Rodrigo up the three steps on to the front porch; just a step away from the explosive. He runs back, and starts dragging the short fat one towards the front door; to the same spot. *It's more difficult than he thought. Should have continued weight lifting after Stanford.* He pauses for a moment to catch his breathe. But with his animal instincts in full play mode, Nick persists, getting the second skunk up the porch steps. *Crap! He's wriggling.* He plunks the heavy body half on top of Rodrigo; then quickly sprints back to the bushes to retrieve his shovel. Leaping back on the porch, with all his force, he smashes the metal down on Julio's head. *No more movement.*

I need to get to Martina; extract her from the house. But how? If I ring the doorbell or knock, and she opens the door, where the two bloodied men lay gagged and tied; she's guaranteed to freak out. Damn! This is one stupid move, but I'm going for it. God, I hope Jessi doesn't show up now. Not yet! He moves quickly to the side window, the one that Rodrigo tried to enter earlier tonight. *That dumb, over-confident thug. He doesn't know how to jiggle a window and pry it open?* Nick perseveres and gets it open with his pocket knife. *He almost forgets that he has it in his pocket.* He extends his left leg and steps inside a bedroom. *Nobody's there.* He whispers, "Judge Wells. Judge Wells. *She'll probably shoot him dead, but what else can he do?* No response back. He moves to what looks like the master bedroom. *Nobody there either; totally dark. The dimmed hallway light saves him from falling on his face.* He moves into the living room area. *Not there* either. She must still be in the dining room. He walks through another hallway. Good. There she is, her head still down on the table. What should he say so she won't be startled? It doesn't matter because he loses his balance, tripping on a shopping bag full of stuff which sits there by the table.

The sound of his body hitting the floor gets Martina's attention. Groggy, she manages to raise her head, darting her eyes from one corner of the room to the other. "Who is that? Who is there?" Her voice is weak. Oh my God, she thinks. Did they leave my dad here? Maybe they decided to get him back to me tonight?

Nick reaches for a dining room chair, and tries to raise himself up, moving with a slow, cautious motion; not wanting to alarm her. He hopes to just ease her into his entrance. He pulls himself up and looks Martina directly in the eye. She looks bad; like her soul's been yanked out of her. "I'm Nick."

She unsuccessfully attempts to pick up the whiskey bottle and throw it across the table. "N-no, please. I-I'm Nick, a friend of Jessi Salazar's. You know her!"

Martina drops the whiskey bottle onto the table. The brown liquid pours out, dripping from the table runner onto the navy blue carpeting. She gives up, and uncontrollably shakes her head back and forth. She pleads. "No. No. I can't talk to you. Leave! Please. My father's life is on the line. Go away! Now!" She screams, rocks back and forth, covering her ears. "Go! I beg you."

He sits down on the chair across from her; and picks up the leaking bottle, putting it back upright. He whispers. "Judge Wells. Your father. Your father is dead. I'm so sorry. I just heard those two Latino thugs confess it. They didn't know I was there. I'm afraid it's true. He's buried in cement under some office building being constructed." He shakes his head in sympathy.

She freezes. Her eyes go even colder. Her soul just exited her body; leaving her lifeless – an empty shell. The chandelier's light catches her dark eyes. For a second, she looks extremely beautiful, like a cover model without a personality; just a face – but a lovely one. Then, the beauty quickly vanishes before his eyes. She looks ragged and lonely; destroyed.

"What? He's dead? But tomorrow, tomorrow, they were giving him back to me." She whines like a little girl, her hands shuffling around, now scratching the table. Broken. She's completely broken, Nick empathizes.

"Listen Judge. We need to go. We have to leave here now." He speaks measuredly; trying to be gentle but he knows that he needs to quickly influence her to follow him. "Right now, Judge! Your house is going to blow up. A bomb has been planted by those two men."

At first, she's startled by the word. Bomb, did he say bomb? "I don't fucking care," she cries. "I don't care." Her head drops back down on the table. She's drained.

He mans up. "Judge, we're leaving now. Those men are outside."

She looks up. Something in his eyes is too much for her to ignore. He's good. An honest man and he's here to help me. She barely gets the words out. "I did it all for nothing then! I did it for nothing. A murderer got away scot-free. No justice."

"Judge. Please. We need to go."

She nods and attempts to rise from her chair. She's drunk; more than two thirds of the whiskey consumed before the bottle fell down on the polished wood tabletop. He comes around the table and helps her stand up. She's shaky on her feet.

"Do you have an alternate door to the outside? We can't go out the front. I'll tell you why later. But first, we just need to unlock the front door. Can we do that?"

She walks out to the living room, barely able to maintain her balance. He follows and helps her along the way. She struggles to unlock the door. Then, like a zombie, she leads him to the door to the outside back garden, from her spacious kitchen. Her hands shaking, she manages to opens it. Once outside, he takes her hand, pulls her with him and briskly runs around to the front of the house, and out to the far end of the path that leads out from her front door. "Don't turn around Judge. Don't." He doesn't want her to see the men bloodied and gagged. Those men are there by your front door, tied up. Just stand here. Kneel down in the bushes. He points to where he was hiding earlier. "I need to do something." Inside she wants to find the sharpest carving knife possible, and run up those stairs to stab them. Stab them a thousand times. Kill them like they killed her defenseless father. But she has no energy. Her brain is jammed. She kneels down and crawls into the area near the bushes.

He turns to make his way back to the two men. "Jessi?"

She approaches him. "Nick! What the hell are you...?" Jessi falls into his open arms. "You knew? How?" He looks into her troubled eyes. It hits her. "You heard every word that man said on the phone last night, didn't you?"

He nods. "Yes."

She notices something stirring right behind him. "Don't move Nick. Someone is... Oh my God, Judge Wells!" Jessi grabs this ghost of a woman, hugging her closely. Her guilt for what she was about to do comes tumbling out of her. Physically and emotionally, Jessi's relieved. She can't stop holding onto the frail, frightened Martina Wells. Jessi looks over at Nick. "What happened?"

"Her father is dead, Jessi. I heard both men discussing it."

"You saw them? Rodrigo, and someone else with him?

Nick nods again.

Jessi's mind races. "Rico. Rico is dead too. I just had that confirmed by the police." Her head hangs. "These terrorists have ruined so many lives in the past few weeks; and now they've killed two good people." Her distress heightens. Will Myrna and Lance be next or is it already too late for them?

Nick takes Jessi in his arms and tilts her chin up to his. "Jessi, those men – Rodrigo and his brother Julio are up there on the porch steps; tied up and gagged." He looks in their direction. "I've knocked them out."

She can make out two bodies piled by the front door. Her head reels thinking about what Nick must have done in the last several minutes – knocking them out, tying them up, gagging them, and then getting the judge out of the house. He is amazing, she thinks; but she's still puzzled by the details of the scenario. "But what about Myrna and Lance? We need to save them."

Nick explodes with emotion. "What we need to do is to get rid of these slime balls. They are killers. And if they survive, we are dead! Maybe not me. But probably after tonight. You – there's no way you'll survive. The judge will be gone! If Myrna and Lance are still okay; they are lucky and that's what we hope. That's what we hope!" He shakes her a little. He wants to make his point. "There is no way out with these guys unless I eliminate them."

The judge sits there on the grass, in the dark; not able to speak, not able to move.

"I think she has alcohol poisoning. I was barely able to coax her out of the house." Jessi huddles on the ground next to the Martina, attempting to console her. She looks up at Nick.

"The switch? The white switch?"

He bends his knees, and gets close to them. "The bomb is set. I watched them do it. It's in the house. The white switch is ready to go. Jessi, stay here with the judge. Okay?"

"W-what do you mean? What are you going to do?"

His eyes give away his plan, what he's about to do, with or without her consent. He's determined now. "Desperate circumstances require desperate measures."

Jessi takes his hand, one arm still embracing Martina. "You love me Nick. I can see it in your eyes. But I don't want you to do something reckless because you love me, and then regret it later."

Something has clicked into place inside him. He can't be talked out of it. "It is the only way. Stay here." He brushes her forehead with his lips and disappears. Martina is shaking again, rocking back and forth; locked up in a catatonic, drunken miasma. Jessi places both arms around the petite judge. A light rain starts to fall.

Nick leaps up the porch steps; approaching the two bodies. Both men are still out cold. His final thrusts with the shovel seemed to have kept them quiet. Stepping over them, he turns the decorative bronze handle, and pushes the front door open. He enters the house, and from inside, he drags the fat one's body into the front hallway. Nick is sweating again. It's so humid tonight. He goes to pull Rodrigo through the threshold and Rodrigo's hand regains life and reaches out to grasp Nick's ankle. Stepping on his hand hard, he hears the crunch and then the muffled groan from behind the handkerchief gag. If his grandmother only knew that her last year's Christmas gift of embroidered silk handkerchiefs were being used now for this devilish deed. After three attempted drags, he finally gets Rodrigo's limp body into the house. The Latino's face is bloodied; his cheek cracked open from Nick's earlier whacks.

Stop thinking, he tells himself. Just focus on task completion. The two bodies are now almost at the living room entryway. He nudges each one to see if they are both still unconscious. No movement. Good. He rushes back through the front door, and sprints back down the dimly lit path. He can see Jessi and the judge, huddled off to the side of the house, in the bushes. "Both of you must leave here now. Run down the street. Go!" He points in his requested direction. I'll meet you there, at the end of the block."

Jessi helps the judge to her feet. "But, Nick...what...?"

"Please Jessi, no more questions. Just do what I ask." His eyes are still warm and kind, but his words are firm. She stops talking. Nick collects his array of stuff from the ground near the bushes, and starts shoving it all into his back pack. He wipes the dirt with his pack to eliminate footprints. Jessi and Martina have started down the street. Nick walks over to the white switch, hovers, almost hypnotically staring at it. There it is. Oh shit. Can I really do this? Suddenly, out of the corner of his eye, he sees tiny Judge Martina Wells rushing up to his side.

Jessi is not far behind her, perplexed as to what the judge is doing. Martina looks down at the switch. "Murderers! Murderers!" Her tears flow. She is disoriented and consumed by the devil. "This switch – it's what they were going to use to kill me? Right?"

"Yes, I'm afraid so, Judge."

She pushes Nick to the side, and steps down as hard as she can with her right foot; making direct contact with the white switch. Flabbergasted, Nick grabs her hand, and starts running back to Jessi. The boom of the blast is alarming, rattling their ears. They look back as they run. They can hear breakage everywhere, windows bursting, shards of glass flying. The explosion has ripped open the roof; the house now consumed in luminescent multi-colored flames. They turn away, and keep running down the street; faster and faster. Jessi holds the judge's cold, clammy hand. The dark sky is illuminated with burning embers shooting out of the two million dollar house. A surreal sight to behold.

Almost two blocks away, Nick swiftly gets them both into his car. "Let's go to my house. We can stay there until morning," he says. "Jessi, okay for you? He can see her in his rear view mirror, sitting in the back seat. The streetlight furnishes just enough of a glow to make out Jessi's silhouette. Her hair is tied back in a long ponytail; her face, grim.

Numb, she can barely speak. "Yes. That's fine." She realizes just how much he was willing to risk for her. There is nothing like the love of a good man, she thinks as she watches the streetlights, and notices a homeless man huddled up in a blanket outside a shoe store.

Martina sits shivering in the front seat. Jessi grabs a blanket folded up in the back seat of the Volvo, and reaches forward to wrap it around the judge.

Nick makes each of the next two streetlights. Looking over at the judge who has almost disappeared under the blue-plaid, wool blanket, he says: "You hanging in there, Judge Wells?"

Tears roll down her sunken, pale cheeks. She nods. In a weak, raspy voice, she speaks out with seething anger. "I killed those sons of a bitches." Nick stares straight ahead and nods.

Silence. Just the humming sound of the engine for the next 30 seconds. "Thank you Nick. Thank you for everything you've done. It's me who killed them. They're gone." the judge whispers. The sound of fire engines speeding past, in the opposite direction, commands their attention. Shrill sirens blaring. Nobody in the car says another word until they are inside Nick's house.

37

THE DOOR OPENS FROM THE WALL

Nick turns on the antique lamp in his living room and crash-es onto his old brown leather chair; another item left to him by his grandmother. His other inherited possession, Pedro, the parrot, perks up as they enter, fully alert in his large cage lo-cated in the corner of the room. "Nicky boy! Nicky boy is home! Nicky boy is home!"

At first, the judge is startled by the sound of the bird. Jessi helps Martina to the sofa as the parrot continues his welcoming speech. "Nicky boy! Nicky boy! Nicky boy is home!"

Nick interrupts. "That's enough Pedro. Quiet now." Nick firmly commands, glancing at his watch and sees that it's 1:30 in the morning. He feels like he's fought a hundred day war. Weary, he struggles to stand up, hands Pedro a goodnight treat that he takes from a box sitting on the side table, and drapes the large flowered cloth cover over the bird's cage. He dims down the lamp. The bird instantly ceases his squawking, curtailing all movements.

Nick looks over at Jessi and Martina. "Judge – I have a mod-est guest room. I hope it's acceptable for you tonight. There's a bathroom just outside. He points in the direction of the bed-room. The small woman is uncomfortably perched halfway back on the sofa like a lifeless, worn out department store manikin;

her eyes hollow, her cheeks sunken. The scent of death hangs in the air. It cannot be ignored.

Jessi's phone buzzes. She jumps, at first, expecting it to be Rodrigo. Maybe what she thought just went down at the judge's house, never really happened; that Rodrigo is still on his maniacal tirade - ready to torture her with yet another threatening phone call. She closes her eyes for a second, and shakes her head. "No, it's not possible. Please God."

She stares down at the cell phone. Not a phone call, but a text from somebody unknown. She clicks it open and reads. "Jess, it's me – Myrna. Sorry I'm texting you so late. I hope it doesn't buzz and wake you. But I wanted to let you know that we got home from Salinas at around 9:45 this evening. It's Monday, so we're home a day later than expected. We had a nice time; but I don't think Rod is the one for me! He's got issues and it's good that I had a chance to get to know him better. Let's get together for lunch tomorrow. My cell phone has disappeared. I think it dropped out of my purse somewhere. My laptop is also gone. Stolen! Weird! Nothing else is missing from my house. No sign of forced entry. I was just throwing out the trash I left before the trip, and ran into my neighbor, Tracy. She let me use her phone for a few minutes so I could text you. What a night! I'll email you when I get to work in the morning. Love you, Jess. Lancelot says howdy!"

Relieved, Jessi sits there on the sofa, thanking God that Myrna is still seemingly unaware of whom she just spent a long weekend with. A degree of relief rushes over her, feeling thankful that Myrna somehow acknowledged on her own, that Rod was not the right "love" match. She turns to tell Nick that her cousin and nephew are both safe. But, he's no longer in his favorite easy chair.

He emerges from the bathroom which he inspected to ensure that it was presentable and clean for the judge. "Jessi, I guess I've hit the wall. I'll be in bed. Goodnight, Judge Wells."

"Nick, please don't call me Judge Wells. Just Martina. Thank you." The voice drifts out from her limp body. Her head hangs, shoulders slumped, unable to manage direct eye contact with either of them. Nick and Jessi lock eyes. In her simple request, they can sense the knife still twisting and turning inside the judge's gut, horror hanging in the air.

Jessi breaks the silence. "Ok Nick, I'll be right behind you, in just a few minutes." She longs to show him her affection, caress him, hold him close. She can't help but notice that he looks so worn out; ten years older than yesterday.

Before he exits the room, Jessi adds. "I just heard from Myrna. She and Lance are home." Nick stops in his tracks, emotionally relieved.

He rushes to her and without a word; he gently takes her face in his hands, peering into her blue eyes. "They're safe?" She nods. For the first time tonight, he smiles, happy to hear this wonderful news. He pulls his tired body up again; heading for his bed.

Jessi helps the Martina get settled in the small bedroom; finding some clean towels in Nick's linen closet. She tiptoes into Nick's bedroom and closes the door behind her. She peels off her clothes, and crawls into bed next to the man who risked his life to save her. They don't speak. They don't make love. They only touch, hold each other as the bright moon shines through the leaded glass, arched-shaped window. It's an old house, full of charm; comfortable.

She runs her fingers down his bare chest; reaches across to his right arm and does the same thing again. Her tender touch feels good. He stares up at the ceiling, feeling rattled about how the night ended up with the judge stamping her foot down on the white switch. He would have done it himself. She saved him from committing murder. He releases a deep sigh.

Jessi can see his eyes in the moonlight. Turning onto his side, he kisses her nose; then her lips. He doesn't need to say I love you. Their bond is unspoken, and yet stronger than any other she's known before. They fall asleep wrapped together.

The clock buzzes; the radio automatically turning on, the disc jockey's voice barking the next song title: "I Can't Get No Satisfaction! It's The Rolling Stones. Come on listeners! Get out of bed and dance to this blast from the past." Jessi jolts awake.

Nick stirs beside her. "Oh God," his head feels groggy. "I should have switched that thing off last night. I'm sorry it woke you." He shuts off the radio. "Clearly not the right song for the occasion." He still has his sense of humor.

"Good morning," he says. He kisses her on the cheek and gets out of bed, grabbing his navy and white striped terry cloth robe from the upholstered chair. "I better feed Pedro before he chews through the metal bars. They can hear his frenzied movements in the cage. "I'll make some coffee for us. I need to go into the office today because my boss is evidently lost without me. I never showed up yesterday. But I saved his ass on the phone with our CEO, which means I can show up at 10 today, and arrive just in time for the staff meeting." Nick exits the room, heading for Pedro, who is now squawking.

Jessi finds another robe hanging in his bathroom. She puts it on and makes her way to the guest bedroom to see if Martina is still asleep, or if she needs anything. The door is ajar. Nobody is there. The bed is made as if not slept in. "Nick," she shouts out. She walks into the kitchen. "Is Martina in here?" He's sitting at the breakfast nook reading a handwritten note. He passes it to Jessi.

"Jessi and Nick. First, let me express my gratitude. You two were so strong. I was the weak one. And the only way for me to re-gain any integrity is to openly confess what I've done. I will not implicate you two in any way. Rest assured. Take care of each other. Martina."

Nick turns on the right, front burner of his electric stove. He touches the note paper to the electric plate and the flame ignites. Together, they watch it burn. He deposits the remains in the sink disposal, and flips the switch. The grinding of the paper saddens him. Jessi takes his hand. "She's doing the right thing, Nick. This disastrous kidnapping ripped her apart. She loved her father so much. Her life was centered around him, as well as the preservation of justice. She went so far off course. Confessing is the only way for her to live with herself."

Jessi walks into the police station and asks to see Detective Bob Downey. Tall and balding, he greets her and repeats how sorry he is for her loss. He escorts her down the street to the San Francisco General Hospital and pushes the button in the elevator to the basement. The dank, musty smell hits her as the elevator opens to the sign above the two giant swinging doors: "San Francisco General County Morgue." She follows behind him without speaking. They pass a young woman who is exiting the small ante room, with a man who wears a black suit. The woman wails and shakes, as the man hugs her shoulders and offers her a handkerchief. Detective Downey moves Jessi past them and through the opaque glass doors to another small room where she can see an electronically controlled entry door to the actual morgue.

The detective stops, and sits her down on the long wooden bench. "If you're open to it, I would like to tell you about how your friend died the day before yesterday. A child and his mother found him in a movie theatre on Market Street; slumped down in a seat near the front of the screening room. He was shot through the head from behind at point blank range. Attending officers also found a wallet on the floor behind him, belonging to someone named Julio Velasquez. Not a savvy thing to do when committing a murder – leaving your wallet at the crime scene. Sure enough, it turns out he's some drug Cartel criminal. A long track record with several convictions. My guys are hunting him down right now. It appears likely that he did what we call "a hit" on Mr. Mendez. Did you know him or hear his name before – this man, Julio Velasquez?"

"No. No I didn't know him. I don't recognize his name."

"Of course, you wouldn't know this guy." The detective shakes his head, sorry he even asked this lovely, grieving woman the question. "He's the scum of the earth. I'll keep you posted on our progress finding him if you wish. Okay for us to go in there now so you can make the identification?

She nods. "Yes, I'm okay. I hadn't seen Rico since we were teenagers in Panama. I met him for that drink in the afternoon, and we were planning to have dinner at his hotel and catch up." She doesn't share that Julio and his brother, Rodrigo have burned in flames at 659 Ashburn, and have surely gone to hell.

"I understand. I'm sorry your time together was cut short. Those are really all of the questions I had for you." The detective slides his plastic card across the sensor. The door buzzes, and unlocks.

"Oh," just one more thing Dr. Salazar." He turns to her.

She almost jumps. "Yes?"

"Is there any reason that you know of as to why Rico Mendez would be a target for murder? Anything you can tell me?"

She shakes her head. "N-no. He was such a kind, good-spirited man. A wonderful career ahead. I-I…"

The Detective touches her shoulder. "Please, I'm sorry. I have to ask the question. Let's go in now so you can get through this, and go home. I can imagine how you must feel. You have my sincere sympathies." He swipes his card one more time for entry.

A plump, balding man wearing a starched, white medical coat greets them. "Detective Downey."

"Hi Arnie. We're ready to see the body. Rico Mendez."

The man looks down at the chart which sits on the long table. He seems to have some sort of limp, as he walks over to a small metal gray door on the wall marked Number 22. Jessi can feel the ghosts circling the room, peering down from the dark shadowed ceilings. He unlocks the door with a tiny key. The door opens from the wall, and he slides out what looks like a gurney. It's a body covered from head to foot in a thick zippered plastic bag. "Dr. Salazar?" She nods. The man unzips the black plastic. The sound sends shivers up and down her back.

She's sees the single dark mark between Rico's dark brown eyes, where the bullet exited the front of his head. Almost collapsing, Jessi reaches for the detective's arm to give her some support. He responds quickly, moving closer to help her re-gain her balance. "Rico," she murmurs. She brushes a wisp of dark hair from his forehead. He looks like a sleeping prince. Then she turns away. Why, why did they have to kill him? she asks herself. He was just an innocent bystander. Why did he have to show up in San Francisco now? Detective Downey puts his arm around her shoulder, then briskly moves Jessi out of the dismal basement, up the elevator to the lobby, and back into the light of day. He walks her to her car parked in the garage; pats her hand, empathizes once again for her loss. Then, he lets her go on her way. She drives one block, parks on a side street and sobs.

38

THE SUN DESCENDS OVER THE OCEAN

Jessi sits in her favorite chair, taking in the incredible vista from her living room window. The immense, burnt orange sienna sun descends on the steel gray San Francisco bay. She closes her eyes and imagines herself sitting quietly on the beach, as the giant setting sun appears to float on the water. The globe of orange seems to catch a big wave, surfing into the shoreline just in front of her. The huge mass slowly makes it way back out to sea and then, once again glides back towards the shoreline. She imagines herself laying down on the sandy beach, her arms and legs outstretched. The glowing, yet muted sun reaches her, covering her like a natural cloak. She feels serene, soothed, like a soft, giant leather kid glove has been fitted around her body. It's like butter touching her bare skin. Returning back to her living room, a sense of renewal overtakes her.

For the first time in almost four weeks since the explosion at the judge's house, Jessi feels alive; almost back on track. During the first week after the ordeal, she had grieved the loss of Rico, overwhelmed with sadness and loss. She also lived in fear, timid to go out in public; worried that at any given moment, a Cartel member would press his weapon into her back, and threaten her or take her life in an instant. Maybe it would happen at the grocery store or at her vet's office as she would unlock the door in the morning. He'd be lurking in the waiting room ready for her arrival. Then, he would sneak up behind her and take her life in less than a second. But nothing like that happened. The Cartel seemed to be underground now. Detective Downey called her three days after she identified Rico in the morgue, letting her know that over fifteen Columbian Cartel members had been arrested in the bay area, all of them in some way related to Rodrigo and Julio Velasquez; including an uncle and cousin at a Salinas dude ranch. They found a meth amphetamine lab in the basement. "The Cartel would now be running scared."

She never heard from the judge again, although she accidentally came across her in public. It was only two days ago. Jessi had just finished a challenging 7 mile run. Exhausted, she stopped in the park, filling her water bottle at the fountain. She was thirsty and tired out. As she took her first gulp of water, she noticed a petite woman sitting on the wooden bench close by, just opposite the playground. It was Martina, feeding the pigeons, a bag of bread crumbs in her hand. She was watching the children play on the monkey bars. Two other children were being pushed on metal swings by their over-zealous parents. Martina was gazing at one little girl, maybe five or six years old, who jumped from the monkey bars onto the see-saw. "Ben, come and play with me! Mommy said you should." It was obvious that Martina was enjoying this simple everyday scene. Jessi could see her chuckling when the little girl was bounced high off the ground on the end of the see-saw, begging the boy to please let her down. He teased his little sister, then finally put her down to the ground, with a hard pounce of the wooden plank against the dirt. The little girl jolted, then giggled and called out to her brother who was already moving on to his next playground adventure "Hey Ben, do that again. I liked it. I like being high up in the air. Please! Please Ben!"

The boy shrugged his shoulders, and turned back to his sister. "Okay. Okay. Stop whining. I'll do it." He shook his head in annoyance, but then grinned, flattered that his sister wanted him to play. "But I'm going to let you down harder this time. You know that Amy. Right?"

Martina sat there, feeding the birds. She seemed happy, her face much fuller than a few weeks ago; almost a pink glow in her cheeks. Jessi had seen the article a few days before, in the San Francisco Chronicle. Judge Martina Wells had been removed from the bench; taken out of her position as Superior Court Judge; relieved from all duties. She had been arrested and was now released, on $20,000 bail. Her case was in review, pending a determination as to whether she would be indicted, with a trial date set or just permanently discharged from the California judicial system. Jessi didn't approach the judge. There was a man sitting next to her on the park bench. With his dark skin, Jessi thought he looked Indian. Nice looking, thick dark hair, wearing jeans and a dark green sweater. Jessi could see his hand tenderly placed on Martina's knee as she tossed the bread crumbs into the circus of pigeons surrounding them. What Jessi didn't know is that the DA, Sanjay Dalla, was sharing the afternoon with the woman he once thought of dating. Jessi's heart warmed by the scene before her; the brother and sister in the playground, and the judge with a friend enjoying the day. She looked up and smiled at an old man who was walking by. He tipped his hat and said, "Stunning day, isn't it?" She nodded, stuffed her filled water bottle into her jacket pocket, and jogged away.

Pandora, the cat, now jumped up on the overstuffed chair and perched on her lap; snapping Jessi back to the sun now beginning its descent on the bay. "Pandora, you sweet kitty. Where's Creature? Where's your brother?" Hearing his name, Creature appears in the living room. He doesn't jump up; preferring to be independent and not follow his big sister around. Pandora starts to play with the long chain which hangs down from the tiffany lamp on the side table. Swatting it back and forth like a fly, the cat is thoroughly entertained. This was indeed, the feline's favorite plaything in the house.

The grandfather clock chimes. 7 o'clock. She had invited Myrna to dinner tonight. They both craved some one on one girl talk. Myrna's friend, Maria would babysit Lance. Time to get dressed, Jessi thought. She was meeting Myrna at the Buena Vista Bar and Grill.

Over the last few weeks, Jessi hadn't shared the truth with Myrna about Rodrigo Velasquez. Her cousin just thought Rod didn't call back after the dude ranch weekend because she had given him the hint that she needed space, and wanted to re-think her goals regarding their developing relationship. She had concerns, and needed to work them out alone. Things were just moving too quickly for her.

Rod received the news just before they exited the freeway in downtown San Francisco. Lance had been fast asleep in the back seat. Rod listened, then nodded, and didn't comment. He seemed to have little reaction. "I understand Myrna. You can call me when, and if you are ready." Then he dropped them off and while she was tucking Lance into bed, he slipped her laptop inside his jacket, calling out to her that he was leaving now. When she came back into the living room, he had already left. Her front door was still ajar. She thought maybe her comments had been too cold and possibly painful for him to hear.

39

DINNER - THE TIPPING POINT

The salty waiter, with the sea lion mustache notices Jessi as she sits down at the bar window table in the Buena Vista. Oh no, not those two laughing hyena women. They're back, he thinks to himself. I haven't seen them around here much lately. Where's the screechy one? This one's probably waiting for her. He stalls several minutes before he reluctantly approaches her. "A drink, Miss?"

She transitions out of her reverie, where she had been preparing for how she might break the news to Myrna about Rodrigo. "A glass of Mondavi Cabernet, please. Thank you."

"Expecting someone else?" He grunts, as if taking an order at some busy bar in New York City. Not very "have a nice day" California charm, she critiques to herself. I guess he remembers us gigglers, and not too fondly.

"Ah, yes. You're a lifesaver. Thanks for reminding me that my cousin was joining. I was daydreaming I guess. She should be here in a moment. Make that two glasses of Cabernet. Thank you."

Surprised at her compliment, he warms up. "Sure thing. Looks like the tourists are starting to clear out this week. I'm happy to get the locals back even if it brings more rain with the change of season. About time." Jessi nods in agreement. He breaks into a grin, happy to have a pretty woman grateful and smiling at him.

Myrna arrives, looking elegant and professional, her hair pulled back in a slick, full shiny brown bun; her bangs short, a new blunt cut. She must have come straight from work on this balmy Friday night. "Looking very chic. New haircut? Makeover?"

"Uh huh. You like it? Actually, I've had a bit of a delay getting here because I was busy with Lance's new puppy. Believe it or not, Lance wanted a dog. Looks like his fears are subsiding. When he asked, I had to jump on it before he changed his mind. Maria, the babysitter, met me at the Presidio Animal Shelter, with Lance in tow. He selected an abandoned border collie, only four months old. The cutest thing. Nice colors. Yellow, gold and white, with a tinge of dark brown around the ears. Seems very gentle and loving. We're calling him Gordy. Lance's idea. Who knows where that came from?" She laughs.

"Wow. That's a breakthrough for Lance."

"Yeh, it's all good, but can you put your vet's eye on Gordy tomorrow – just to be sure he's in A-1 condition?"

"Hmmm. For my usual fee." Jessi beams happiness for them. "How about an afternoon with Lancelot? That's my fee."

The usually grumpy waiter returns and places two hefty sized glasses of red wine on their table; then retreats after flashing another smile in Jessi's direction.

"Impressive Jessi. Did you bribe him to honor us with this new friendly behavior?"

"All in the sex appeal. When ya got it, use it" They both giggle, but in a subdued tone, carefully containing themselves so as not to alert their favorite waiter, and click him back to his standard persona. They like this new version.

"You know, his name tag says Gus; but we never call him by his name. We never call him anything. How often do we frequent this restaurant? We've probably been here over a hundred times, and every time it's been him serving us. It's like we're strangers but we really have a relationship that we choose to ignore."

"You're right. Myrna, I've re-connected with my father."

"Oh my God. That's incredible. You've been denying he exists for so long now."

"I talked to him on the phone yesterday. Called the hospital in Panama City. I thought it would be difficult getting in touch, but they instantly connected me to him. He was just about to leave the hospital for home. Denny's friends, Tikko and Cora were there, ready to escort him. His diabetes is still serious, but now they're hoping to not have to amputate his foot after all. When I heard his voice, I just melted. I've missed him so much. He was my idol, my hero; and I was his princess."

"I always knew that you still loved him. But every time I mentioned Denny Salazar, your father, you would give me such an angry mug. So, I stopped bringing him up. To me, he was still my brilliant Uncle Denny. I remember him fondly, the few times I met him as a kid."

"I was in denial, completely rejecting him when I still loved him so much. I hope it's not too late to forgive him and make amends. I realize now that sometimes you can't help who you fall in love with even when it will ruin your life and possibly the lives of others close to you. That's what happened to my father. He fell in love with Carina. I fell in love with Stefan. He was the absolute wrong man for me. I couldn't resist him. He made me feel alive even though I was stressed every day of that relationship. Jealous all the time; in an unhealthy loop. I think he wanted me like that so he could keep control over me. Pull my strings."

"Yes, it just happened to me with Rod. It wasn't love. I was totally infatuated. But, I realized it before it got out of hand. Something about Rod wasn't right. I could see that Lance noticed too. There was some sort of creepiness behind the great sex and the charming veneer. The things we sacrifice for feeling loved; feeling sexy; feeling desired. The fairy tale."

Jessi shivers when she hears Rodrigo's name come from Myrna. She deserves the truth. "Myrna – there's important information you never knew about Rod."

"Well, there's probably several things I didn't know about him. Actually, part of me is happy he hasn't called me after the ranch weekend; although it did make me feel like a cheap trick. I mean I know I broke up with him, but it caught me by surprise that he didn't even try to talk me out of it. At least call me after a few days. I confess; I do miss some of the things we had." She rolls her eyes and shrugs her shoulders.

"Myrna, you're better for it. Can I share some information about Rod that I haven't told you before?"

Myrna's eyes widen with cautious curiosity. "Okay, but how would you know anything more about him than I already know?"

"His real name is Rodrigo Velasquez, and he's a member of a Columbian drug cartel."

She sips her wine. "Don't be ridiculous, Jess."

"I know. It sounds insane. Myrna, sometimes we know subconsciously things about a person as we're starting to get involved with them. Bad things. A sign flashing inside our gut. Maybe for a nanosecond, it hits us each time we're in their company. But we choose not to acknowledge these second thoughts; our eyes and ears filtering out all the signals and subliminal messages. We sit up higher in the saddle, and continue riding that wild horse, the one that makes us feel free. But something is 'off'; not quite right."

"Bingo, that's exactly what I felt with Rod; but what's this stuff about a drug cartel? Nonsense, right? You were kidding."

"It's the truth. Remember how stressed I was only a few weeks ago; everyday since my birthday? It was Rodrigo, your ex-boyfriend. He was blackmailing me. He took Dr. Pepper and I think he killed him."

"Dr. Pepper is dead? Jessi!"

"I didn't want to tell you. This nightmare started when I accidentally witnessed Rodrigo and his brother abduct and shoot an old man while I was gazing out the Carrington Grace restaurant window at my birthday dinner. Nick was in the restroom and the dining room was empty – except for me. I became the endangered witness; someone they had to hunt down and manipulate to keep me quiet."

"This happened at the Renaissance Hotel with Nick?"

Jessi nods. "I'm so sorry Myrna. I didn't put it all together until you were in Salinas at the ranch with that gangster. I hadn't realized that the evil man turning my life into a living hell was the same man you were dating. While you were at the ranch, Rodrigo phoned me and told me he had you and Lance in his custody. He threatened to kill you both if I didn't agree to his demands. Honestly, I was too scared to tip the boat. If he knew I was even trying to contact you, he would have hurt you both. He said he wouldn't harm you if I cooperated. What he wanted was... Listen, that's all you need to know. The rest is better off left unsaid."

"All I need to know? All I need to know." Myrna loses her composure. Tears form in her eyes. "Rod? I was set up because he was targeting you? Basically, Lance and I were kidnapped by a ruthless criminal. Him pretending to be attracted to me, sweeping me off my feet and getting close to Lance? It was a ruse and I was an idiot. And he took full advantage. Lance figured it out at the ranch. He heard Rod mention your name on the phone. He was speaking quickly in Spanish. I thought Lance misunderstood. Kids can do that. But the little voice in my head was nagging me. Oh my God! What a fool I've been."

"He was the devil Myrna."

"Was?" Myrna freezes. "What do you mean? Was?"

Jessi swallows hard. "I believe he was killed when plotting to take someone else's life. He had already murdered two other innocent people. One of them was Rico."

"Rico, from Panama is dead? And the man I was falling in love with is dead, too?"

Jessi nods. Myrna sits back in her seat. Her next sensation is to feel the sting of the bullet she dodged with Rod, or is it Rodrigo – whoever he is or was. He masterfully deluded her; like a magician plays the crowd. Like the mosquito attacks the human flesh; coming out of nowhere, he lands and sucks the blood of his victim who never detects the nasty bite until the insect is long gone. Tears stream down Myrna's cheeks. Her heart strings strain when she thinks of all the things that man did to her, what she willingly let him do.

"Lance and I could have been murdered. That's what you're saying?"

"Myrna, both you and I have reached our tipping point. Me, getting over the horrific experience of Rodrigo and his brother. You, hearing about what could have happened to both you and Lance, if things went in a different direction. Neither of us will ever be the same again. But we can both move forward with dignity." Jessi gets up and moves to the other side of the booth, sliding in next to her cousin. She takes Myrna's hand, squeezing it – understanding how much this cataclysmic news must be affecting her. No more details necessary, she thinks. Myrna doesn't need to know about the judge or about Nick coming to the rescue in the midst of crisis. Maybe another time; years from now.

The two cousins stare out through the smudged restaurant window, in silence. The San Francisco cable car just opposite them, now making its famous turn-around at the end of the line. They watch as the conductor prepares to go right back over the same hills but on a new journey, with a new set of passengers, who giggle and chatter, thoroughly excited about what's to come.

Since she was a preschooler, Myrna had dreamt about a handsome prince sitting tall, atop a beautiful silky white stallion, galloping through the woods, over the mountains, across the valleys, in search of her; his one true love. She had grown up brainwashed by Walt Disney, Cinderella, Rapunzel and Snow White; turned inside out into believing that her primary goal in life was to be desired by some man. Not an ordinary man, but an Adonis – an alpha man. This fantasy continued into Myrna's twenties and thirties. She was in love with romance.

The skies have turned darker in San Francisco. Myrna can still make out the white caps on the navy blue bay waters beyond the lit up cable car. Myrna leans her head on her cousin's shoulder. They both listen to the conductor clanging the bells loudly; signaling that new passengers can now board the to start the ride over the steep hills, and into the foggy night.

40

THE RETURN OF THE NATIVE

He stands on her doorstep, places the cardboard box down on the ground just behind him, and rings the doorbell. He's anxious about seeing her tonight, hoping to convey his need for a bigger commitment. He wants her all to himself; exclusivity. They've become much closer over the past few weeks; almost inseparable. Intimate, sharing their hopes, dreams, fears and regrets. Jessi now talking openly about her father; how she dealt with the hurt, how she's happy to re-connect; and make plans to visit him in Panama.

What happened on that razor's edge of a night at 659 Ashburn sliced and diced both of their worlds. The dark side of life had been tossed up in their faces like the freakish wind of a hellacious tornado. An incredibly strong bond was now forever forged between them; but what about love? What about love? That was his question. He needed to lay it on the line. Whatever Jessi's reaction, he'd just have to live with it.

The door opens. "Nick. Sorry I took so long to answer. I had to get the tri-tip and the baked potatoes out of the oven. Ready for a delectable home-cooked meal?"

"My stomach has been growling since early this morning. I resisted filling it with junk food all day, so that I could fully enjoy tonight's feast. A bottle of vino for us." He hands her the bottle of Mondavi Cabernet. "And, I also have a yummy dessert I brought along with me." He turns around, and picks up the silver cardboard box; the lid topped with a large red satin bow.

"Yum. What is it? A giant cake? A very deep crusted apple pie? Hmm?"

He holds the package out before her. Some movement comes from the box.

"Is it Pedro? Did you decide to bring him along for dinner?" She laughs. "I wonder how Creature and Pandora will deal with that."

Her two cats look up from their matching food bowls. As he holds up the box, Nick signals for Jessi to remove the rectangular lid. A small, silky-haired dark brown head peeks out. He energetically jumps to the floor, heading straight into the kitchen, like a small gust of wind.

"Dr. Pepper? Oh my God!" she screams. Her thinner, but clearly recognizable dog turns from the kitchen, and runs into Jessi's open arms. The delighted Yorkshire Terrier licks her face profusely, like she's his favorite flavored dog bone. Then, he wriggles out of her arms, and jumps back onto the wood floor; heading straight for the two cats. An instant pet re-union. The chase is on!

She can see the wide bandage on the side of his little body where the hair had been shaved away, but his injury doesn't seem to have slowed him down. Only when he eases his pace, does Jessi notice a slight limp derivating from his back right paw.

"Nick, how in the world...?" She's at a loss for words; and crying tears of deep appreciation. She sits down on the sofa staring across the room at Pepper, the pet she thought she'd never see again. She sits in silence for another minute; taking in her pet's return. "He's alive! But where did you find him? How? You are Houdini." She springs up from the sofa and sprinkles kisses all over Nick's face.

"Yep, he's got a slight limp. His bandage can come off tomorrow; but then you're an expert on that. Anyway, that's what Sally Rafferty told me."

Jessi slides onto the living room area rug. Dr. Pepper immediately jumps onto her legs, his tail wagging, his spirit as perky as ever. He settles down just above her knees. He places his front paws under his head, happy to be home at last.

"Sally Rafferty?"

"That's the woman who found Dr. Pepper, almost dead under a bush near Presidio beach. He was covered in blood, barely breathing. Took a gunshot to his side. She rushed him to an emergency vet; but not yours." He smiles. "Now, that would have been something. Then, she took him home. I guess his ID tags had fallen off. No way of knowing who he belongs to. No chip, Jessi?"

"No. Guilty as charged. I had been meaning to do it. I was just so busy; kept forgetting. Ridiculous, isn't it?"

"Sally is a hairdresser who lives down in San Jose. Once she got Pepper home and he started to recover, she contacted her local animal shelter to let them know about finding this lost and badly injured Yorkie. A good woman. Animal lover."

"I thought he was dead." She snuggles her dog. "Killed by that sadistic maniac. I can't believe he's okay. Looks like the shot missed his major organs. Thank God. You lucky little rascal!" She pets his head. Pepper sits up regally, thoroughly relishing his home coming.

"How did you connect with Sally?"

"I just had a hunch that maybe Dr. Pepper wasn't dead, and we shouldn't give up on him. If he was alive, then he had to be in an animal shelter or with some kind person who was caring for him. So, over the past two weeks, I've contacted over 25 shelters in the surrounding counties. No luck. Then yesterday, I was sitting at my desk in my office, staring out the window on Great America Parkway, and I thought what the hell. Why not give it a try? I hadn't checked the shelter just a half a mile from my office. At lunchtime, I drove over to the shelter. Pepper wasn't there but I talked to the staff person on my way out the door. Rebecca raised her eyebrows and told me that she'd personally call me back. Evidently, there was a woman who called in several days before about finding a Yorkie in San Francisco about 3 weeks ago. The dog had been hurt badly. She promised to call me this morning. I didn't want to tell you just in case it was a false alarm. And voila! When Rebecca phoned me back, she didn't need to say much before I knew she had Pepper. I could hear him in the background, that unmistaken little 'ruff'; his sort of yappy signature doggie bark."

"Hey, watch it! That's my dog you're talking about!" She scoops up her shrunken dog in her arms, raises him high in the air, and brings him down like a hovering UFO.

Nick scoots down on the rug to sit beside Jessi. "Once that bandage is removed, the fur will grow back, right? Is that how it works for dog injuries?"

Jessi laughs. "Well, first off, Yorkies don't have fur. They have real hair." She runs a handful of her dog's head hair through her fingers. "Here, feel it." Nick touches it, making exaggerated, funny faces, as if he's luxuriating in the sensation of feeling the Yorkie's fine hairy coat.

"Ahh, real hair. Ooh! Feels divine! I guess that explains his new coif, and the tiny red bows in his hair, gifted by Sally the hairdresser. I thought that was a limp from his injury; but hey – maybe that new walk he's acquired indicates a doggie gender identity crisis. Hmmm."

"Animal sarcasm will get you nowhere. With that outburst, I think it's time to eat." Pepper takes the hint, leaping from her outstretched legs. "And yes, Pepper will have a nasty scar, but most of his hair should grow back, and pretty fast. Looks like 15 or so stitches. How about some vino first?" She moves to get the wine opener and glasses from the kitchen. Popping the cork and pouring, she places the two full glasses on the coffee table. "Let's allow the wine to breathe, just a bit." For a second, she thinks of Stefan, his overconfidence, his "I'm better than the rest of the world" smirk. She shakes her head.

Pepper skips over to Nick, who wraps him in his arms, cuddling the dog affectionately. "You're such a Casanova, Pepper. How do you do it? Tell me your secret."

"Hey, no guy talk behind my back." She takes the dog from his arms; then turns Dr. Pepper around to face Nick. "By the way, have we told you how much we both love you?"

"That's 'thank you for the doggie rescue' talk, isn't it?"

She grins, and hands him the Cabernet. Swirling her glass of wine, she demonstrates. "I'm volatizing the esters. Oooh la la. Hey, let's toast to the truth, shall we?" Clink. "To be precise, Dr. Pepper loves you for bringing him home to me. And I love you because I just do! If you'll have me, I'll be yours for a long, long time, Mr. Daniels."

He's speechless, unsure of what he just heard. But her eyes clarify her feelings. He grabs her, and kisses her.

Her cell phone rings. "Oh, I forgot to tell you. I'm on call for St. Andrew's emergency room tonight; advising the attending vet interns."

"No problem.."

"Dr. Salazar, here," she answers.

Nick occupies himself, playing fetch with Dr. Pepper. "Hey Pepp, here ya go boy." He throws the fuzzy green octopus all the way into Jessi's bedroom. Pepper is excited, jumping onto Jessi's bed, his paws trampling all over her laid out clothes. Nick notices Jessi's large black suitcase open on the floor, a few things already folded inside. "Now that she's confessed her love, she's disappearing into the sunset? I've got the worst luck with women I love, don't I?" Nick plops himself down just next to the array of what looks like summer shorts and halter tops. "Hmm. Is it a planned trip to Hawaii I see before me?"

"Dinner is served," she shouts out. Dr. Pepper reacts to the announcement with repeated jumps as Nick holds up the octopus, teasing him; raising and lowering the toy in opposition to the dog's soars into the air.

"Come on boys. Stop the horsing around in here." Jessi stands at the bedroom door, her hands on her hips.

He pulls her onto the bed. "So, you're in love with me, and now you're ditching me for some tropical island paradise?

Already? Are you setting a speed record for the shortest gap between professing undying love, and then disappearing into the ozone? I'd say this suitcase, and that assortment of skimpy clothes, definitely require some sort of explanation."

"How about if I tell you all about it over some Caesar salad, and tri-tip? A fair trade?"

"No can do. I'd like the prognosis now, if you don't mind, Dr. Salazar.

"Well, I've accepted a short term assignment in Panama – just for a month, to study the flying pattern behavior of jungle parrots. I'll be tied up only three hours a day, and then do report writing for another thirty minutes each afternoon." Nick falls back on the bed; his fears confirmed.

"I have Saturdays and Sundays off; guaranteed. Tough assignment, eh? And the results of my study will be featured on Animal Planet – Parrot Patrol in Panama; an hour long television special. They'll be filming segments of my work on some of the days; but they promise me lots of free time. And, they're locating me in Boca del Toro; just minutes from where my dad still resides." Nick brightens, happy for her.

"I'll be staying at a family friend's resort. It's called Rainbow Lodge. Oh God. I'll need to get Myrna to look after Dr. Pepper. She's already said okay to the cats. Or, what if Myrna takes the cats, and Sarah looks after Pepper?"

"Or, Dr. Pepper could hang out with me," Nick adds.

"Yes, I guess so," she says hesitantly. "I leave in six days. I'm going to scatter Rico's ashes in the rainforest. It's the right thing."

She looks down, then takes his right hand holding it palm up.

"You see this? This is your lifeline. She slides her finger across his palm. "Notice how the long line branches off into two short lines, and then down here they join up again. That's us - together."

She closes her eyes just for a moment as if in prayer, then smiles up at him. "I know it's a long shot, Nick, but is there any chance you might come to Panama with me? I'd like the man I love to be there with me, supporting me on all counts."

Nick's face turns a crimson color. It's what happens to him when he's euphoric. He wants to bounce up and down on the bed just like the rambunctious Dr. Pepper. "I am definitely smelling what you are cooking – on both Panama, and the tri-tip. I'm ravenous, Jess." He brushes the two dark curls out of her eyes. "The fact is that I've just earned a five week sabbatical; an extra paid vacation. I already hinted to my boss about taking the time off."

"Well then - you better start packing, Mr. Big Shot."

THE END

30142023R00146

Made in the USA
Charleston, SC
05 June 2014